AN IMPOSSIBLE TASK AND A VILE SOLUTION

BONE KNIGHT
BOOK 7

TIM PAULSON

Cover design and internal illustrations by Mark Smith Illustration

First Edition: March 2022

Ikkibu publishing

OTHER WORKS

Arcane Renaissance series:
Path of Ruin
Betrayal at Goliath Gate
Wrath of the Risen God

Bone knight series:
A Grim Demise and Even Worse Resurrection
A Doomed Fight and Not So Great Landing
A Hard Truth and An Unwise Decision
A Lost God and A Hostile Land
A Daring Plan and A Cold Shoulder
An Agonizing Day and A Dread Knight
An Impossible Task and A Vile Solution
A Brutal Clash and A Bitter Rival
A Grave Threat and Ultimate Illumination

**Join Tim's mailing list at www.paulsonwriter.com
and receive a free Arcane Renaissance novella.**

1

BRASH AND EMBARASSED

Thunder's rumbling roar echoed from the battered walls of the fortress and the many nearby airships as the Midnight swerved away from the side of the ruined tower. Rain poured in sheets from the thick clouds above, obscuring swathes of the night sky and drenching Max and Arinna as they climbed down the ladder into the ship. Trina was there waiting for them, already shaking her head.

"What did you do to her?" the plague doctor groused as she took Arinna by the hand. "This way, I'll take a look at that wound for you."

"Me?" Max stammered in reply as his armored feet clanked against the ladder rungs.

"You... are beautiful," Arinna said.

This made Trina pause. "What?"

Max dropped to the deck beside Arinna and followed her gaze up to the ceiling where Mytten was hanging upside

TIM PAULSON

down above them. The spider's legs had grown back and her chitinous body seemed to shine like he'd never seen before. "She is, isn't she?"

Thank you, Max.

"Oh... the spider!" Trina said. "She molted. Nearly scared me to death."

Now that Trina mentioned it, Mytten did look bigger.

"I haven't seen a spider of her breed in centuries," Arinna said, still staring at Mytten. "I thought they'd been exterminated. Where did you find her?"

"I didn't," Max replied. "A dark elf I met did. She died defending her village from the light and left Mytten to me."

Arinna nodded solemnly. "So they haven't taken everything from us."

"No," Max replied, removing his armored helmet. "They haven't."

A loud clang shook the entire ship, nearly knocking Max into the wall.

"Get up front and help Tela get us out of here!" Trina snapped.

Max looked to Arinna. "She'll be alright?"

"I can't answer that until I get a chance to take a look," Trina replied. "Go."

Arinna put a hand on his upper arm, leaving a streak of black blood. "I'll be fine," she said as yet another bang made the ship tremble.

She did not look fine but Trina was right, there wasn't much he could do for her so he ran to the bridge.

Max was greeted by nothing by an empty console. A clinking sound drew his attention to the right near the door. The automaton was there on the floor. The creature's metal arms were wrapped around its knees and the whole thing was shaking like a timer for a party game.

"Don't worry clanky," Max said. "I'm sure it's not that bad."

"It is!" Tela shouted. Her usually cheery voice sounded strained. "There are ships in every direction and the ones that aren't shooting at the tower behind us are shooting at us!"

Max watched the world outside of the forward viewport rotate in front of him as the ship banked hard. A half second later a bright ball of white fire shot by, illuminating the entire cabin and much of the sheets of rain in front of the ship.

That's right, it was raining hard. How was it possible the other ships saw them so well at night? It had to be those flood lights they used.

"Tela, are our lights on?"

"No, they aren't!" a stressed out Tela shot back. "Trina said they should be off so we're harder to shoot and I agree with her."

Tela banked again, just missing the spire of a familiar looking tower. It looked like the same one Max had used to get Arinna out of that freaky convent.

"Get ready to turn the lights back on, but first we have to go up. Straight up."

"What?" Tela replied. "But weaving through the fog in between these buildings is the only thing that's kept us from being torched."

"Just do as I ask. Head straight up into the storm. There are thick clouds up there. Get to them. They'll be the perfect cover. I'll make sure we're not shot in the meantime."

"How are you going to do that?" the automaton asked. It was the first time the thing had spoken in some time and, Max was surprised to realize, it had spoken in the common tongue, not high demonic.

"You can speak... eh... never mind. You want to help?" Max asked it.

The creature's bird-like head looked up. "How?"

"The only two human-shaped friends I have are currently indisposed. Can you operate a weapons station?"

The creature seemed at a loss, his head bobbing. "I... I don't believe that's listed in my directives."

"Do your directives tell you to prevent your own destruction?" Max asked.

The metallic head nodded emphatically.

"Then you'll figure it out," Max said. "Follow me. Tela, power up the guns!"

"You've got it!" Tela said, sounding like some of her hope had returned.

Max pulled the automaton out of the bridge and around a corner to the central ladder. "You take the bottom gun, and I'll take the top. It's simple, just like a joystick back home. You point the red dot at the center of the bubble at the bad guy and press the trigger."

The automaton looked up at him, the metallic irises of its glowing eyes contracting slightly. "What's a joystick?"

"Figure it out, or we all go boom!" Max said and started climbing up.

The automaton rubbed its metal hands together and started following him.

"No!" Max yelled back down. "You go down the ladder to the other gun!"

"Oh... oh yes," the creature said. "I see."

Max rubbed his gauntleted fingers across his boney temples.

The whole ship shook again.

"Whatever you're going to do, please do it quickly!" Tela called from the bridge. "They can see us!"

Max yanked his way up to the top gun as fast as he could, quietly humming the theme to the tie fighter attack as he strapped in and grabbed the stick.

"Here we go baby," he said as the Midnight's upper gun bubble turned into position, exposing the single light cannon that jutted from just above Max's spherical cockpit. Max had tested these guns on the trip over to Reylos, blasting a couple of trees into cinders. The shots weren't as big as those fired by the bigger ships, but they were faster, which was something.

The giant pair of search lights ahead and above him was something too: a target. Max aimed the gun and fired. A burst of three small spheres of golden light shot from the barrel above him. They fired out in a loose line slamming into the bow of the ship ahead. The blasts of holy fire exploded, boring large smoking holes into the metal clad bow of the Clathian vessel.

Max could see immediately why holy fire was so popular as a ship-to-ship weapon, it cut through the metal like nothing. As Max watched, a huge explosion erupted from the left side of the enemy ship, illuminating the rain with an orange glow as the ship belched flaming cinders and black smoke. There was a moment where it seemed nothing would happen, like the ship was frozen in place, but then it began listing to the side.

One down.

"Don't get cocky Max," he told himself as he used the foot pedals to track his weapons blister to the right, searching for another target. There was a light clicking from some gears down by his feet, but the movement was otherwise silent and surprisingly smooth. Max had to admit the mechanisms in this ship were pretty ingenious. It was like steampunk but without the steam. What would you call that, magic punk?

"What do I press?" said a mechanical voice from far below.

Max leaned over to the ladder hole. "Sit in the seat! The stick in front of you has a small button. Press it!"

"Oh!" the automaton said from below. "I see."

"Great!" Max yelled back. "Now do some damage, and to THEM, not to US."

"Yes!" the bird headed robot replied.

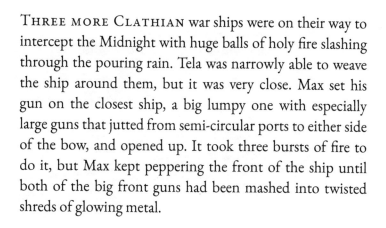

THREE MORE CLATHIAN war ships were on their way to intercept the Midnight with huge balls of holy fire slashing through the pouring rain. Tela was narrowly able to weave the ship around them, but it was very close. Max set his gun on the closest ship, a big lumpy one with especially large guns that jutted from semi-circular ports to either side of the bow, and opened up. It took three bursts of fire to do it, but Max kept peppering the front of the ship until both of the big front guns had been mashed into twisted shreds of glowing metal.

It helped that the Clathian ships were so pathetically slow. It was like shooting hot air balloons with a rocket launcher. The things would try to move away from the shots, but they weren't very maneuverable. When he saw the remaining two turning away, Max was sure they were home free.

"We got 'em!" he shouted. "It looks like they've... had... enough."

"What?" Tela called from the bridge below. "Really?"

No. Not really. The Clathian ships were turning their sides to him, exposing rows of cannons he didn't even know they had.

"Tela! Dodge the ship!" he yelled down the ladder tube.

"But you said go straight up into the clouds!" Tela shouted back.

"I know what I said! Just do it!" Max said. He was pulling his trigger as fast as he could. One, two, three salvos of his faster, smaller shots launched out, raking the other ships, but the armor was thicker on the sides. His gun wasn't enough to get through it and that was going to be a problem.

The Clathian ships unleashed hell, firing two full broadsides at the Midnight. Dozens of huge glowing balls of fire launched in their direction coming in like a flaming wave.

"Tela!" Max shouted. "Dive! Now!"

"Ok!" Tela replied.

The Midnight plummeted back toward the ground, swerving to the right in a sort of corkscrew. Even with the crazy maneuver three of the incoming shots came uncomfortably close to the ship, with one grazing them enough to burn a slab of the hull away to Max's right, shaking the entire ship as it did.

Max spun his turret and fired again and again at the ships, knowing they were reloading for another massive salvo. It didn't seem to be making any difference though. His shots would land and burn glowing smoking pits into the Clathian armor but he couldn't penetrate it.

"I can't get through their armor!" Max called down. "Is there any extra... you know... juice... for this thing?"

"I don't know what you mean!" Tela called back in a happy but strained sounding voice.

"What in the name of Gazric are you two doing?!" Trina shouted from below. "I'm glad I thought to strap her down because we would both have been on the floor!"

"We're trying to escape!" Max said, pulling the trigger again.

"I think I got one!" the robot called from below. "Oh... no I didn't."

"Whatever," Max called back. "Just keep shooting at them."

"Tela, I need you to fly more smoothly!" Trina said.

"No!" Max called down in response. "Tell me how to make these guns more powerful!"

"How many times have I told you: I'm a doctor not a technician?!" Trina growled.

"Thanks for nothing then!" Max shouted down.

The guns on these things were based in magic weren't they? Maybe there was some way he could pump his own magic points into the system. The Clathians were going to let loose again any second. It was worth a shot.

Max! Don't pump your magic into the ship. It will explode.

Mytten? Arinna is talking to you?

Yes! She says to use your magic on the ship, like it's a thing. She is telling me to ask if you have any spells of concealment.

Actually... he did. Would it let him equip the Shadow Staff as a Dread Knight? There was only one way to find out! Max brought up his equipment screen and switched from the Flesh Ripper to the staff. No buzz! It worked!

Quickly he used the weapon to cast Ruse, pointing it at the ship. There was a hiss and a flash of black as two other versions of the Midnight appeared nearby.

"Now!" Max yelled.

"Now what?" Tela called from the bridge below.

"Go up again, straight up into the clouds! As fast as you can."

The whole ship shuddered, pressing Max into his seat as it broke out of the corkscrew drive and pulled up at the steepest possible angle, leaving the two other Midnights behind. They'd pulled up just in time too. The Clathian ships had just unleashed a second wave of fire balls that instantly obliterated one of the clones of their ship.

"I had no idea this spell would work on an entire ship," Max said.

Arinna says it won't work for long, but it was a good choice.

"Tell her thanks, Mytten," Max replied.

She can't hear me, we're not bound.

"Then give her a thumbs up or something."

You know I don't have any thumbs.

"Yeah... I'm sorry about that one," Max said. It had sounded funnier in his head.

The last thing Max saw before the Midnight finally ascended into the swirling gray mass of clouds that hung over Clathia, was the final collapse of the central tower of the fortress of Gelra. Hopefully the disgusting mass of black goo that had once been a man, was now burned and crushed into oblivion, like he deserved.

Max crawled down from his gun station, pausing at the center to cup his gauntleted hands and shout to the automaton.

"You can stop shooting now. It's over."

"It is?" the creature asked.

"Yep. Come back up here and help me decide where we go next," Max replied and stepped into the bridge. "Tela, just level off here, and maybe head north for a bit."

"I sure will!" she replied, clearly relieved that their ordeal was over, at least for the moment.

Max was relieved too, Arinna was finally here. Though, he wanted to see her again. Just to be sure she was still there, of course. The last time he'd let his eyes off her in this ship she'd jumped out the back. He'd personally seen to the destruction of the creature that made that possible, but Max still felt a bit leery. And... if he was being honest with himself, there was another reason: he liked her.

Mytten was waiting for him outside the bridge, still hanging on the ceiling. She looked stuffed into the top of the hallway given her larger size.

"You keep growing like that and we're going to need a bigger ship," Max told her. "Where are they?"

In my room.

Max nodded and proceeded down the hall, clanking his Dread Knight armored feet across the metal grating of the ship's deck as he went. As he casually glanced at the few small rooms that led off from the passage, he couldn't help but think he was forgetting something. Wasn't there something else here? Or maybe it was something that ought to be there but wasn't? Odd.

Max arrived at the smallest of the rooms, the one just big enough for Mytten to sleep inside the huge cocoon plastered against the ceiling that she'd made for herself out of webbing. However on the floor of the room, Max found Trina pressing a poultice against Arinna's stomach.

"How's she doin' doc?" Max asked. "Will she live?"

"She's... uh... Yeah, I think so. She's healing that's for sure, at an accelerated rate. Uh... are you... a vampire?"

"You could say that," Arinna replied. "It's close to the truth."

Trina frowned. "Not a fan of straight answers are we?"

Arinna threw her head back and laughed. Max caught a glimpse of those pointed teeth. They'd returned just the way they were when he first saw her, as had the green in her eyes. Though as he looked at her, the emerald hue didn't seem quite as bright as before.

"No, I suppose I'm not," Arinna said. "It's a bad habit I picked up a while back."

Trina grimaced, looking annoyed. "She'll be fine, bone boy," she said as she stood up. "I suppose I'll leave you to... get better acquainted." She winked at Max.

"What's that supposed to mean?" Arinna asked as she sat up, one single questioning eyebrow raised.

Trina paused at the door, grinning impishly. "Maybe you should ask Max."

Max sighed.

2

A NOBLE RING AND AN UGLY MEETING

Arinna peeled back the poultice from her stomach, revealing pure clean flesh which she proceeded to prod with a finger. Max watched. The girl's flesh was extremely white, too white.

"So you are undead," Max said.

She looked up at him and shrugged before getting up with a little groan. "Ugh... still hurts some."

"But you feel pain," Max said.

"Don't you?" she asked.

Max nodded. "Yeah, sometimes. Pure water may be my least favorite thing here."

"Terrible stuff," Arinna replied.

"The worst," he said.

"So?" she said, folding her arms.

"Uh... what?"

"What did the girl mean when she said that?"

Max suddenly felt the urge to flee, to hit the latch and jump right out the back of the Midnight. He would get Trina back for forcing this conversation on him.

"And don't play dumb," Arinna said. "We have a great deal to do."

"A great deal? I thought this was the deal!" he said. "Vish told me to find you and free you and you're free!"

"Don't change the subject," she replied, tapping a single finger against the flesh of her upper arm.

Damn.

Max grit his teeth. "Fine..." Why was this so hard to talk about? "I... am... betrothed."

Arinna frowned. "So?"

"Well I... I thought..."

"You thought I was hitting on you?"

"No!" Max said. "I mean... I don't know. I kind of hoped... eh... I mean... uh."

"Well I was, a little bit, but what are you talking about?!"

"It's on my sheet!" Max replied, reaching for his wrist. "Look!"

Arinna held up a hand. "I know Vishellus gave you a nasty bent, you don't have to go into it."

Max paused. "Huh? What's a bent?"

"It's that thing at the top of your status screen that you're about to show me," she said. "I know all about it. Vishellus gave you the most difficult one, you probably shouldn't have made fun of his eye."

"He deserved it. He was being a pompous ass," Max said.

"He's a demon. That's what they do. You can't be too angry at him though. You made it this far. You found me, even with the anguished bent."

Max tilted his head. "What do you mean anguished?"

"That's the one you have," she said, pointing to his wrist. "It gives you access to all the classes but with a hefty stat penalty. It's a wonder you survived at all."

"That's interesting," Max replied, "because that's not what my screen says." He turned it to face her. "Look."

A skeptical Arinna reluctantly obeyed and her eyes widened. "What?! Betrothed? Why does it say that?"

Max stared at her. "I thought *you* would know!"

"But it doesn't make sense..." she said, turning away, a hand at her chin. "Unless..."

"Unless what?" Max asked.

Arinna looked to her left, toward the door. "You can come out, doctor. No need to eavesdrop."

Trina appeared from around the corner, looking sheepish. "I... uh... I was just..."

"Can it," Max told her. "Arinna... What were you going to say?"

Arinna turned back to face him, her eyes moving up and down his armor.

Max suddenly felt very self conscious.

"What's that ring you're wearing?" she asked.

Max raised his hands. "I've got a lot of them," he said. "It's been the only reliable way to offset the penalty to my stats."

"That one," Arinna said as she leaned in and grabbed his hand, pulling it up close to her face. "This is a signet ring! You're nobility!"

Max was speechless. "B-but..."

Trina laughed. "As if... Next you'll say you two are related."

Arinna nodded, letting Max's hand go. "That's quite likely. Few noble houses of the dark remain. The design on that ring is made of two halves, one is of my house and the other is of the light."

Trina's mouth was hanging open. "So... that pile of bones is your cousin?"

"Could be a half brother, or a nephew," Arinna said. "Long ago my father thought he could broker a peace between the light and the dark by marrying my sisters to Cerathia's sons. Six of my eight sisters were married off that way, two later died under suspicious circumstances."

18

"I haven't heard any of this," Trina said. "It's not written anywhere."

"Few know," Arinna said. "Even fewer know that the remaining four of my sisters betrayed the dark and left." She looked back at Max. "He could be one of their children."

"Wait! Stop!" Max said. "I can't listen to this. I'm from Earth. I was brought here by Vish. I work at a coffee shop, or I did. I'm just a human... guy."

"But didn't you say your father had been here?" Trina asked. "You were raving about his paintings back at my school."

Max looked at her. "You remember that? You called me crazy!"

"I remember everything," Trina said, hands on her hips. "And it was crazy... at the time."

Arinna's eyes narrowed as they bored into Max's face. "I thought you looked familiar. Who is your father?"

"He's just... he's an artist... he paints things like... like what happens in this place," he said, looking down at his hands. "And there's something else."

Arinna's eyebrows rose, waiting.

"He taught me things. As a boy he gave me a game this place is based on. We played it together, like a lot, and he told me bedtime stories about griffin riding knights. I even know how to fly one. That's how I got back to the Midnight during that battle in Reylos."

Arinna pursed her lips, her fingers were at her chin again. "I see. So your father might be one of Cerathia's sons and your mother one of my sisters. It explains why my father wanted him."

Max shook his head. "No. That's not possible. My mother is just a woman... I... I haven't seen her in years."

"Is your father overbearing? Perhaps, self centered?" Arinna asked.

Max stared at her. "I thought I told you. He's an artist. What do you think? That doesn't mean he's Cerathia's son. That's insane! If that's the case why would Vish have recruited me to find you?"

"Because of her sister, who is your mother," Trina said. "It's very simple, try to keep up, won't you?"

Max shook his head again. "I told you... no... that's not possible."

"Her hair would be dark, right? Don't all of Gazric's daughters have black hair?" Trina asked, turning to Arinna.

"You don't know his world." Arinna responded, shaking her head. "Women there routinely change their hair to suit their whim."

"There are potions like that here too, but they're viciously expensive," Trina said. "Only the richest families can afford them but usually they change everything, not just their hair."

"How do you know about my world?" Max asked Arinna. "Have you been there?"

"Yes," Arinna replied, her green eyes staring off wistfully. "A long time ago."

"How is that possible?" Max replied, pointing a gauntleted finger in her direction. "You laughed at modern references I made... but I was told you've been held captive for hundreds of years. Those can't both be true."

"They can, and they are," Arinna said. "It's complicated."

"Try me," Max said.

Trina was staring at them both.

"What?" Arinna and Max said in unison.

"Uhm... you two..." she smiled.

"Go on!" Arinna snapped. "Don't stop now."

"Yeah!" Max added. "Your foot's already half in your mouth."

Trina's eyes widened and she giggled. "You're... you're quite funny."

Arinna folded her arms again, donning an annoyed expression as her head tilted back toward Max. "Regardless, your task is not complete."

"What are you talking about?" Max replied. "You're free. That's what I was supposed to do, right?"

"I can't just release you from your bond, only the dark king can do that," Arinna said. "And my father is not coming back."

"What?" Trina said. "King Gazric? How do you know?"

"Max gave me a letter from him," Arinna replied with a sigh. "That's what he said... among other things."

"Maybe it was a fake letter? Like a ploy or something," Trina suggested.

"So what?" Max asked. "If he won't or can't be king then you be queen. This is an airship. I can fly you straight to castle Dracula or wherever it is you live and drop you there."

"It's not that easy," Arinna said. "Not even close."

Max shook his head slowly. Of course it wasn't. "So what then? What do we have to do?"

∾

BRITTNEY'S EYES CRACKED OPEN. It was dark. Her face was wet. She was being rained on... why?

Oh, right, that skeleton. What a dork. He would be gone, or he should be, but she looked around for him anyway and there was nothing. Nothing but rain and the smell of burning.

Her head was throbbing. Stupid sleep powder. She'd unequipped her wakening ring so it would work, but now remembered why she'd bought it. Magic sleep always gave her a hangover.

As she sat up, she groaned, rubbing a temple with the thumb of her pure white sun steel gauntlets.

Somewhere nearby, someone made a noise.

"Who's there?" she asked, flipping up the visor of her helmet. The divine sky knight armor was such a pain. The visor was impossible to see through and it pinched her, like everywhere.

A distant bolt of lightning flashed a pulse of white, revealing something on the deck, down by the ship's back end. Whatever it was... it definitely wasn't human. The shape was odd. It jogged her memory somehow. Were those wings?

"Vita?" she asked. "Is that you?" The angel had spent too much time with her and had been forced to return to the halls of Akasa. Had Brittney slept long enough for her to return? That seemed unlikely somehow. The shape was too large to be Vita.

"Phoebe?" Brittney called. Hadn't she unsummoned the Seto eagle? She was sure she had.

I am here, but it is too soon. I cannot be summoned again.

Brittney nodded. "Ok, thanks," she replied, standing up. "Whoever you are, show yourself. I've got a headache and I feel like I gotta ralph. I'm not in the mood for games."

"Liar," said a soft male voice, just behind her right ear.

Brittney spun around. No one was there.

"I'm serious, dude," she said as she summoned her lance into her right hand and the... hey! Garem's amulet had been wrapped around the wrist joint of her right gauntlet, now it was gone.

She turned around again but was blinded by bright beaming lights of a passing airship. "Hey!" she stammered, stepping. "Give it back!"

Wind swirled around her, spraying her face and eyes with tiny droplets of rain.

"Fool," the voice said again, this time to her left.

Brittney swung her lance, lashing out, but the blade found only air.

"Stop it!" she said. "You're pissing me off!"

Then, in a flash, brilliant light poured into her eyes, forcing her to squint and use her right gauntlet to shield her eyes. A form hung in the air before her, a tall man with a weirdly shaped body and long blonde locks that hung down to his waist. He was wearing a loose-fitting robe of pure white with a long golden sash covered with glowing runes; however the vast majority of the light was coming from the white feathered wings that sprouted from both sides of his back. Each feather was like its own high powered light bulb, pulsing with a sort of musical electricity that pierced into Brittney's eyes like a sharpened tuning fork.

"Kneel mortal. Beg for mercy," he said, his thin human-like arms outstretched to either side, palms up. "Do so and I may grant it. Do not and I shall return to our lord Garem with your corpse."

His power was so great, she could feel it. The urge to kneel was growing in her with every second that passed. This wasn't just any of the angels. It had to be one of the council of light, an archangel.

Brittney could see the amulet in the creature's right hand, wrapped by thin fingers. Could she take it back from him? Probably not.

Before she'd finished her thought, Brittney realized that her right knee was already touching the metal of the deck, that her weapon had been stored in her inventory, and her helmeted head bowed. It had just happened, somehow.

"Good, now tell me of your transgressions, daughter of humankind, stranger to our world, so that I may absolve thee."

Brittney didn't want to, she wanted anything but to admit what she'd done, but her lips started moving anyway.

"I... I allowed the dark warrior to escape," she said and elation flooded her, filling her with a warm wholesome feeling of peace and love.

"How troubling. Why?" the angel asked her.

"Because... I don't think he's a bad guy... He was just trying to help her. He thinks the light is evil."

"How interesting. Do you agree with his assessment?"

"I... I have doubts."

"I see. Why?"

"The Clathians. Their leader was doing terrible things. He was-"

"Irrelevant," the angel hissed. "Your task was to deal with the dark one. You failed."

"But... Yes. I failed," she replied.

"You admit your failure.. You feel ashamed, do you not?"

"Yes," she replied. Even trying to think hurt. The light was so overwhelmingly bright, even in the rain, even reflected from the surface of the ship beneath her, it cut her, straight through to her soul.

"Given your penitence, you shall receive my blessing of mercy," the angel replied. It reached forward, putting a single finger on her helmet. "Come."

There was a white flash and everything changed. No longer was Brittney kneeling on the deck of a damaged Clathian airship in the dark of night. Now she was in the center of a raised marble platform, surrounded by sculptured columns of pure white, under a bright cloudless blue sky. Pennants of gold and white billowed from flags. The symbol of the shining sun of Cerathia was everywhere, on every flag and even engraved on the platform below her.

There were priests of light also. They too wore white and stood in a circle surrounding the platform. The oldest and most ornate of them approached, his head lowered. In his hands was a golden cup but instead of approaching the angel, who now floated to Brittney's right, he came to her. The man bent and offered her the cup.

Only now did Brittney realize she was still on her knees. Only now it wasn't just one, but both, and her hands were already reaching for the cup.

"Take this cup and drink from it," the angel stated. "This is the blood of our everlasting covenant. Cerathia's gift to Fohra, that she has shed for you all."

Brittney's gauntleted fingers closed around the gilded goblet, filled with the softly glowing white gold blood of the purest creatures of light, of angels. As she did this something stirred deep within her, a powerful fright that quickly grew into panic. It was made far worse by the fact that her body was still. Her lips were frozen. She was like a doll, a marionette, going through motions planned by others.

"Be not afraid mortal," the angel said. "This will allow you to survive the transition."

Then before she could say or do anything, she was drinking. It felt like pure heat flowing into her body. It was like the time she'd broken into her father's expensive liquor cabinet and downed an entire glass of scotch... only about a thousand times worse. The burn only started in her throat but it continued on, filling her entire body with a horrific searing sensation. It felt like her flesh would burn away and she'd be nothing but bones, like that skeleton.

"The way is open and this hero of light has been prepared. She now joins Cerathia above you all. Rejoice!" the angel said.

"Rejoice!" the priests cried as one.

Then symbols embedded in the floor around her began to glow. She hadn't even noticed them before but now they were plain as day as were others running up and down the columns that surrounded her.

There was a brilliant flash and she watched as white flames erupted from below her. In only moments they grew into a great holy conflagration that surrounded her and the angel as well. The priests were chanting something but she couldn't make it out because the roar of the fire was so loud.

She was being consumed by holy fire. It hurt so much. Why did it hurt so much?

3

A SCRUFF HUNT AND AN
ORNERY OWL

"We can't fly to castle Kharan Khul. The land of the dead is on a different plane entirely. The only way to get there is through a portal made for that purpose," Arinna said.

"So we find one then," Max said. "Where's the nearest one?"

"They're all gone," Trina said. "Melnax told me about this. The light had them destroyed."

"Yes and no," Arinna said. "They had to leave at least one."

Trina frowned. "Why?"

"Because the light and dark realms are connected," Arinna said.

Max and Trina both stared at her, their mouths agape.

"It's true. We are two sides of the same coin. My father used to say it often, but I never listened to him. I thought I knew better," Arinna chuckled bitterly.

"So a portal that takes you to one can go to the other," Max said.

Arinna nodded, "Exactly. If the light destroyed them all they wouldn't be able to enter this plane at will. That would make it very hard to control the people here."

"So where is a light portal then?" Max asked.

"I don't know," Arinna said. "You might not realize this but I've been held in confinement for a little while."

Max nodded. "Yeah, I get it. What does it look like? Is it something we might have seen somewhere? I've seen some crazy crap in this place."

Arinna smiled. "I'm sure you have," she sighed, trying to think through his question. "I don't know... it doesn't look like a door so much as a sort of circle of power. Powerful ancient runes arrayed around a central point."

"So like Stonehenge, kind of," Max said.

Arinna nodded.

"I don't know what a Stonehenge is, but I think I might know where that portal is," Trina said.

Max and Arinna looked at her.

"Maybe," Trina continued. "My father is a member of a powerful guild of engineers. He's traveled all over the kingdoms of light to work on various projects."

"You're not telling us he worked on the portal, are you? That would have been hundreds of years ago," Arinna said.

"No," Trina said. "But when we had to go to the floating city of Ghrellen when I was a child, I remember his talking about how he was supposed to re-build a bridge around a powerful magical object surrounded by tall columns. He was annoyed because they had to use big equipment and they'd been told that if they broke a column the consequences would be serious."

"Ghrellen... Isn't that the same trip where you lost your airship?" Max asked.

Trina nodded. "I'm impressed you remembered that."

Max shrugged. "Me too. So Ghrellen then. Is that what I'm hearing?"

"We can't just go there!" Trina said. "That's a core kingdom, part of the trinity cities."

"So it'll be well defended?" Max asked.

Trina nodded. "Incredibly. Especially now. I'm sure they'll know Arinna has escaped."

"That's right," Arinna replied. "They will be waiting for us."

"We'll figure something out," Max said. "I'm not about to give up now."

Arinna smiled, "Thank you! I was hoping you'd say that." Then, before Max could even react, she leaned in and kissed him on his right cheek bone.

"Uh..." he said.

Trina giggled.

Max was about to say something else when something clanked against his left leg. He looked down to see the automaton knocking its metal knuckles against Max's armor.

"Uh... hey... robot," Max said. "What's up?"

"You said we'd decide where the ship should go," the robot said.

This made Trina jump back with surprise. "He can talk normally?!"

Max nodded. "Yep, I guess he was holding out on us."

"A demonic automaton!" Arinna said, bending down to pat the creature on its head. "I haven't seen one of these in so many centuries! I thought they were gone."

The automaton seemed to like the pats and leaned into it.

"I was taught they only existed in museums," Trina said, "but we got this one from some dark pirates."

"The Sky People still exist?" Arinna asked. "That's not surprising I suppose. They were always resilient. I can't tell you how many times the light exterminated the pirate clans only to have them crop back up seemingly out of nowhere."

"Actually, the Black Skull pirates are waiting for us right now," Trina said. "We have a rendezvous location up the coast."

The way Arinna was petting the automaton reminded Max of something... something important.

Scruff!

"Where's Scruff?" Max asked, looking around. "I didn't see him when I came in..."

"Oh..." Trina said, her eyes dropping to the deck. "About that."

He's gone.

"Whaaaaat?!" Max shouted.

From outside the room, the spider pointed toward the back of the ship with one of her long legs.

They jumped out of the ship after you.

Max stared at Trina. "Mytten says-"

"I know!" Trina snapped. "They jumped! I was unconscious at the time. There was nothing I could do and I had my own problems."

"You couldn't go back for them?" Max asked. "You couldn't even look for them?"

"No!" Trina said. "I told you... we got boarded and-"

"You got boarded? By who?" Max asked.

"By whom," Arinna said.

Max stared at her. "Did you just correct my English?"

Arinna did a kind of half-smile at him.

"What's English?" Trina asked.

"I..." Max looked back and forth between the two women. Both were staring at him, waiting. He didn't have time for this. "I need to find Scruff and his little buddies. They depend on me. They're the most loyal friends I have, except for Mytten."

Trina frowned. "Hey!"

"How can we find them? Where could they be?" Max asked.

Arinna tilted her head. "What is a Scruff?"

"Uh... they're dungeon crawlers. Tentacles and teeth, and that's about it," Max replied.

"Ah," Arinna said, putting a finger to her chin. "Those creatures have an excellent sense of smell. It's likely they tracked you through the ocean. You found me on the beach, then we went into the cave-"

"Right!" Max said. "And we burned everything to death in there."

"Including me," Arinna said. "But that's alright, it wasn't your fault. Then I ran away."

"After kicking me in the chest," Max added.

"And you caught up with me on the beach."

"Wow, you two," Trina said, shaking her head.

They both stopped. "Hush!" Arinna said.

"We're trying to think this through," Max said.

Trina rolled her eyes.

"Then the Clathians stole you," Max said.

"And you fell into the water again," Arinna added. "Then what happened?"

"Uh... I was pretty pissed. I walked back out onto the beach... Oh! I killed this Slayer who's been following me since my first day in this place and I stole his airship."

"What happened then?" Arinna asked.

"The ship was a trap, it took me way out into the ocean and crashed."

"So they probably couldn't have followed you after that," Trina said.

Max took off toward the bridge. "Tela!" he yelled.

The ship turned hard to the right before diving down beneath the clouds. Max switched to Dark Summoner so that the Shadow Staff would have greater power with his higher stats. It wasn't long before the chain of barrier islands along Clathia's eastern coast came into view. They had to follow them south for a while before they came to the island Max and Arinna had been on.

"What's that?" Trina said. "There's a light."

"It looks like a campfire," Arinna said, leaning in.

"Huh," Max said. "Let's see who it is. Tela, bring us in backwards, I'll come down the cargo ramp."

"Absolutely!" Tela answered cheerily.

The ramp slammed to the ground and Max stomped down the metal surface to find that the single figure that had been sitting next to the campfire was now trying to hide behind a nearby bush, poorly. He was holding a sharpened stick like a spear, only it wasn't nearly big enough and he just looked silly.

"Get back!" he called.

Even though the dawn was soon to come, Max could still see well enough to tell something had been going on here. There was a ring of partially burned sticks arrayed around the campfire, like a kind of half-assed protective circle.

"By the grace of Gazric, what are you?" a frightened voice asked.

Max laughed. "Your worst nightmare."

"Go away! I didn't want to summon you or anyone. I just want to be left alone... please! I beg you!" the voice said. The voice was unfamiliar to Max, it sounded male, but a little bit haughty and obnoxious. It reminded him of Vish and not in a good way.

"I didn't come for you," Max said. "I'm looking for someone."

A loud hiss came from Max's right. It was followed by several others. Only seconds later, Scruff burst from the brush to his right. Even though the crawler was now easily two feet larger than before, Max immediately knew it was him. He bent down and opened up his arms for a hug.

Max! Max!

Several other smaller dungeon crawlers burst from their own hiding places and they all trundled at top speed to crash into Max's skeletal body, wrapping their tentacles around him and slathering his bones in slimy gooey licks.

"Oh lord! What are those beasts doing?"

"These guys," Max said, patting Scruff and his smaller clones, who had also grown by quite a bit, "are my friends."

"Just keep them away!" the voice called. "They've been attacking me since I got here. Only the fire keeps them at bay. I can't sleep... I can't even close my eyes or I get poisoned!"

"Reken?" Trina asked as she stomped down the open cargo bay door. "Is that you?"

The creature let out a little shriek of surprise and fell forward in the sand, dropping his makeshift spear. "Oh please! No! I know what I did was terrible... I'm so sorry! Please... Please don't torture me any more."

"Torture you?" Trina asked. "Max what's going on?"

Max stood up, completely covered in writhing dungeon crawlers. Now that Scruff was the size of a large dog, his limbs could wrap Max's body almost completely, making it look like he too was made of tentacles. He was strong enough, even as a Dark Summoner, that the weight of the creatures wasn't a problem, which was nice.

"I'm reconnecting with my pals. What do you think is going on?" He pointed a bony thumb in the direction of the prostrate creature, who looked to be some kind of bird person. "Do you know this guy?"

"We've met," Trina said.

"Did you find them?" Arinna called from the ship.

"Yep!" Max called back. He turned back to the groveling creature. "Look, buddy, if you know Trina that's enough for me. You can catch a ride with us if you want. Clathia is pretty crazy right now. It's gonna get ugly for people of the dark. We're heading out of this place. I'd suggest you do also."

"Max... I'm not sure that's a good idea," Trina said.

"Oh glorious night! I'm saved!" the creature cried as tears welled in his eyes. "Thank you so much. You... you wouldn't have any food would you?"

Max shrugged. "I don't eat, ask Trina."

"But.... Max!" Trina called after him but Max was already heading up the ramp. "Arinna, meet Scruff and Scruff two and Scruff three, and Scruff four and Scruff five."

"They're adorable!" she replied, smiling. "They really like you."

"Or maybe I just smell like a dead carcass," he replied.

Arinna chuckled. "I'm sure that helps!"

They were in the sky and heading toward the rendezvous only a few moments later and shortly after that everyone convened again on the bridge.

"Why are we here?" Trina asked, looking sullen for some reason.

The owl-like bird creature Reken, who it turned out was called an ullu, was standing next to the doctor, devouring a large lump of cured meat. "I assume our illustrious skeleton captain has orders for us," Reken said.

"Actually," Max replied, gesturing to the woman to his left. "I'm not in charge here: she is."

Arinna nodded. "Thank you Max. As some of you may not know who I am, let me state it here for the record. I am Arinna, daughter of Gazric, King in exile of the dark."

At this the ullu's yellow eyes widened and he did a spit take. A chunk of meat flew from his mouth and hit the wall before sliding to the floor where it was instantly snatched by a loitering dungeon crawler.

Trina frowned and used a fist to thump the bird man in his left shoulder.

"Long was I last in line for the throne of the dark, but now that my sisters are gone, I am all that remains. Though my father and I have not always seen eye to eye, we do agree on some things," she said, glancing toward Max. "As such, I intend to return to Uhksaan, the land of the dead, where I will assume my father's mantle and claim the throne as queen."

The ullu clapped his free hand against the side of the meat he was holding. "Hear, hear! I for one am all for it!"

"None of that is going to be easy," Trina said, sounding annoyed. "Assuming we even get to the portal, we'll have to activate it."

"I know how to do that," Arinna said, "more or less."

Max looked at her, "More or less?"

"I've seen it done," Arinna replied, "but I'm not a necromancer."

"Why does that matter?" Trina asked.

"Because that's the kind of magic we need to forge a path to the plane of the dead," Arinna said.

"But you're a god, aren't you?" Max said. "Can't you do anything?"

Arinna's green eyes cast down. "Yeah... about that."

"What? What's happened?" Max asked.

"I may be a god, but while I'm here I'm subject to the rules of this world. I have a class like anyone else and levels... or... I did have levels."

Trina's eyes widened. "They stole your power?"

Arinna nodded. "Yes. That's what the Clathian was doing prior to his attempt to kill me. He was using a scion to drain me."

"Vish said something about that. How bad is it?" Max asked.

"Well... I'm currently level one, skill one."

Max was floored. This entire time he'd been expecting that when he got to Arinna everything would be easier. "Crap," he said.

"I learn fast though," Arinna interjected. "I promise I won't hold us back."

"What class are you?" Trina asked.

"Grave Blade," she replied.

Trina frowned. "But that's..."

"A prestige class," Arinna said, with a shrug. "Apparently the scion couldn't undo what I'd unlocked."

"What else do you have access to?" Max asked.

"Rogue, Assassin, Ronin, and Dark Samurai," she replied.

"Wow," Max said.

"You are," Trina cleared her throat, "very focused."

"On murder," the ullu said through a mouthful of meat. "Goddess of death is right."

Trina chuckled a little, then her face changed and she looked angry at herself. Max was seriously starting to wonder what was up with her.

"This isn't a disaster," Max said. "We can get you levels. I've got a few things up my sleeves for that."

"What sleeves?" the bird man asked. Now that Max had a good look at him, he looked more like an owl actually.

Max looked down at his cloak and boots. He hadn't gotten anything specific to wear as a Dark Summoner or Dark Mage. His rib cage was still hanging out. It would be good to remedy that sometime soon.

"It's a figure of speech," Arinna said. "It means he has some ideas."

"I also have some equipment," Max said. "I don't know how much of it you can use, but I liberated a great deal from... ah... from the temple where I became a Dread Knight."

"That's a great start," Arinna said.

"We need to decide what we're going to do," Trina said. "There needs to be a plan. 'Get to the portal and jump in' isn't good enough. We need more than that."

"I agree completely," Arinna replied. "It will be heavily guarded. Even if I regain some of my former strength we'll be up against the light's best. They'll do anything to prevent my return."

"There's a group of ships up ahead!" Tela announced. "I believe it's our friends."

"Thank you Tela," Max said.

"And it looks like they're under attack!" Tela added with no small amount of excitement.

4

PARTY ON AND BE EXCELLENT TO EACHOTHER

Max turned around to look out the forward viewport, shielding his eyes from the morning sun that was just peeking over the horizon to his right. On the ground ahead were three funny-looking airships. They were sleeker than any he'd seen so far but they were currently inert with no one around.

"Where?" he asked. "I see some ships but that's it."

"Look to your left," Tela replied. "Do you see the fire?"

Max couldn't, but he could see a small column of smoke rising from the center of a small stand of trees.

"I see it," Arinna said, putting a hand on Max's shoulder. "Maybe I can earn a level or two."

Max nodded. "Sure. Set us down, Tela. Let's have a look."

"I'll stay here and mind the ship," Reken said, raising one of his clawed avian fingers.

"Sounds good," Max said. He and Arinna left the bridge toward the back of the ship, heading for the cargo bay.

"I'll be staying behind," Trina said. "Please leave Mytten here also."

Max turned back. "Why?"

"There isn't time to explain fully," Trina replied, "but suffice it to say that Reken has already tried to steal this ship once. I'd rather he didn't get another chance."

Arinna's eyebrows raised. "I see."

Max looked up at the huge spider perched on the ceiling above.

I agree. He is untrustworthy.

"Alright," Max said, turning to Arinna. "Looks like it's just us."

Tentacles almost ripped Max's legs off from both directions. He looked down to find Scruff and his pals holding on for dear life.

"Ok! Ok! You guys can come too," he said.

Max stepped out of the back of the Midnight into relatively open terrain with only a few sparse trees. There was grass, tall grass that waved in the hot breeze. Even with the sun barely above the horizon the heat had already taken hold. If Max actually had any flesh it might be bothersome, Scruff, who was currently hanging from Max's back, was panting loudly. As were the two other smaller dungeon crawlers that had stuffed themselves into his rib cage. The others had glommed onto Arinna. Actually, that made him wonder about...

Arinna had already waded into the tall grass. She saw him looking at her and paused.

"What?"

"Uh... I was wondering if you're gonna burn up in the sun," he said.

"No," she replied and forged on in the direction of the smoke ahead.

"So you're not a vampire then? Or maybe you're that special kind that sparkles," Max said.

"Har har," she said. "That's not how it works here. Vampires and werewolves are different from the stories on Earth."

"I know about werewolves," he said. "I met several."

"Good," Arinna said, trudging forward through the brush. The gray leather armor he'd taken from one of the unfortunate failures at the Dread Knight temple fit her very nicely. She'd called it Dusk Leather armor and apparently it was tier three equipment, significantly better than the black leather he'd been using as a Breeder. That wasn't too surprising though, he hadn't really had time to dig through everything he got there.

Though what would really be great, now that he thought about it, would be to get back into that dragon hoard. There had been an unbelievable amount of stuff in there.

Actually, that made him wonder how the dragon they'd met was doing. It might be a good idea to check on him, maybe soak him for some more cash. Would he want plastic surgery? Perhaps a smaller nose horn? Could be worth investigating.

For weapons, Arinna had taken a short bow with arrows and a familiar looking sword that she called a muruul. It looked a lot like a katana, except the blade was a little shorter and the back edge was serrated. Arinna said it was usually part of a set of two: the muruul ri, but the second weapon was missing. Grave Blade was looking kind of like a Ninja, which would be super helpful, if he could get Arinna some levels.

"Oh... actually," Max said.

She turned back, annoyed. "What now?"

This made him pause.

Arinna frowned. "Sorry. I'm a little impatient. I haven't killed anything in a long time."

"Will you join my party?"

"I thought you'd never ask," she said, smiling a little.

"Well... I just... you know... want to be able to see your stats and stuff."

"Sure, let's go," she said.

Max tagged along behind, pulling up his display.

"Add Arinna to party," he said. After all the crap he'd been through, it felt good to say that.

Arinna has joined the party.

"Arinna status," he said.

Dutifully, his display came up.

Status	Arinna		
Level	1	Grave Blade Skill	1
Health	11/11		
Magic	1/1	Affinity	Wanderlust
Skills		Magic	
Veil of Shadow, Blur, Lethal strike, rekindle			
Strength	14	Attacks x 1	7
Agility	18	Accuracy	74%
		Defense	5
Vitality	9	Evasion	9%
Mind	5	Magic Defense	3
		Magic Evasion	4%

"Ouch," he said.

"Yeah I'd rather you didn't look at that," she said.

"No worries," he replied. "I've been there."

Actually he'd had it much worse. Even at level one, Arinna had no negative penalty to her stats. He didn't have big numbers for quite some time. More importantly, Max knew exactly how fast prestige classes like Grave Blade powered up. Soon she would be ripping paladins apart with her bare hands. He was looking forward to seeing that, like a lot.

Even better, Arinna had rekindle, the same ability he had that brought him back to life after he died. That was very good to see. The last thing he wanted was to lose her to a stray crossbow bolt in some throw away battle and then be hunting around for a demon scale. It didn't mean she was invulnerable, but it was a big help.

Max summoned his Shadow staff into his right hand. If things got hairy he could use it on Arinna and give her some breathing room. Given his level, his own health was more than high enough to deal with whatever they were likely to encounter out here in the countryside and as a Dark Summoner he had access to all his spells and all his summons.

Bite! Bite! Bite!

"Absolutely, guys," Max said. "You can bite 'em all."

"Shhhh!" Arinna said. She was crouched up ahead, only a small part of her ahead above the grass.

Max hadn't even been paying attention. Oops.

She gestured for him to join her so he crouched and approached.

Arinna pointed ahead. They'd crested a rise and were now looking down a smooth slope of grasses toward the stand of trees they'd seen on approach. There was only one problem though, one small change from how it had been before. There was a huge guy standing over the trees. No, not like a seven foot NBA center, like a forty to fifty foot tall giant dude. The guy was wearing regular clothes like any normal sized person would, only they were just as huge as he was and he was using a stripped tree trunk to prod into the woods.

It looked like there were regular size people hiding in between the trees and they were hurling fire bombs at the huge guy's feet. Fires had burned circles into the grass in several places, but each time a new bomb was thrown, the giant would stomp it until the fire went out.

"I'm bettin' our pirates are in those woods," Max said, quietly.

"I thought giants were extinct," Arinna said.

"So that's a giant," Max said. "Are they weak to anything?"

She looked at him. "What do you mean?"

"Uh... I used a tiny potion to go to an Arachnian village. While we were tiny, physical attacks were useless and even weak hits did huge damage, but magic worked like normal."

"You've been busy!" she said.

"Yeah, well... I didn't exactly know where you were."

"No," she said, looking back down the slope.

"No, what?" he asked.

"No, they don't have any weaknesses," she replied. "A giant's skin is stronger than dark steel and twenty times as thick, their strength is incredible and they're faster than they look."

"So nuke it with magic?"

"Natural resistance to all magic," Arinna said. "Though they don't have a troll's regeneration, they're better in every other respect. When I was a girl, they formed the spearhead of my father's most devastating armies."

"So this guy might be on our side?"

"No," Arinna said. "They left the dark more than a thousand years ago. Giants are part of the light."

"Crap."

WELL, once again it was time to figure something out. His specialty. Max stood up and started walking toward the giant.

"You stay here," he said. "I've got an idea."

"Max!" Arinna said. "What are you doing? He'll smash you flat! His attacks can do thousands of damage."

"Maybe he's just cranky," Max yelled back over his shoulder. "You think of that? Maybe he's got like a hang nail the size of a coffee table."

She ran up next to him.

"Hey!" Max said. "You get back there. You're level one!"

"Sorry," Arinna replied. "but you can't order me around. If you're going, so am I."

Max shook a boney finger at her for a moment, but gave up. She was right.

"What are you going to do?" she asked.

"I have no idea," Max replied. "I'm winging it."

"You're crazy!" she said, but she was smiling.

"Crazy like a dead fox," Max replied. He was about half way down the hill now, the giant could probably hear him. "HEY TALL GUY!" he bellowed. "HEY! OVER HERE!"

The giant was ignoring him. It continued to use the stripped tree trunk to poke into the small stand of woods. The action reminded Max of a child poking an ant hill.

"Alright, I guess we need to get his attention in a different way."

Max stored his staff and brought his hands together to summon a Bolt lance, aiming it carefully. The blue lightning shot a straight line that went right in front of the giant's face.

"Shot across the bow," Max said. "That's got to get his attention."

"I'm not sure we want his attention," Arinna said.

The huge head turned toward Max and Arinna. Two gigantic gray eyes the size of basketballs looked straight at them for a fraction of a second, before turning back. The giant resumed his prodding.

"COME OUT A THERE!" the giant bellowed. The noise was deafening. Max was really glad he didn't actually have eardrums.

"Maybe we can shoot him with the ship's guns?" Arinna wondered, her hands on her hips.

Max looked at her. "I like how you think." He held up a boney finger. "However, I'm holding out hope for a peaceful solution."

Arinna chuckled. "I don't know why... but..."

Max shrugged. "Humor me." He fired another bolt lance at the giant, but this time he aimed for the creature's left leg. The blue lightning cut a neat line through the fabric of a monster-size pant leg, making a hole big enough to drive a truck through.

"That got his attention," Arinna said.

The giant's brow furrowed as he looked down at his still smoking slashed pants. Then he turned toward them.

"STAY OUT 'A THIS!" he roared. "IT'S NONE 'A YER BUSINESS!"

"YES IT IS!" Max yelled back, both skeletal hands cupped to the sides of his lip-less mouth, for all the good it would do. "I CAME HERE TO MEET MY FRIENDS!"

"GO AWAY SKELETON!" the giant yelled. "WE DON'T WANT YER KIND HERE!"

"Well that's not very nice," Max said. "That's undead discrimination."

Arinna chuckled.

"Should I continue cutting his clothes apart?"

"He's not really leaving you much choice," she said. "Though I still don't know why you're purposely annoying him."

"That makes two of us," Max said as he fired a third bolt lance. This one he aimed at the giant's left arm, slicing part of the cuff from his baggy shirt. The magic wasn't even leaving a mark on the creature's skin. Apparently whatever resistance this guy had, it was strong enough to completely nullify a tier two spell from an upgraded class. That was fine though, Max wasn't trying to actually hurt him.

"I SAID LEAVE!" the giant shouted. Or maybe he wasn't shouting, maybe that was just how loud his voice was because he was so huge. "STOP RIPPIN' MY CLOTHES!"

"Can't do that," Max said, clearly a third Bolt lance was in order.

As Max was charging up the spell, another small bomb flew out of the forest. This one landed right on the giant's left foot. As he was wearing sandals, something Max hadn't noticed until this moment, the bomb exploded on the big toe, setting alight the hair that grew on its top.

The hot foot. Classic.

"OW! OW! OWWWW!" the giant whined as he stomped in a small circle, shaking his foot. Every time the creature's colossal feet slammed the ground it felt like a mini quake.

Max let loose his lightning bolt, but despite its speed the shot missed the jumping giant completely. Arinna was right: those things could move fast when they wanted to.

"You're pretty quick as a Grave Blade, would you scamper off into those trees and tell them to get ready to run?"

"Now you're telling me to run toward the danger?" she asked.

"No, I'm asking you to do something useful," he replied, "politely."

"You don't have to get snippy," she replied. "I'll do it. Just don't get yourself crushed into bone dust."

"No promises," he said.

Arinna rolled her eyes and took off running down the slope. Even at level one her movements were hard to follow. She seemed to naturally blend into the grass around her, even moving in time with the blowing wind that rolled across the plains that surrounded them. The Shadow staff, given how poorly it worked in daylight, would have a marginal help at best.

Max took a second to check his magic.

348/416 MP

"We're good," he told Scruff, who had pulled himself up to hang his mouth over Max's right shoulder. A long line of drool was dribbling onto Max's clavicle. "Oh you want a taste of that big guy huh?"

Smell good.

By which Scruff meant the giant smelled rotten like the rancid things Scruff preferred to eat. Max hadn't noticed it before, but the crawler was right, there was a sort of sweet scent in the air. The smell of the smoke had masked it somewhat. As a Dark Summoner Max didn't share his creature's senses in the same way as the Breeder.

"What do you think that is?" Max wondered.

Bite!

Bite! Bite! That was the other two in Max's rib cage chiming in.

"Alright, well we don't have time for a round table on this," he said. The giant had gotten over his singed toes and was now bending over to pick up his tree trunk. Any second he could notice Arinna. "I guess let's try Thundercrack... wait," Arinna had said resistance to magic damage and physical damage but the old First Fantasy games had a third type.

He started running, straight at the giant.

"HEY! LOOK OVER HERE!" Max yelled as he ran as fast as his mediocre agility score would allow. At skill level thirty-seven he was only slightly faster than Arinna at level one. Nuts.

The giant wasn't paying attention. He was rearing back for a wide slash with his tree trunk.

"I SWEAR I'LL CUT YOUR PANTS APART!" Max screamed.

That got him.

A very angry looking giant whirled in Max's direction and lunged. In the span of only a few seconds a gigantic left hand had closed around him and was lifting him into the sky at incredible speed.

729 damage received.

"Ow!" Max said as he was brought up in front of a gargantuan face.

"NO!" the giant roared, his hot breath washed over Max, blowing the hood off of his skull. "I WON'T LET YA!"

The fist closed tighter, crushing him.

1119 damage received.

"Dude," Max said. "You need to brush your teeth."

Bite! Bite! Bite!

"OWWWWWWW!!!" the Giant shouted as his fist instantly snapped open. Max fell forty or so feet to crack into the ground below.

13 damage received.

The first thing he did was look up to where the giant was rapidly shaking his hand, trying to dislodge Scruff and his two tentacled comrades as they bit deeply into his flesh.

A hand grabbed Max's elbow, pulling him to his feet. It was Arinna.

"You're back," he said.

"They won't do any damage to him," she said.

Max waved his hand. "I don't care about that," he replied. "They're currently pumping his ass full of some nasty poison."

"Ah," she said. "Status damage."

Max nodded. "Exactly. I thought about putting him to sleep with a powder, but that way we couldn't negotiate."

"You're not going to be able to negotiate with him," Arinna said. "He acts like a spoiled child."

"Teenager, actually," a man's voice said from nearby.

5

TOO MANY STEPS AND A VERY
FRIENDLY PIRATE

The pain was ending, as was the blinding light, and Brittney found herself on her side on a floor covered with discarded paper. Though it was clearly hard underneath, she guessed some kind of stone or brick, the papers were plastered together so completely that it was impossible to tell for sure.

She looked around. She was in some kind of hallway. It was long and thin and seemed to go on forever. A quick glance behind showed the same. Endless in both directions.

"Cool beans," she said, pushing herself up.

It felt weird here, like she was super light. It made getting up difficult. Her legs felt wobbly, unsure what to do to carry her forward. Just the slightest move made her careen in the wrong direction.

Was this the land of the angels? If she was back home, she might call it heaven, but she'd been here in Fohra long enough to know better. The angels here weren't like the ones that watched over your shoulder and helped you find your way in life, like that TV show she used to watch with her mother when she was a little girl.

Those had been good times for her. The angel show and that other one with the girl in the old west. The two of them had set up together on the couch and eaten grilled cheese with sweet pickle slices hidden inside and canned tomato soup. Back when her mother had been sober.

Things were starting to come together in her mind. She'd been brought here. That creepy angel had done it. They'd forced her to drink that gross metallic gunk. Then she'd burned.

Brittney inspected her body. She wasn't wearing armor anymore, that had been replaced by a white sleeveless tee and Jordache jeans, her jeans. It was like she was back at home. Only she wasn't. Not even close.

There was a sort of dry wind running through the hallway but it didn't make any noise. Nothing did. Except for her own voice and her feet as they scuffed against the paper laden floor, there was no sound coming from anywhere.

"I do not like this, Sam I am," she said, partly just to hear something. "I do not want green eggs and ham."

This was new. Brittney had been a chosen warrior of light, what they called a Sikari, for more than a thousand years of Fohra time. Never had she been brought here. As far as she knew, no one had.

Maybe, if she looked around, she could find her own way out.

Above, there was a ceiling but it was at least thirty feet up. There appeared to be some pattern up there, or maybe some pictures, but she couldn't make out any of it. Actually, now that she looked up she saw doors. They were about twenty feet up and spaced pretty evenly but there was no way to get to them. They were just stuck into the wall, with no ledge, no ladder.

She thought about trying to jump. Her body did feel lighter. Maybe it was possible.

Brittney sighed as she walked over to the wall of the hallway. "What did they do? Forget about me?"

"Oh no," a voice replied. "We would never do that."

Brittney turned around but there was nothing there... well... maybe? There was a sort of lightness there, a kind of moving transparent something, like a film of plastic wrap suspended in the air.

"Who are you?" she asked. "Why did you bring me here?"

"My name is not for the ears of your kind," came the reply.

"I see," she said. "You're an ass, just like Garem."

"Your distaste for the emperor hasn't stopped you from repeatedly trying to lay with him," the voice said.

Brittney folded her arms. "Who cares?" she replied. "I can hate a guy and still want to fool around. I'm a nineties girl."

"Revolting," the voice replied.

"Why can't I see you?" she asked.

"What you see here is only what your tiny human brain can comprehend."

She kicked some papers. "What I see looks like a train wreck. Do you guys ever clean?"

"Be silent," the voice said. "Your hearing will begin soon."

"When is soon?" she asked. "And what do you mean by hearing?"

There was no answer, only a soft pffft noise as the plastic cling wrap evaporated.

Brittney sighed angrily. Stupid angels.

Wait a minute, she was here in angel town, Akasa or whatever they called it. It seemed like the light had a hundred different names for the same thing. Wouldn't Vita be here? All Vita ever did was yak about rules and procedures. If there was anyone who could explain things, it was the flying puppy angel.

"Vita!" she called, turning around in a circle. It was still the same in both directions. One long perfectly straight hall, that went off forever.

There was no response either. There wasn't even an echo. Freaky.

She touched her right wrist, expecting to see the display. Nothing came up.

"What?" she snapped. "What the hell is going on?"

Brittney couldn't take it anymore. She started walking. She didn't even care if it didn't go anywhere. She just wanted to be moving. It helped her think.

The paper crunched under her converse tennis shoes as she walked, trying to focus. Why were they having a hearing? Oh... oh, no!

She remembered. That asshole angel had forced her to confess that she helped that skeleton.

"Dammit!" she snapped.

No doubt he'd use the same power in her hearing and make her tell Garem the same thing. He'd promised to send her home as an old woman.

Brittney frowned. Would that be so bad? She'd been in this world a long time. She missed a lot of things, like her favorite shows, Cali beaches, skiing in Utah, and renting videos for a cozy weekend. All of that stuff was back on Earth.

The entertainment here sucked. If you didn't like watching self absorbed nobles prove their strength by fighting weakened monsters or hearing people talk forever about how awesome Cerathia was, you were out of luck. Though Brittney hadn't ever actually seen the goddess. At this point she was starting to wonder if that woman was a figment of everyone's collective imagination.

All her favorite things were back at home, but even if she returned would things be the same? How old would she be when she got back? Eighty? Ninety? It would be like twenty forty or something. Everything would be different! People would probably have flying cars and big fat computer chips drilled into their skulls.

Ugh, gross.

No. She didn't want to go back. Brittney had more power here than she'd ever had at home, even in her dreams. She had to get out of this endless hallway before the angel came back. Somehow.

"Hey, girl," a voice whispered.

Brittney stopped, dead. "Huh?"

"Quiet!" it said. "Keep walking for another two hundred and thirty two paces, then turn right and walk straight into the wall."

Brittney frowned, "What?"

"Shhh!" the voice replied.

"Vita?" she asked. "Is that you?"

There was a soft chuckle. "No. Now do it."

"I..." she said, but trailed off, unsure what to say. She didn't have any choice did she? It was either wait around until cling wrap angel came back, or listen to the mystery voice and try to actually do something about her situation.

So... how many steps? Shit! She'd forgotten!

She opened her mouth to ask.

"Two hundred and thirty two," the voice whispered, sounding a little irritated. "Now start walking."

"Ok," she said and started. There were so many steps to count. Why did they expect her to do that? What a horrible task! She didn't even count sheep! Now wait, she was going to lose count, she needed to stop thinking about counting and just count!

Uh... where was she? Right: twenty-seven. Keep counting. Just keep counting Britt.

It felt like eons went by while she counted and counted, but finally, she came to the end.

Two hundred and thirty-one. Two hundred and thirty-two.

Brittney turned right, stepped toward the wall... and she was someplace else.

Instantly the world had changed around her, and not for the better. Now she was in a cramped closet sized space. Every inch of space in the room was filled with discarded, yellowed old papers. They were plastered to the walls and ceiling, stacked in piles as tall as she was, stuffed into shelves, and of course, coating the floor. Directly in front of her though, was a dingy looking desk and at that desk sat a figure wearing a thick oversized trench coat. Long blonde hair hung down from a small head, all the way to the floor.

"Where is this?" she asked. "Who are you?"

"I'll be right with you," said a soft child-like voice. This was not the voice she'd heard before.

"Vita?" she asked.

"I said, one moment," the voice said. "I just need to finish this."

Brittney realized there was feverish scribbling going on at the desk. She leaned in, trying to see what was going on.

The scribbling stopped. This was followed by an exasperated sigh.

Brittney got the message. She leaned back again and the scribbling continued.

This was taking so long! What the hell was this place? Argh!

"You," the voice said softly. This was followed by a flourish of several other scribbles. "Are very impatient."

Then a paper slid from the desk and flew through the air in the tiny room, swirling twice before it slapped against the wall near the ceiling and there it stayed.

With a creak, the chair began to turn and with it came the sound of clinking chains. Sitting in a chair, was what looked like a frail old woman. Like the angel Brittney had seen in Clathia, this one had long platinum blonde hair but it was frayed and graying and her eyes were like nothing Brittney had ever seen. The irises were pure white. The only way to tell they were there at all was the soft golden outline that ran around the outside edge and at the very center.

She wore a simple white tunic and over that, the huge coat, which made it look like she was one of three children that had been standing together inside the closed coat, trying to pass as an adult. She was so small in stature that her feet, clad only in simple sandals, didn't touch the floor, but the most surprising element of all was the golden shackle connected to her right ankle.

"You're not Vita," Brittney said.

The angel frowned. "Yeah? What tipped you off?"

"Hi!" Max said, turning to his right toward the middle-aged man jogging in their direction. Behind him was a woman, also jogging, but holding her skirts up as she did. The two of them looked like they'd just walked right out of a fairy tale. "Would you be the woodcutter and this is your wife?"

The man laughed, his thick black mustache fluffing up and down as he did. "Not much wood around here, is there. There'll be none if Rogald has his way," he said, nodding toward the giant who was still shaking his hand. In the background one of the dungeon crawlers lost its grip and was flung hundreds of feet off into the distance. "You were right about one thing," the man added, gesturing toward the woman coming up behind him, panting. "This is my wife, Grentella."

The heavy-set woman immediately pointed a thick finger at Arinna. "How dare you call our boy spoiled! Why I've half a mind to strangle that scrawny neck of yours!"

Max looked at Arinna, who seemed just as surprised as he was.

"Now, now Grenty, let's try an' be civilized," the man said, stepping in front of his red-faced wife. "Mr. Skeleton. Would you be kind enough to call off your little beasts?"

"OWWWW!" Rogald bellowed, though his speech was slurring. "DAH! THEYYYY POISONNNNED... MEEE..." Then the giant's eyelids fluttered and everyone ran as he crashed to the ground, hitting the side of their hill like an anvil dropped into a pile of sand. There was an enormous thump and the ground seemed to shiver for a few seconds afterward. No one was crushed though, which was good.

"I'm sorry about the poison," Max said. "It was all I could think to do. If you can guarantee your...ah... boy... will be calm when he wakes up, I can provide you with antidotes that should cure him."

"Oh!" Grentella exclaimed with frustration. "He went and got his clothes all torn up! That boy!"

Arinna poked Max in his shoulder.

"Uh... yeah," he said. "That was me. I was trying to get his attention off of whoever he was trying to kill in those woods."

"Why would you tear up my poor boy's clothes!" the woman demanded. "Do you have any idea how hard it is to keep them mended as it is, let alone clean!"

"I take it them pirates are your friends then," the man stated.

Max nodded. The giant's huge mouth was hanging open. Drool was running out of the corner of his mouth like a small stream. "How much antidote is it gonna take?"

"I'd say thirty, perhaps more," the man said.

Max nodded. Well there goes half the stockpile. "Sure."

The man nodded as he walked over to the giant's open mouth. "My name's Ordan," he said as he pulled a small vial from a pouch at his waist. Then he used a dropper to put a single drop of the liquid in the vial on the very tip of the giant's tongue. Instantly, the monstrous body began to shrink. It took only about thirty seconds for the giant, cut up clothing and all, to become a relatively normal looking teenage boy.

"You're all giants!" Arinna said.

"You shut your mouth missy!" Grentella snapped.

Max looked from the others back to Arinna. "Seriously?"

"Hand over the antidotes," Ordan said. "Then, why don't you come and break bread with us in town."

"I don't eat," Max said. "We really have to get going."

"I insist," Ordan said. He nodded toward the stand of trees where several heads were peeking out of the brush. "And bring your friends."

Max looked to Arinna. She shrugged.

"Ok," Max replied as he summoned the many, many antidotes he'd promised. "Sure."

Ordan and Grentella ministered to their son while Max explained the situation to the pirates. They were a little reluctant at first, many were carrying items they'd liberated from the town, much of which was food but Max assured Caerd they would not be harmed. He wasn't completely positive about that part, but he figured the pirates had pretty much made their own bed by stealing from a sleepy village in the middle of nowhere.

Did they know nothing of RPG tropes? When you came upon a village like this there was always something funky going on, otherwise why even have it? Plus, Max really wanted to hear these people's story.

So about thirty minutes later Max, Arinna, all the dungeon crawlers, and the pirates followed Ordan and his family into the town. The place had no protective wall and was surrounded instead by scores of fields brimming with all kinds of growing things. There was even a pen full of sand colored cow-like creatures with thin curly horns that Max heard someone call gogs.

The townsfolk didn't seem curious so much as upset. They glared from behind homemade fences as Max and his company passed. Oddly, every family seemed to have several girls, often three or more.

"These people don't seem very friendly," Caerd said.

"You just raided this place, of course they hate us!" Max replied. "We have food on our ship. Why didn't you just wait?"

"The doctor said she was flying into the center of Clathia's largest city to go looking for you," Caerd replied. "The odds she would return were not large."

"Yet you waited," Arinna said.

Caerd beamed at her, stroking his thin beard. "I told her we'd wait and we did. I'm a man of my word..." He leaned in closer. "However, I don't believe you and I have met."

Max opened his jaw to reply but Caerd was already talking again.

"Because I'm certain a creature as arresting as you could never escape my memory."

Here we go. Caerd apparently styled himself a bit of a Casanova. That was interesting given Trina had basically been drooling over him before. Apparently she wasn't his type.

"Buzz off," Arinna replied flatly.

The wrench carrying pirate Shaena snorted with laughter, followed by several others.

Caerd frowned. "Surely you jest," he said. "I've spent much time in the company of your kind. If you're feeling thirsty I can help you with that. I have..."

"Enough," she said. "Stop talking before I tear your lips from your face."

Caerd's eyes were wide, but not with surprise so much as... maybe interest. Not good. But it made sense. The guy was a tactician. His whole deal was figuring out creative ways to win. The bigger the challenge, the more he wanted to beat it.

"The lady has spoken," Max said, stepping between them. "That's the end of it."

Caerd did not respond, but he stared at Max for an uncomfortably long time before his expression suddenly changed and he continued on like nothing had happened.

Ordan was waiting in front of a house near the center of town. It had a thatched roof and wasn't any bigger than any of the other houses; however unlike the rest, this one had a small wooden sign out front with a little crown carved into it.

"Come on in, all of you," Ordan said with his sullen looking son standing behind him. "My wife's going to prepare a meal. Just take a seat at the long table inside."

Max couldn't help but notice how the teenager kept staring daggers at the pirates. Whatever they'd taken from him, it had sure pissed the kid off.

"Thank you for your hospitality," Arinna said as she entered.

Ordan simply nodded to her as he did to all that passed into the house. Did he know who she was? If he did, he wasn't showing it.

However, when Max went to enter, Ordan held up a hand. "Your creatures. If they stay outside, will they cause trouble?"

Max looked down at Scruff who had been trundling along beside him. The creature seemed to deflate. "Well?" Max asked.

No.

"No biting."

No bite.

"Promise?"

Promise.

"Ok," Max said. The crawlers flopped up against the side of the building, looking quite hot and dry. "Could you ask someone to throw some dirty water on them or something? The poor guys look parched."

Ordan nodded. "I will."

They all sat around the rustic table. Max and Arinna sat together, eating nothing, while the pirates ate like mad men and women. Luckily only eight of them had gone on the raid, the rest had remained on the ships. If there had been any more, Max would have worried they'd eat every crumb of food in the entire town.

"I'm sorry about them," Max said, thinking of Raeg. "I don't think they've ever eaten."

Arinna smiled. "You've made quite a life for yourselves," she said, addressing Ordan but as she said that Max couldn't help but notice three girls of varying ages peeking into the great room from the kitchen. Even more interesting, the three had green, purple, and silver eyes. Colors of the dark.

The man nodded slowly. "Indeed, we have. Don't worry about the food, my lord," Ordan replied, brushing his mustache with the back of his hand. "We have plenty here. This land is good to us."

"Why did you call me lord?" Max asked.

"You wear the signet ring of a lord of the dark. You travel with lady Arinna, daughter of Gazric himself. What else should I call you but lord?"

Caerd's mouth was hanging open as he stared at Arinna.

"Call me Max," he replied. "I'm just a skeleton trying to get a lady back home."

Ordan chuckled bitterly. "You will find that difficult, I'm afraid."

"That's what we've been told," Arinna said. "I'm pleased you haven't treated us as your enemies. Does that mean you've decided to come ba-"

"No," Ordan said quickly. "It means we no longer take sides in the wars of others. We live in peace here, unmolested by the armies of either side."

"Well... Dah," the teenager said, anger reddening his face. "That's not all true!"

"It's true enough," Ordan replied sharply. "Excuse my son. He's young and foolish. Now, speaking of my boy, if the pirate captain would be so kind as to return the item he stole, we can declare this matter settled."

"I thought you only took food," Max said, looking at Caerd.

Caerd held up the bone he was currently gnawing the meat from. "I didn't actually say that."

"I'm happy to pay for whatever they took," Max said. "I have gol."

"Money?" the teenager shouted, slamming a fist on the table. "I don't want money! I want Willa's heart!"

6

A WARM LOCKET AND A COLD CASE

Arinna's eyes narrowed. "Could someone please tell us what's going on?"

"It's a brass locket, shaped like a heart," Ordan said. "It's my son's."

"I didn't take that," Caerd said through a mouthful. "Shaena?"

Shaena was using a huge wooden spoon to drop a pile of some kind of mashed vegetable on her plate. "Hmmm?"

"Locket," Caerd asked.

"Ahhh... yeah," she said and slipped a hand in her pocket. "Oh... it's gone."

"LIAR!" the boy said, standing up and knocking his chair backward. His mother, who happened to be walking behind him with another tray of food, stuck out a foot to stop the chair and pushed it back like it was nothing.

"Sit down Rog!" Ordan said. "If you get upset you'll pop off again and I swear this time those poisoned beasts will be the least of your worries. Do you hear me boy?"

The teenager balled his hands into fists. "Yeah, Dah," he grumbled.

"I'm not sayin' I didn't take it," Shaena said. "I love jewelry. I just mean it's not here now. It probably fell out while we were trying not to be stomped to death."

"That's what you get for stealin' from us!" Rogald said, angrily. He shook his head, sighing heavily. "We'll never find it now, Dah."

Max held up a single boney finger. "That's not necessarily true."

"What do you mean?" Ordan asked.

It took a class change and a wardrobe change, but after brunch was over Max, now a Scavenger, followed the thumping sound of his item seeking Rummage ability, right to the brass locket the teenager had been looking for.

"That's it!" Rog declared, tearing the item free from Max's fingers. "Oh thank you, lord skeleton! Thank you so much!"

"Uh, sure," Max said.

Ordan was standing nearby. "Now please leave," he said. "Your people have had their fill. Anything else they've stolen they can keep."

The teenager was walking away, cradling the locket like his own child. Arinna saw it too and approached Ordan. "What is that to him?"

"It's none of your concern," he said. "Now all I ask is that you go in peace. Do not speak of this place or the nature of the people here. Giants exist no more. We like it that way."

"As you wish," she said.

The walk back to the ships was full of burping from the various pirates, except for Caerd. The pirate captain was brooding at the back of the group. Max had an idea why.

"Are you really Arinna?" Shaena said.

"Yes," she replied.

"Do you grant wishes?" the pirate asked, looking a little sheepish as she did.

"Who told you that?" Arinna asked.

"My mother," Shaena replied. "When I was a lil' girl she told me that Arinna was our hope and that when she returned, all our people's wishes would come true, that we'd once again rule the skies."

Arinna smiled wanly. "I hope so," she said.

"I believe in you," Shaena said. "You saved us from a giant who would've pulped us into fleshy jelly. You got my vote!"

"I didn't really-" Arinna started but Max cut her off.

"It was amazing what she did," he said. "She's a natural leader I think."

"I agree!" Shaena said.

Later, when they'd returned to the Midnight, Arinna stopped Max at the entrance to the cargo bay. "You didn't have to say that," she said. "I know it wasn't my idea to talk to the giant, it was yours."

"I know," Max said, "but I don't care. I'm not here to hog the glory. You're the queen, I'm just some skeleton."

"No," she replied, smiling. "You aren't."

"Hey!" a young voice called.

It caused Max and Arinna to turn around as one. There they found a young girl peeking around the bay door.

"I remember you," Arinna said. "You were at the meal in the village."

The girl nodded. This was the one with the violet eyes.

"Is everything alright?" Max asked, suddenly concerned. Anyone who would go to a skeleton and a dark god for help was serious.

"My brother... Rog... he's... he's forbidden to ask... But... Can you help him?"

Arinna approached the girl, taking a knee before her. "You're not a giant are you."

The girl shook her head. "No... I... I'm a Clathian. My mother brought me here so... so..."

"So they wouldn't make you nokara," Arinna said.

The girl nodded.

Arinna looked back to Max. "The dark is strong in this girl," she said. "The Clathians knew it."

"If the giants are hiding Clathian children," Max said, "it's only a matter of time before they're found out."

"Willa didn't come back," the girl said. "She brings people to the village... girls like me. But she didn't come back this summer. She and Rog were gonna marry!"

Arinna nodded. "I understand. You want us to look for her?"

The girl nodded. "Please! Please for Rog. He's mean sometimes... but he's a good big brother."

"Big is right," Max said.

"We'll help," Arinna said. "But how can we find her?"

The girl pointed at Max. "Just use him!"

Arinna frowned. "He can't find people dear, he's a Scavenger. He can only find things."

"Oh!" the girl said, looking down at her feet. Then her face brightened. "Wait! The locket!"

"We already found the locket," Max said.

"Willa had one too!" the girl said. "Hers was just like Rog's, only it was made of black iron."

"A little black heart," Arinna said softly. "How precious."

That reminded Max. He had a gift for Arinna sitting in the party inventory and now that she was in the party, she had access. Sooner or later she would see it and the surprise would be lost. Still this didn't seem like the right time.

She turned back to Max. "You can track that, right?"

Max nodded, though he felt almost nothing, maybe the slightest twinge toward the south. "I'm not getting much. I don't have a lot of levels in this class, we'll need to get closer."

"You'll do it?!" the girl asked, her hands clasped together.

"Yes," Arinna said. "As much as I want to go home. I have unfinished business with Clathia."

"Thank you so much!" the girl said. She lunged at Arinna and hugged her. For a second, from the sick look on her face, Max thought she might be distressed, but after a few seconds, she leaned in and hugged the girl back.

"Now go home," Arinna said as the two parted.

"Thank you! Thank you both!" the girl blurted as she left.

Arinna stood, turning toward Max. "Are you Ok with this? I kind of made the decision for both of us."

Max chuckled. "Are you kidding? I rarely turn down a side quest, for better or worse. If I had a problem, I would have said so. Besides, you're part of the party, you get to make choices too."

She nodded. "Ok."

"Oh!" Max said. "Before I forget. This is for you." He summoned the violet scarf made of Arachnian silk into his skeletal hands.

Arinna approached him. "You... got me a gift?"

"Actually Trina grabbed it, but it was because I wanted to get one. I just wanted... I..." Suddenly he felt very embarrassed. He handed it over.

She took it. "It's beautiful," she said, wrapping it around her neck. It completely covered the last vestiges of the scar from her near beheading at the hands of that Clathian, which was a nice bonus. "Thank you."

"Alright. I'll tell Trina," he said.

"Tell Trina what?" Trina asked. She was wearing her plague doctor mask and carrying a glass jar filled with many small crawling things.

"What is that?" Max asked her.

Trina stopped, her mask pointing at Max. "That ullu had so many ticks... It was unbelievable."

"Yow..." Max said, recoiling instinctively even though he had no blood.

"I've never seen it so bad! It's a wonder he's still alive!" Trina continued. "Now... What did you need to tell me?"

"Arinna and I have a mission in Clathia. There's a village that's lost a person."

TIM PAULSON

Trina's mask nodded. "I see, so that's why you're a Scavenger again."

"I can take care of those for you," Arinna said, pointing at the jar filled with engorged ticks.

"Oh, thank you," Trina said, handing it over. "Should I tell Tela we're lifting off?"

"No," Max said. "We aren't too far north of Gelra. Taking the ship back just invites another attack from the many they have down there."

"So... what?" Trina asked.

"I have a wyvern," Max replied. He's pretty beefy. He can carry Arinna and I down there tonight. We'll have a look, and be back, hopefully before the sun is up."

Bite?

Max looked down to see Scruff trundling into the Midnight's cargo bay. He had two of his smaller selves hanging onto his own back.

"No buddy," Max said. "You're too big to bring with me."

"If you bound him into a cattan, you could take him anywhere," Trina offered.

"Yeah," Max said. That would probably be a good idea, eventually. "But right now it would help me more if you stayed here and helped Mytten keep an eye on that bird guy. Can you do that?"

Scruff nodded.

"Good."

"When you come back, bring fuel," Trina said. "Tela says we only have enough to make it half the way across the ocean. The pirates are fine, they're planning to leave tonight. I spoke to one of them while you were gone, hoping they had extra fuel, but they said they don't."

Max nodded, "How much do we need?"

"Five drums will do it. More if you can get it."

"Ok," he replied, turning around. "I'll see what I can-" Max stopped.

Arinna had returned from outside the cargo bay. The jar in her hands was empty. Max might have thought she'd dumped it outside, if it weren't for the small trickle of blood running down from the corner of her mouth.

"What?" she asked.

MAX AND ARINNA left that night, but later than they would have liked because Dwayne wasn't yet fully healed after his ordeal with the Clathian army, and that girl Brittney. However, after Trina patched him up, Dwayne was only too happy to carry them both. The flight was relatively short, only about an hour had passed before they saw the lights of the city and the ruined tower fortress nearby.

Now that rain wasn't pouring down he could more clearly make out the damage to the fortress. Extensive wasn't the word. The thing had been trashed. The entire top half was just gone. Even with the torrential downpour that had just gone through, some places glowed from still smoldering embers.

"There are many airships," Arinna said into his ear hole. She'd wrapped her arms around his chest rather than his waist, since he didn't really have one.

"Yeah," Max replied. "But most of them are near the fortress. We don't need to go there." The thumping for the little black iron pendant had started about ten minutes ago and it was definitely coming from the town, down by the docks.

"Why would a country that mostly moves things with airships still have the docks next to the sea," he wondered aloud.

"This is an old city," Arinna replied, "settled before there were such things."

He nodded. "But they could change it right? It's a really low point and if there's an earthquake out in the ocean everything would be wiped."

"Things have a momentum to them," Arinna said. "It's not so easy to change how you do things."

"I guess," Max said. "Dwayne, down right there. See that storage area near the parked airship? With the ring of lights?"

See it, bro.

"Great, land there," Max said.

The wyvern began turning in a circle, preparing to land, when Arinna let go of Max's chest.

"I think I see something," she said. "I'll find you down there."

"What?" Max replied, but she was already gone, dropping from the wyvern's back. She grabbed the end of a long flag as she flew through the air and used it to swing in a graceful spiral before landing perfectly on the roof of a building.

Max sighed. He didn't realize he'd been holding his breath the whole time. And she called him crazy! She didn't have a heck of a lot of hit points yet.

"Oh well," he said. "So much for landing."

Bro?

"Don't worry about it Dwayne," Max said, patting the wyvern on his thick scaly neck. "You did good. Dwayne come back."

The wyvern beneath him dissolved into a poof of smoke, reforming as a cattan in Max's right hand. He stored it as he fell a couple hundred feet to the ground, smashing through the wooden shingled roof of a decrepit dockside storehouse.

57 damage received.

He sat up just in time to see about eight hundred rats and assorted other creepy things scuttling away from his noisy entrance.

"Sorry for dropping in guys," he said, chuckling to himself as he stood, looking around. The place was full of crates, old beat up ones. It seemed this storehouse hadn't been used for a while. Maybe shipping wasn't doing so well in Clathia. Being run by a bunch of nuts tended to do that.

Arinna hadn't said which of the two things they were looking for she'd seen, so he didn't know whether to use Rummage to follow the pulsing toward the fuel, which was to his right, or the pendant, which was to his left.

"Crap."

Even worse, he was currently a Scavenger with no usable weapons and only the old black leather armor. He had a heck of a lot of health though, and his stats weren't terrible. He had two agility at least. That was better than zero, though not by much.

Dammit. He'd meant to remind Arinna that he was basically defenseless as a Scavenger, but she should know that right? Maybe this was some kind of test. No. She hadn't seemed like that kind of person. Maybe she was just... kind of impulsive.

He sighed. Awesome.

He should think a second though. Whatever she'd seen it had been from the air. It was more likely that would be the fuel. It wasn't easy to spot some tiny pendant from hundreds of feet up. The only question was: should he go after the pendant or try to link up with her?

It was probably better to go after the fuel first. They could link up and search for the girl's pendant later. As sad as it was, Max was pretty sure they'd find the pendant and no girl. The Clathians probably killed her and if she no longer had the pendant, there was no way to find out.

So, the fuel was to the right.

"It was down here, brother," said a man's voice. "Like a crash from above."

Max froze. Uh oh.

"It's an old building," replied another. "It may have fallen on its own. But you're right, by the grace of the Goddess, we should check."

Max grit his teeth. Damn! It was dark in here and they'd see his eyes for sure. Max started moving in the opposite direction, as quietly as he could in the black leather boots. If it wasn't so annoying, it might be funny. Here he was, with more than a thousand health, scuttling away from a pair of low level dudes, just like the rats.

Luckily, there was a hole in the side of the building. Max slipped through, emerging into a tight alleyway full of coiled tie ropes and big wooden spools to wrap them on. He thought of the black iron pendant again. The thumping was louder and quicker. If he was getting that close, he might as well look for it.

Max followed the alley until he came to another alley. He took a right, following this one and making sure that however he went, the sound kept getting faster and louder. Soon he came to another dilapidated warehouse. This one looked even worse than the one before, more than half of the building's front had collapsed. The rusted metal gate was roped off to prevent entry but Max was thin enough to slip through with a little wiggling of his skull.

Inside, the condition of the building didn't improve. Much of the ceiling had caved in, leaving it open to the stars above, and the recent rain, which had turned much of what had once been a packed dirt floor into thick, viscous mud. Max had to be careful with every step he took that his boot wasn't sucked from his foot. That wasn't easy when there wasn't any actual flesh on your feet.

Still, the thumping kept getting louder and louder, until he was standing in the middle of the largest and deepest puddle. Above him was only sky.

"Alright, I guess it's down here," he said and squatted to fish his hands around in the muddy water. At least it was dirty enough down here that the rain hadn't created freshwater puddles. Not that a few points of damage was going to kill him, but still.

Then his boney fingertips clicked against something hard. Max knelt down, filling his boots with muck and dug both of his hands in, using them as sieves. On the second pass, he got it.

Out of the mud came the little black iron pendant. It was the same shape as the other one, only the chain was broken. He stored it in his inventory.

"Well," that's one down.

Max looked around. No one else was here. There were no bodies that he could see, though they might be under the water. Scruff would probably have been useful here. The creature's senses would have easily detected any rotting flesh.

"CSI Clathia reporting," he said, swishing his hands through the water in circles around himself. "We found the victim's belongings, but no body."

He sighed, and stood up. "Oh well." Max did not relish the idea of telling the kid his girlfriend was probably dead.

"You found it!" Arinna said from behind him.

Max jumped nearly a foot, splashing down in the mud and spraying it in a wide circle around him.

Arinna laughed.

Max turned around to see her crouched on a rafter on the other side of the building where they were still intact.

"Good job," she said, still smiling.

Max stood up, shaking the mud from himself. "Yeah, but she's not here," Max said.

"That's Ok," Arinna replied. "I already found her."

7

HAVE MERCY AND SAVE THE GIRL

"You're old," Brittney said, trying not to sound disgusted, but probably failing. "And you're not a puppy."

"Ha!" the old woman said. "Every one of us here is eternal. Age is meaningless. If you don't get that, maybe I should throw you back to the wolves."

She frowned. "Then why do you look like that? What am I even doing here?!"

The old woman extended a single finger. "Shut your mouth and listen, and listen good. If you do not follow my instructions to the letter you will not go home, not as a young girl or an old woman, not at all. You will die. Do you hear me girl?"

Brittney paused. "Yes."

"Good," she said. "Zadkiel informed you of your hearing."

This was not a question, but Brittney answered anyway. "Yes," she said.

"The hearing will be run by the four principalities of Akasa. Zadkiel will present his case, including information from your own mind. He will force you to testify against yourself. It will be impossible for you to lie. Do you understand?"

"What?" Brittney snapped. "It's... It's like a trial?" Her daddy had been a lawyer, hadn't he? Or was he a business man? God that had been so long ago. The only thing she remembered for sure was that he always said there was nothing more important than having a good lawyer in your corner. He used to say that a lot actually.

"B-but... do I get a lawyer?"

The old woman laughed bitterly. "Oh, you'll have an advocate, certainly. They will not help you. I promise you that."

"Ugh!" Brittney said. "Can't I hire someone?"

"We don't use money dear sweet idiot girl. The only things that matter here are rules, that is all we have. It is all we know." She gestured at the papers everywhere around her. "They are everywhere."

"I... I..." Brittney was starting to feel sick.

"All is not lost, if you do as I say, exactly as I say."

"Ok," she replied.

"You will be found guilty of treason against the light," the old woman said.

"But-"

"It is already decided, inescapable. Be silent. We have only moments before they discover you've been taken."

Brittney bit her lip, nodding.

"You must not deny the charges against you. For your own sake, you must admit your guilt and beg the mercy of the court. Do you understand?"

"I... Yes," she replied, but her mind was still reeling. This kind of thing happened to other people, not to her. It was wrong! It was unfair!

"There is a second item, even more important than the first. It is critical that you do not mention the scion."

Brittney frowned. Scion? Didn't... Vita say something about that? "Why?"

"Don't ask questions. Tell me you understand!"

"Yes! I understand!" None of it felt right though. Why should she admit she was guilty? It was stupid to stop the skeleton from saving that girl. The Clathians were terrible people and their leader was a revolting pig. She hoped very much that he died horribly. If the skeleton hadn't done it, she would have done it herself.

A hot wind was swirling around her, ruffling the papers on the floor and the walls and the ceiling.

"Our time is over. Heed my words, girl," the old woman said. "Do NOT argue. Mercy, ask for mercy."

"But... What about Vita?" Brittney asked. "She was there! She saw that man. She-"

In a fraction of a second she was back in the endless hallway.

"-saw... the..." Brittney stopped. "Shit," she said.

Not more than three seconds passed before there was a bright white flash and Brittney found herself standing in the center of a ring of bright lights. Fear filled her as memories of many movies about alien abductions flooded her mind. She tried to struggle but she couldn't move anything, not even a finger.

"Be still," a voice boomed. Or was it a voice? It felt like it came from everywhere at once, from below, above, behind, even inside her.

Her mind quieted instantly, like turbulent waters suddenly stilled. It felt unnatural, just as it had when that angel had forced her to tell him the truth. It was as if her very thoughts and feelings were not her own, but everyone's, to dig through or change as they pleased.

From all around her there was a sort of buzzing noise. The sound grew and grew until she realized it was humming. Thousands of voices, hundreds of thousands, all together in a perfect union, humming the same long note that lasted and lasted, growing in strength. Did they never need to take a breath? Her ears were full of it, overflowing with that pure, powerful sound.

By contrast, her eyes could see only white. It was as if a screen surrounded her, like a movie screen before the start of the picture, only everywhere. The only exception were the lights. They were above her, that much she knew, and arranged in a perfect circle, pointing at her.

Then, without any warning the white screen suddenly disappeared and the world around her revealed itself. There was only one word for it: horrifying.

Brittney was suspended above a tall pillar. Around her the ground fell away into a gray formless nothingness. The ring of lights was hovering above her, circling slowly to her right. They seemed to come from nothing as there was no ceiling that she could see that fixtures might be attached to. Beyond the lights, instead of a ceiling there was only a kind of sky that filled the space above her. Brittney wasn't sure how, but it felt wrong. There was no blue, only a sort of grayish yellow, and instead of a bright sun, there was only a vaguely brighter spot directly above her.

More was being revealed to her as the moments passed. Now, directly ahead she could see a tall ornate bench that seemed to rise out of the emptiness. There were four seats lined up in a row, with a fifth, higher and behind them. Light beamed down from above, illuminated four seated figures but it was so bright, it was hard to even see them, let alone figure out who they were.

Then, her eyes caught sight of something else. Farther away, completely encircling her, were stands, just like a sports stadium. They were filled with creatures of various kinds. Even though they were much farther away, since the stands weren't washed out by insane amounts of light, she could actually see the onlookers and they were nothing if they weren't creepy. Some had wings, some didn't, but all seemed odd in one way or another. They were too old or too young or too thin, and they all wore simple fabric draping, like Romans in the old movies.

Ahead, a hand raised and the humming from the stands ceased, leaving an eerie silence to settle over the multitudes.

"The high court of Akasa is now in session. Presided upon by the four divine principalities: Naliniel, Makenarien, Dekaliel, and Benethen. May the light shine forever!" the voice boomed again.

"Forever!" the multitudes shouted in unison from their seats. Brittney thought of surfing. The sound felt like a wild wave, crashing over her, knocking her off her board and beating her into the sand. She just wanted to come up for air, but she couldn't.

"We are here to depose Sikari Breylara, also known as Brittney. At this time, this is only a preliminary hearing," the voice said.

Brittney wanted to ask who was speaking and what she was accused of, but her mouth wouldn't move, nothing would, so she waited.

"Archangel Zadkiel," a voice said. This was a new one, a deeper, more gruff tone, someone up above. "Please state the charges for the record."

"Of course, principality," Zadkiel stated as he floated forward to Brittney's right. This time he wasn't transparent but looked like he had back on the ship, a weirdly thin man with long hair. He wore long flowing robes now though, they draped from his body like a bridal train, trailing along behind him as if blown by an unseen wind. "Sikari Breylara is accused of treason against the light."

Onlookers gasped and others whimpered with surprise.

"I will present evidence forthwith," Zadkiel continued, "that, though she had the power to destroy him then and there, this human girl conspired with the dark warrior known as Boneknight to destroy the light fortress of Gelra, and free the unspeakable horror and last vestige of dark power, Arinna, daughter of Gazric, butcher of angels."

Brittney frowned. Butcher? Seriously? It looked like most of these guys could break a wrist trying to butter bread.

"Thank you, Zadkiel," said another voice from above. This one was softer, almost feminine. "Will the advocate come forward?"

"Yes, principality," came a response from Brittney's right. She'd been hoping this would be Vita. Vita would know she hadn't conspired with anyone. Vita would know that the worst she did was let him go and... and... he'd tricked her. That was why! The dark warrior had tricked her!

Unfortunately, it was not Vita who fluttered forward.

~

"IS SHE DEAD?" Max asked as he sloshed through the mud.

Arinna laughed. "That's a rather indelicate question, don't you think?"

Max shrugged. "People don't usually just drop highly personal items in mud puddles. I've watched enough Batman cartoons to know that."

Arinna dropped from the rafter, landing lightly on the ground. He saw that she was already wearing the violet scarf which trailed behind with an almost living grace. Oddly, it seemed to have changed color a bit.

"That's weird," he said. "It looks like your scarf is getting darker."

"Is it?" she asked, nonchalantly. "Look up and you'll have your best clue to the girl's location. Otherwise, follow me."

Max did look up, but all he saw was the stars, through the hole in the... No way.

"That's right!" he exclaimed. "Where is she?"

Arinna grinned and took off into the dark. "This way, do try to keep up!"

Max couldn't even come close. Two agility was nothing compared to hers. It was all he could do to keep her in sight, though that was probably just because she let him. They ran through dark alleys, slipping by terrified dockworkers and porters who fell to their knees in prayer when they saw them, if they didn't try to take a swing. Funnily enough, they more often tried to hit Arinna who zipped past first and then saw Max and his glowing green eyed skull running after her and they bolted.

The building they came to was huge. It was no wonder she'd been able to see it from the air. She must have known what they were looking for from the beginning. Max hadn't even thought about it, but now that he had, it made total sense.

The chain that prevented entry had been slashed and the doors left wide open so Max just waltzed in, stepping over the bodies of two Clathian guards Arinna had already killed. The girl was impressive, and she did need the experience.

As soon as he stepped inside he saw her. Willa was chained to the ground, all forty or so feet of her. The chains wrapped her body and were connected to huge metal stakes embedded in the ground. Max ran around Willa's large hand, where two fingers had been denuded of their skin, toward the girl's head. It looked like she was asleep. It also looked like the Clathians had been cutting parts from her head too. Half an ear was missing and a section of her nose also. Nearby there was a table covered in blood and metal containers of various sizes.

"They're experimenting on her?" he asked, rage boiling up.

Arinna appeared at his side, slipping out of the dark. "Not like in your world. More like, gathering ingredients for potions and items. Giants are classified as monsters. Their skin and bones are poten-"

Max held up a hand. "Ok, stop! We've got to get her out of here."

"Agree!" Arinna replied. "She's under the influence of a high level sleep spell. They used it on me all the time during my... captivity," she said, her face hardening. "Arrested torpor. It combines sleep and paralysis. It's very hard to dispell."

"Hmmm," Max said. "Will it wear off?"

"Eventually," Arinna said. "However... I killed the guards I saw but I missed two others. They ran. I'm sorry... I'm not used to being so low level."

"I'm not thinking it's going to be that way for long," he replied, casting his eyes around the building. Lines of drums were arrayed against the wall, but six were missing. "Oh... that's a lot of fuel. I see you already took what we needed, plus a little extra."

"Can't be too careful," she said.

"I hear that," he turned around, taking in the look of the place. Just looking at it all made him angry. "Did you look around for any of that potion the giants use to make themselves small?"

"I did," she replied. "But I didn't find any. I assume you're not feeling any either."

"No," Max said. "Rummage isn't giving me anything."

"I hear them coming," Arinna said. "There are dozens of them."

Max glanced back at her. "Really? How?"

She looked to the side. "Uh... vampire senses," she said quietly.

"Oh!" Max replied as he walked over to one of the fuel drums. "So you *are* a vampire."

"It's... it's not a big deal," she said.

"If you're downplaying it, it is," he replied and kicked the drum over. "I'll be asking you why later." Then he went to the next one and did the same. A thick white liquid, that Max was pretty sure was unicorn blood started glugging out onto the floor of the warehouse.

"You can ask all you want. What are you doing?" she asked him.

"I'm sick of this place," Max said, "and I really don't like these people. I'm going to give Clathia something else to remember us by."

Arinna looked to the giant. "The fire shouldn't harm her, but it would burn off the rest of her clothes, such as they are. I'd rather not take her home like that."

"What level would you say she is?" he asked.

"She's young, probably only two or three-hundred years. Maybe level four," Arinna said.

Max shook his head. "Ok... That's kind of what I'd hoped, I've got an idea. It could be totally crazy, but it might work and I don't have anything that I know for sure will wake her up before the Clathians get here... so it's all I've got."

"If you're going to do it," Arinna said. "Now is the time."

"Alright," he said. "We've got tons of sleep powder in our inventory. That should help."

"Unless they have a mage or cleric with them," Arinna replied.

"Thank you, Mary Sunshine," he said. "Just buy me a few minutes. I've got to change my class but it's been a while, it should be fine."

She was gone before he'd even finished his sentence.

Max thought for a minute as he stared at the spilled fuel leaking out onto the floor. The stuff was flammable, that was for sure, but it didn't have a strong smell like gasoline.

"Maybe this will work then," he said. Did he still have those candles? It turned out he did. As he thought of them, one appeared in his right hand, black candle from Bob's old place. Max placed the candle in the center of the still spreading fluid and stood there staring at it like an idiot.

"Shit," he said. "I have no way to light it."

The moment he said the word 'light' the little black candle started on its own.

"Ha!" Max said. "Well that's useful." He turned back to the literal sleeping giant. The sounds of weapons clanging was coming from outside the building. Arinna had begun her murdering spree.

"No more dicking around," he said and brought up his display. He unequipped the armor and switched back to Dark Summoner. No wonder Arinna had recommended it, it was very flexible, like being a Dark Mage and a Breeder at the same time and a nice bonus to magic points to boot.

Hello Max.

"Uh... hi," he said. It was that creepy entity he'd bound before... the one with the contract.

I am not creepy.

Max did not respond.

Can I kill the giant?

"No!" Max said. "I'm trying to save her."

I know. Your plan is sound.

"Uh... thank you?" he said. "Is that all you wanted to say?"

Do not tell Arinna about our contract.

"What? Why?"

Just don't.

"Or what?"

You know what I can do.

"Is that a threat?"

More clanging from outside.

Yes.

Max sighed. "I don't have time for this." he turned around to face the giant. She was now glowing with a faint blue-green aura.

Don't tell her.

"No promises!" Max said. "Just go away." He paused. "Bind Willa."

Willa added.

Good. That was the first part. The second was something new, something he hadn't ever done before.

"Create cattan Willa," said.

Unable to comply. Necessary element not present.

"What?" Max asked.

More clanging from outside the warehouse, and shouting too.

Arinna receives 3 damage.

Arinna receives 2 damage.

Arinna receives 4 damage.

"Dammit!" Max said. "Create cattan Willa," he said again. It had to work. He read the book. It hadn't mentioned any other ingredients.

Unable to comply. Necessary element not present.

"Shit!"

I can tell you what you're missing.

"Then do it!" he snapped.

Promise me you won't tell her.

"You said my plan would work!" he said.

It will. You have everything you need.

Arinna receives 1 damage.

Max grit his teeth. "Fine. I promise I won't tell her about you, but I want to know why."

That wasn't part of the deal.

"Well?" Max asked.

You must hold a core in your hand. The flawless Stone of Death. Summon it, then try.

"Ok," Max said. When he thought of that item it appeared. It looked just as it had before when he'd pried it from a cradle of black lava rock: a smooth translucent green sphere. Holding the sphere in his hand as a summoner was much different than it had been before. As a magic wielding class he could feel the power emanating from it. This wasn't just some gem. This was a fire-hose of power, aching to pour out.

"Create cattan Willa," he said.

The green sphere glowed and tendrils of green light emanated from it. They reached out for Willa and where they touched her body seemed to evaporate into gas. The chains that had held her body released and clanged against the floor. The gas then coalesced and rushed at Max, funneling in a curling channel down until the palm of his left hand. At that same moment the light left the sphere in Max's right hand and it disintegrated into black sand. All that was left in the end was a little bone.

The shape was right, but... bone? Whatever, he stored it anyway. He sure hoped the girl would heal on their way back.

Conversion successful.

Max suddenly felt very drained. How much MP did that cost him?

3/416 MP

"All but three?" he exclaimed. "Damn!"

"I hope you're done!" Arinna yelled from outside.

"Almost!" Max replied, turning around. The candle was only barely burned down. He wondered if it responded to other commands.

"How about fall over?" he asked.

Dutifully, the little black candle tilted and fell. There was a great poof as the white fuel exploded. The entire warehouse filled with flames at the same time that Max was blasted off his feet and halfway across the room.

238 damage received.

8

A DANGEROUS SECRET AND A TERRIFYING TRUTH

Max sat up, fire all around him. "Ok, yeah. I was a little too close to that."

"Come on," Arinna said, grabbing his elbow. "More of it is about go."

She pulled him to his feet and dragged him out of the building as it collapsed around them.

Clathian soldiers and Clathian Commander defeated!

Arinna has gained a level of Grave Blade!

Arinna has gained a level!

You've gained a level of Dark Summoner!

You've gained a level!

"I assume you've got her," Arinna said, but she didn't sound super sure about it.

"I do," Max said. "Though... it was a little weird."

"You can tell me on the way," she said as she grabbed him by his spine and dragged him up the side of a building like a sack of dirty laundry. "Is this high enough?"

Another series of explosions drew his attention. Apparently the fuel wasn't the only flammable item in the vicinity of that warehouse. The fire was spreading quickly to other buildings, causing more explosions as it engulfed them in flames. Max could even see a pair of grounded airships on fire.

Defiler unlocked.

"Ho HO!" Max exclaimed. He'd wondered how you got the class upgrade for Scavenger. It seemed wrecking stuff was the way to go. He wasn't actually a Scavenger now, but he had been when he set that candle going. Maybe that was how it worked?

"Are you even listening to me?" Arinna asked.

"Huh?" he replied. "Oh... sorry. What did you ask?"

"Is this high enough for the drake?"

"Wyvern," Max said, "and yes."

"Then let's go," she said. "Airships from the fortress are already moving this way."

Max summoned Dwayne's cattan and the two of them flew off into the night.

"What's the problem?" she asked.

Max thought about Neline the arcane entity and her bargain. There were few red flags bigger than when someone says: "Don't tell." Maybe he could work it somehow that Arinna could guess it.

No.

Argh!

If you make her guess, I will consider our deal broken.

Maybe that wouldn't be so bad.

Yes it would. Trust me.

Max sighed.

"What?" Arinna asked again, "Where are you Max? Why are you ignoring me?"

"Uh..." Well, there was the other thing. "Willa."

"What about her?"

"To turn her into a cattan I needed a power source other than my own mana."

"I see," Arinna said. "Is that bad?"

"I don't know," Max replied. "The cattan is different. I've never seen one like a bone before. I was hoping you would know."

"I'm not well versed in the intricacies of magic. That's my father," she said.

"Ah," Max replied. "But you knew what that spell was."

"I know a lot about what was used on me, yes," she replied curtly.

"I'm sorry," he said. "I forget that you were held for so long. I bet you'd just like to relax."

It was her turn to sigh. "There's no time for that."

"How are you doing Dwayne?" Max asked the wyvern.

Good, bro.

"You don't have to say bro at the end of every sentence," Max said. "That's... That's too much."

Sure, bro... uh... Sure.

Arinna laughed. "What are you teaching these poor summons of yours?"

"I don't know sometimes," Max said. "I'm like a dog chasing cars."

"You wouldn't know what to do with it if you caught it," she said, finishing the quote.

Max turned to her, his jaw hanging as his green eyes illuminated her face. "How did you know that one?! How is that possible! You've been in captivity for... what? Hundreds of years?"

"Time between our two worlds is..." she frowned, obviously searching for the right word. "I don't know... weird? broken? It's hard to explain. Vishellus understands it better."

"He's MIA," Max said. "I should maybe sleep and see if his girlfriend contacts me again."

Arinna chuckled. "You mean Darsana."

Max nodded. "Yeah, she's been relaying messages from Vish in my nightmares."

"I don't imagine that's a lot of fun," Arinna replied.

"It's not my favorite."

Here, bro... eh.. Max.

"Thanks Dwayne," Max said. "We're approaching the village."

"I hope they don't hate us for doing this," Arinna said. "It wasn't any of our business."

Max shrugged. "Let's find out."

Dwayne dived beneath the clouds, arriving on the outskirts of the giant's village with several hours left before dawn.

"Dwayne, come back," Max said. He was worried the people of the village wouldn't know they were there. That wasn't a problem. They hadn't even started walking when torches appeared in the distance.

"Maybe we should just wait for them to come," Arinna said.

Max nodded. "Yeah."

It didn't take long for Ordan and several others to arrive, including his son. The man did not look particularly pleased to see them again. Neither did the five others behind him, mostly men. They were the only people Max had seen who would come out of their homes at night to meet with a skeleton and a dark goddess and not bring a single weapon.

"What brings you to our town so late at night," Ordan asked calmly.

"I come... to ask for your forgiveness," Arinna said.

"For what?"

"One of your little ones came to us," she said. "And... instead of asking your permission. We went looking on our own for the girl called Willa."

Max summoned both items into his hands. The little black locket dangled, so it was seen right away.

Rog gasped. His hands went to his face, trying to cover his grief.

"I take it you found her then," Ordan said solemnly.

"As it happens," Arinna said, smiling. "We did." She nodded to Max.

Max threw the cattan at the ground behind him, the only space open enough for a giant to spawn at full size. There was a gigantic explosion of black smoke, but then Willa was there.

Though he'd used the stone of death to make her cattan, Willa seemed just as she had before. She still looked a little worse for wear, her fingertips hadn't fully healed yet, nor had her nose and her eyes remained closed, but otherwise she looked normal. Even though he had no lungs, Max held his breath, hoping the girl would open her eyes.

"WILLA!" Rog shouted, his voice breaking with emotion as he ran past his father. Tears rolled down the boy's cheeks as his potion gave out and he grew, stumbling forward as his limbs exploded in size.

Then... the girl's eyes fluttered.

"Rog?" she said. "Is that you?"

Rog fell to his giant knees beside her, cradling her head in his lap as he embraced her. "You're alive!" he cried, his great voice echoing in the darkness. "EVERYONE! MY WILLA IS ALIVE!"

Max was sure he saw tears in Ordan's eyes as he approached and gathered both of them into his arms, hugging Max and Arinna together.

"Thank you... so much!"

There was much celebration after that. The giants cried and held each other and sang songs together. Max and Arinna were invited to stay until morning, but they begged off, saying they had a great deal to do, which was true.

As they turned to go, Ordan was there, standing in their way. His wife was beside him.

"We can never repay you for this kindness," she said.

"Do you plan to take the girl with you?" Ordan asked.

Max was startled. "Willa? Of course not."

Arinna poked him in the arm. "She's bound to you, a summon."

Max chuckled. "Oh, that. Release Willa."

Willa released.

"You would give up a giant so easily?" Ordan said.

"She's not a thing," Max replied. "I don't care what the classification is. Monster or not, no one is ever going to be on my team against their will."

Arinna looked at him then, her eyes glittering green in the light of a torch, and she took his arm. "It's time for us to go," she said. "Think on my offer, Ordan."

"I will," he said.

When they'd walked a ways, Max asked her. "What did you offer Ordan?"

"I told him that he and his people were welcome among the dark, that things would be different than they were with my father," she said.

Max nodded. "Ok. For a bunch of monsters, they sure seem like nice people."

Arinna laughed. "We'll need more than nice to win this fight."

"I know," he said. "I know."

After that they walked back to the Midnight. Arinna held on to Max's arm the whole way as the stars sparkled above them and the insects trilled and chirped. For the first time in a long time, Max felt... home.

BRITTNEY WATCHED AS A TINY, feeble old angel fluttered forward to her left. The creature's wings didn't seem to work quite right as they would miss a beat every once in while causing it to drop.

"I am here, principality," the angel said weakly.

"Do you have any statement regarding the accused?" said a smooth male voice from above.

"Only that I believe this girl is a human, and... as such, ought to... be afforded the comfort of a chair to sit up. Otherwise she may not be able to provide proper testimony."

What?! That was it?

"Your suggestion is noted and acceptable," said the soft feminine voice.

A simple wooden chair appeared beneath Brittney. It moved upward until it pushed into her legs and butt. It did feel better to sit, a little. There was only one problem with it... the chair wasn't on anything! It was just floating in the air! How could she be comfortable sitting on a floating chair with like a hundred spotlights on her?

"We will now begin the deposition," said the first voice from above, the gruff one. "The human will be disallowed from speaking untruths. Please proceed."

"Yes, principality, as you wish," Zadkiel said, as he approached her.

Brittney tried to struggle again. She fought with all her might, but nothing happened. She wanted to punch, to kick, to scream, but she couldn't. She couldn't do anything.

Zadkiel leaned in close, sliding his thin fingertips along the side of her cheek as he whispered. "Now you will tell them all why you deserve to be burned to ashes."

What?

His fingers slide along her cheek, down to her neck and up to the edge of her ear. She felt something... a sort of pain but deep inside, in the back of her mind.

"She is ready!" the angel proclaimed. "Child of humankind, tell the principalities of your crime. Tell them you spoke with the dark warrior."

"I did," Brittney said. The words just came from her. She had no control of them.

There were gasps all around.

"What did he speak of?" Zadkiel asked.

"He asked me to let him save Arinna," Brittney replied.

"Your task was to destroy him, was it not?"

"Yes," she replied.

"Who gave you this task?"

"Garem."

"And what did you do?"

"I let him go."

Another cascade of gasps from the angels watching, followed by many shouts. Some said 'traitor', others 'betrayer.'

"This undead horror had killed many pious soldiers of light, you knew this?"

"Yes," she said.

"Yet, you allowed him to leave?"

"I did," she said.

Zadkiel turned to the great bench before them and bowed. "That is all."

"Damning! Monstrous! Horrific!" voices shouted from all around.

"Advocate Ganielle, do you have any questions for the accused?" said the smooth voice.

"No, principality."

"If I may, principality," Zadkiel said, floating forward. "I have a request."

"You may," said the feminine voice.

What was going on? Brittney was supposed to be able to talk wasn't she? She'd only answered the questions... She'd never been allowed to say anything on her own. How was it possible?

"I move that, given the gravity of the charge, this hearing be advanced from preliminary to sentencing. The human's guilt is self-evident."

No!

"What of you, advocate?" asked the gravelly voice.

"I concur, principality," the old angel replied.

There were cheers from the stands.

"So be it!" said four voices in unison. "Guilt is pronounced forthwith. Before we move to sentencing, the Sikari must be given the chance to speak unfettered. Make it so Zadkiel."

"Of course principality," the angel replied as he once again hovered in Brittney's direction.

Stay away! You horrible thing! I hate you! She wanted so much to scream but could do nothing.

Again, he came too close, his long thin hair hanging from his thin dispassionate face. She wanted to punch him so hard. That thin nose would surely snap like a pencil. It would be so satisfying too.

"I knew this day would come," he breathed into her ear. "I've been waiting for it. Now I'm going to free your voice. Go right ahead and tell everyone what you really think of the light. No one will stop you."

He pressed a finger against her temple and released it. She felt it go. It was like a gag had been removed. She wanted to swear so much it hurt, but looking at that horrible angel's smug face filled her with rage, a powerful force that channeled into one single desire: revenge. She would not forget this moment, not ever.

"Speak human, or say nothing, that too is your right," said the smooth voice from the bench above.

"I choose to speak!" she said, clearing her throat. It hurt so much to even contemplate saying this. As crazy as it seemed, somehow she knew. What Zadkiel had said cemented it in her mind. This was right. This was the only way. "I... I admit wholly to the charges against me," she said.

Gasps.

The look on Zadkiel's face was priceless. His jaw was hanging open.

"I throw myself on the mercy of this court," she said, laying it on as thick as she could. "I beg you... mercy."

"This! This is a lie! She's been coached!" Zadkiel shrieked, his voice cracking like a teenage boy.

"Be silent Zadkiel," said the gruff voice.

"The guilty has admitted her crime and asked for mercy. By law we must commute the sentence."

"By law," said another.

"By law," said the last.

"The sentence cannot be death," said the first principality. "It shall be commuted to a lower level. Given the crime is treason, there is only one option."

"Scouring," said the next.

"Scouring," said the third.

"The human is Sikari no longer. All her belongings shall be taken. All her levels shall be removed. All her skills and classes shall be revoked. She shall be Nothing."

"Nothing."

"Nothing."

"Nothing."

Brittney tried to cry out, but her mouth wouldn't work. The chair was gone. She was floating upward. Something was coming from above, a bright light and at its center a horrifying apparatus of metal arms with needles and claws, clamps and shackles. It grabbed her legs and arms. Needles pierced her, claws ripped her.

An orb appeared in front of her, hovering. It pulsed, heat poured in through her eyes, burning the inside of her brain. She couldn't believe the pain... never had she felt anything like it. She was sure her skull would explode from the pressure but it didn't. She wished it would, but it wouldn't. Anything to make it end. Why wouldn't it end?

Finally, she was able to scream and scream she did. After an eternity of pain, the light stopped, and Brittney fell. She tried to keep her eyes open. There were... people there... weren't there? She... what was going on?

Everything went dark.

Then something poked her in the nose.

"Wake up, Sikari," said a soft voice. "We don't have much time."

Whatever it was, it poked her again.

"SNOOZE!" she grumbled, slapping the area in front of her face. Of all the things she'd expected to feel when she did that, a squish, wasn't even close to the list. Her eyes shot open to find her palm slathered in powder blue goop.

"Ewww!" she said, trying to push herself away while shaking whatever it was off of her hand. The stuff wouldn't come off, and worse, she didn't move backward more than a few inches before her head hit something hard.

Brittney turned around. It was a wall. Just like the others in this place, its surface was plastered with papers covered with some kind of writing. It felt like the writing might be angelic... but... but she couldn't understand it. They'd taken that too.

While she was staring at the wall, trying to understand. The goop had dropped onto the similarly papered floor where it was pulling together.

"Ugh!" Brittney said, "Stay away!"

The blue collected into a single pool and then extruded itself upward, creating a human shape. The blue faded into a soft bluish skin tone. It was a girl, a six inch tall girl wearing a tiny white dress with a very short skirt. Two bug-like wings sprouted from her back.

"A pixie?" Brittney stuttered. "But... they don't have those here!"

The girl frowned. "They used to... ugh! There isn't time! Come with me Brittney, I've got to get you out of here before they come for you."

"What?" Brittney replied, looking around. How was she supposed to get out? There wasn't just one wall around her, there were four, all identically covered with papers. "Get out how... No!" she said. "No, you're wrong. I don't have to run... do I? They said they weren't going to kill me."

"There are worse things than death," the pixie replied in her soft voice. "You're a human in Akasa with no job and no papers. You're an illegal alien!"

Brittney just stared. "Say what now?"

"You need to move fast before they catch you and throw you out. Come on!"

9

LOOTED AND SPEWING

"Alright," Max said, as the Midnight pulled away from the ground. He and Arinna and Trina had gathered on the bridge. "Where the heck are we going?"

"If there's a portal in Ghrellen," Arinna said. "That's where we need to go, but there's no way we'd make it there now, even if we had the fuel."

"I agree," Max said. "You're still too low level and we're flying a stolen ship with Kestrian markings. Even if we're lucky and we can round up everyone we met before we found you, that's not even close to an army, so there's no way we can just smash our way to the portal. We'll have to be crafty about it."

"We'll need a Smuggler," Trina said. "Caerd may know someone."

"They told us where they're going?" Max asked.

Trina nodded. "Yes, since they now have three ships, all stolen from the Nelarians, they're planning to head south west to the kingdom of Barapha."

Arinna shivered involuntarily. "That's cold down there."

"They're not going there yet, they don't have the fuel. They're heading east first, to the Reylosian coastal town of Poe."

"Poe?" Arinna asked. "I haven't heard of that town."

Trina shrugged. "No surprise. It's new but it's surprisingly prosperous, perhaps because it's far enough away that the rest of Reylos forgets about it. That's what my father thought, anyway."

"So they're just getting fuel there?" Max asked. "And there aren't any giants or hidden monsters lurking that will get all of them killed?"

"No," Trina replied. "Poe might be good for airships, but otherwise it's pretty boring. They'll get the fuel."

"Actually, how are they paying for it?" Max asked.

Trina's eyes went to the side. "Uh... I... gave them our money."

Max stared at her. "You what?"

From the corridor outside, Max heard the ullu Reken, laughing. Apparently, he'd been listening in.

"They needed money and we had it," Trina said.

Max checked his screen. Yep. The gol count was now at zero.

"All of the money?" Arinna asked.

Trina nodded.

"Don't you think that was a little bit foolish?" Arinna asked.

Trina bristled. "While you two were off doing.... whatever... I had to make a decision regarding the welfare of our friends and I did. If you'd been here you could have objected, but you weren't, were you?"

Max held out his hands. "Whoa, whoa... let's not get upset. You didn't give any items away did you?"

Trina shook her head. "I couldn't, actually. They were all grayed out because you were too far away. I treated a few minor illnesses and they left."

Max sighed. Thank goodness. If she'd given away any of his high tier armors or great-swords he might have cried.

"You should not take from the group without consulting the others," Arinna said, her lips pressed into a line. "That's common sense."

Trina's eyes narrowed. "So is helping your friends, or so I thought."

"We're getting off track here," Max said. "Tela is waiting to hear our destination. Trina, how long are the pirates going to be at Poe?"

"At least two weeks," she replied, still staring daggers at Arinna. "They want to take on supplies, purchase weapons, and hire some crew. The Nelarians took everything they had."

Arinna stared back, unflinching. "That takes two weeks?"

"Yes," Trina replied. "It does. I told them what out mission is. They're not bad people. They want to help us."

"Is there time to venture..." Max stepped over to the wall where he'd told the automaton to draw a crude outline of this world's continents. "Korin," he said. "Point to Poe."

The bird creature's head tilted. "That identifier is not in my list of locations."

"It's here!" Trina snapped, pointing a finger at a spot near the center of the map. "And we are over here, just across the ocean at the town of Ettyn."

"Ok," Max said. "I see... is there time for us to go back to the south to check on Ceradram, and maybe check the mountains for a goblin tribe?"

"It's a shorter trip across the ocean here, as long as we're careful not to be seen by Nelarians," Trina replied. "Maybe a couple days?"

"Correct," Korin the automaton interjected. "I estimate that distance would take 1 day, seventeen hours and seven minutes of direct travel at the typical cruising speed of this vessel."

"But Ceradram is more than twice that distance. It would eat a lot of time and we'd be flying over the entire nation of Reylos, see?" Trina said. "I think it's a waste of time. We should stay near the pirates. They're the closest thing to an army we have and they're in debt to me, I freed them from the Nelarians."

"What about Rik?" Max asked. "We should check up on him, shouldn't we? He's in the same mountain range as Ciara."

"I told you before, Max!" Trina said. "The Valcas mountains are gigantic! They stretch up and down that whole continent! Even if we assume they're still in the southern quarter of it... it's impossible to find anyone there."

Max and Arinna both looked at each other at the same time.

"Do you know anything?" she asked.

Max nodded. "I do!"

"Then we can do it," Arinna replied. "We'll just have to get you close enough for it to work, maybe we could even raise your level a little, and mine too."

"Oh!" Max said. "I know a place where we can go for that. Do you get skill experience for melee attacks?"

She nodded. "I do, and for avoiding attacks."

"Perfect! I've got a friend you should meet."

"What are you two talking about?!" Trina grumbled.

"Should you tell her? Or should I?" Max asked.

Arinna turned to Trina. "Max knows an item the goblins have. He can use Scavenger to point us in the right direction."

"Not the goblins, actually," Max said. "There's a turs Shaman with them and she has a carved wooden token necklace that I should be able to find. I remember it vividly."

"A she, hmmm?" the ullu said from the hall where he was leaning against a bulkhead. "For a man with no flesh, you sure have a lot of females around you."

Max's head whipped around. "Hey!"

Reken's clawed hands went up. "It's a simple truth, is it not?"

"Now do you understand why I don't like him?" Trina asked.

"I'm starting to," Max said.

"I disagree about going back to Ceradram," Trina said. "We should stay with Caerd... er... with the Black Skull pirates. They'll be waiting for us at Poe... I kind of... told them we'd be joining them there."

"Mmmm Hmmm," Max said, turning back to Trina.

She frowned. "What's that supposed to mean?"

"Tela, do we have the fuel to head back to Ceradram?" Max asked.

"I believe so, but only just," Tela replied.

"Good, start heading that way. If we need to stop and grab some fuel at Rose we can," Max said. "I'm sure they'll be super happy to see us, but I'd like to stop at a particular location after that."

"You've got it!" Tela chirped.

Trina did not look happy as she stalked out of the bridge. Max figured she'd get over it eventually, or he hoped so anyway. They would be reconnecting with the pirates soon enough, assuming they had told Trina the truth, and not just taken her money and ran for it, a distinct possibility.

Sleeping quarters had become very cramped in the Midnight with all the new passengers, it made for a difficult few days of travel. Despite their obvious friction, the two females decided to stay together, which was fine. As it turned out Arinna preferred to sleep during the day, so they could share the same space. Reken forced Max to return Mytten to her cattan but still took possession of Max's room anyway, saying it was impossible for him to sleep in a location covered in webs. This forced Max to spend his time either on the bridge, one of the thin hallways, or the cargo bay; most of the time he chose the latter. The funniest part being when Reken had walked into Max's room, not noticing the sleep sign until he dropped to the deck with a thump, out cold.

On the second day of travel Max happened upon Trina in the cargo bay, fishing out some stored items for something she was doing.

"Hey," Max said. "I don't mean to override you. I know you want to spend more time around Caerd."

Trina seemed to ignore him for a moment, before finally she sighed and turned around. "I don't like or trust that obnoxious ullu, but you brought him aboard anyway. I do like the pirates, but you force me to come halfway across the world when we don't even need to."

Max felt they needed to, absolutely. He'd found a new token and a staff for Khilen, and it had been a while since they'd seen the goblins and the people of Ceradram. Maybe someone there would have some useful ideas on how they could get to the portal.

"I hear you," Max said.

"It doesn't feel like that," she said. "Haven't I helped you with everything you wanted to do? We even found her! I just wanted to spend a little time with..."

"Caerd," Max replied.

She frowned, looking away. "Yes."

Should he tell her that Caerd was hitting on Arinna? Somehow that didn't feel like it would be helpful. She probably wouldn't even believe him.

"We will get back there," Max said. "I promise."

Trina nodded, still sullen. "If you say so."

"I do," he said.

She walked off, carrying an armful of herbs, but at the exit to the bay Trina paused.

"What?" he asked.

"Your betrothed has already asked me for potions, twice," she said. "Maybe you should talk to her about that."

"Uh... sure," Max said.

When she'd left he looked down, bringing up his display, flipping to the equipment screen where the countdown was. He had twelve days left.

They were spending four just going to Ceradram. A straight shot back to where the pirates were would probably be three, assuming they didn't spend any time chatting in Ceradram but they would, so probably another day for that. Training Arinna up would probably add another day. That would leave him with just three to fly to the core. That might be enough, from what he remembered about the distance on the map, but it would be close.

Max sighed. Crap.

～

"BRITTNEY! You need to stand up, right now!" the tiny blue girl shouted.

Brittney frowned, rubbing her head and realizing that her hair was a frizzy mess. "Ok... fine! Just stop yelling at me!"

"This way!" the pixie said as she shot up into the air and buzzed toward a nearby wall. Then she was gone.

Brittney wobbled her way to her feet, trying to make sense of what had happened. No, it definitely wasn't there anymore. Had she dreamed it?

Then a tiny blue head popped out of the wall. "Come on!"

Brittney scowled at her. "What are you talking about! That's a wall!"

The pixie made a face. "Of course! Of course they would leave this to me. Just walk ahead. There isn't really a wall here. You're blind but there isn't time to fix it."

"I can see you and the wall just fine!" Brittney snapped. "See?" she added, pushing against the papered wall but to her surprise her hand went through and suddenly there wasn't a wall there, there was a hallway.

"What? What just happened?" she said.

The pixie grumbled, rolling her eyes. "You can't trust those eyes here, they're made for the mortal plane. Just close them and hold onto me. Walk the direction I pull you, and do it quickly!"

"Huh?" Brittney said, still processing the tiny blue girl's statement. Her eyes were wrong?

The pixie flew out of the wall and turned around. "Put out your hand!" she snapped.

Brittney pressed her lips together, angrily. "Fine!" she said and extended her right hand. "But if you pull me off a cliff I swear I'll find you and make you suffer!"

"You have a rage problem," the pixie replied. "Has anyone ever told you that?"

"Shut up!" Brittney said as the tiny creature pulled on her hand. Brittney closed her eyes, took a breath and walked.

"A little faster, don't worry, I'll steer you," the tiny voice said.

Then something that felt like a phone book thumped into Brittney's forehead hard enough for her to see stars.

"Ow!" she said. "What the hell was that?"

"Sorry!" the pixie replied. "You're taller than I thought you were. Just don't open your eyes right now."

It was already too late, Brittney's eyes were wide open, staring into a space that made her stomach swirl like a toilet bowl. Everything was floating everywhere. There were walls hanging in the sky and weirdly shaped people and monsters walking upside down and file cabinets and papers everywhere. It was like the most boring library in the universe had exploded and was frozen in time four seconds later. It made her brain ache just to look at it so she shut her eyes again, squeezing them tightly this time.

That didn't really help though, she felt her gorge rising in her throat. She was going to throw up.

"No puking! I told you not to look, you idiot!" the little blue girl said. "This is the worst place for the mortal blind. Swallow that down! We'll be back in the hedge soon."

"But... how?" Brittney asked, doing her best to force her stomach to relax. It had felt like they were moving straight the entire time, but maybe they hadn't? No... wait, the creature had been pulling her hand in different ways, but Brittney hadn't been able to even think about whether those ways were left or right or up or down. Did those things not exist here? What was wrong with this place?

Thinking about these things made her stomach churn even more.

"I'm... gonna ralph!" she groaned. "Please!"

"Humans!" the girl replied. "Just hold on for a few more seconds."

"I... can't!" Brittney said... the hot liquid was rising. She was gagging, fighting it as hard as she could but...

"Bleaggghhhhh..." The puke sprayed out like a fountain, hitting something hard with a wet sploshing slap.

Brittney put a hand out to steady herself and found a metal bar of some kind. She held onto that for dear life as she retched again, bringing up little more than bile. She couldn't even remember the last time she'd eaten anything.

"Ugh... you smell!" the tiny girl said from somewhere near Brittney's right ear.

"I'm not gonna apologize," Brittney said, spitting phlegm onto a pile of weirdly shaped papers. "A Cali girl never does."

"Classy," the pixie grumbled.

"Heh," Brittney replied, retching one more time but there wasn't anything to bring up so she just waited it out. "You better believe it."

"Can you see this hallway?" the tiny girl asked.

She was pointing ahead somewhere. Brittney squinted. "I think so," she replied. It did look like a hallway, except, maybe shown at an angle. It was like a fun house though, the sizes of things didn't seem to match up. "Why is this like this now? It wasn't before."

"They had blinders on you before your hearing. It's standard," the pixie said, as if everyone in the whole world knew that and Brittney was just some idiot who'd wandered in off the street. Though, she had to admit, it was sort of true.

"I change my answer... I can't really see it. What I see doesn't look like a hallway."

"Close your eyes then, and feel the walls," the creature replied.

Brittney didn't wait this time, she didn't argue, she closed them. Immediately, everything started to feel more normal. There was a floor under her feet. It felt solid, and that metal railing she was holding on to was still there and still.. wait... now it was moving.

There was a rumble like someone had just sat on a selection of the lowest keys on a grand piano. It startled Brittney into letting go and stepping back.

"I'm sorry sir, she didn't know," the pixie said.

Hot wind moved around Brittney as something very large moved away but she didn't open her eyes. She knew that would only hurt her.

"It's not polite to grope people you don't know."

"No shit!" Brittney replied, swatting her hand in the direction of the voice. She missed as there was no satisfying slap. "Why didn't you tell me what that was?"

"Be glad he didn't notice what you did to his tail," the pixie replied.

Brittney winced. "Just take me out of here," she said. "Please."

"Just follow my voice," the pixie said. "The broker's right down this hall."

Broker? That wasn't a friendly word! Brokers did things for money and as far as Brittney knew, she had none. Did she even have clothes on anymore? Quickly she checked. Yes... jeans and a tee, phew.

"This way... come on," the voice called. "Oh... duck!"

"Huh?"

SLAP!

Something wet clapped right against the right side of her face. It felt like a mop, only made of.. like rubber strips covered in something that smelled a lot like taco sauce. This gave her the strong urge to open her eyes again, but she didn't. She didn't want to know.

"Sorry! She's new!" the pixie called out again. "Keep coming Brittney! We don't have all of eternity for this!"

"I KNOW!" Brittney snarled through gritted teeth as she willed herself to start moving again. One step. Two steps. Three. Five. Ten. Thirteen. Uh... What was she at?

"Ok, turn right and reach out your hand. You'll feel a knob, pull it open."

She did reach out, but what she felt wasn't a knob... it was more like the handle of a knife. "What do I do with this?"

"You turn it!"

Brittney turned it, feeling a mechanism move inside the door. The sound was big, like the mechanism was everywhere, even inside her own head. That was a weird feeling.

"Good, push the door," the pixie said.

Brittney did and she entered a... normal room.

"Oh thank God!" she said, falling to her knees, tears in her eyes. "Nothing's moving. It's all.. normal."

Then a door opened and a crocodile in a lab coat stepped into the room.

Brittney sighed.

"Is this the one?" the crocodile asked as it approached Brittney.

"Yes," the pixie said.

The creature flipped a little lens down from a metal band on its head which it used to inspect her face. "Mmmm," it said. "I see."

Brittney was too stunned to even back away. "Wha... What?"

"Standard price?" he asked the pixie.

"No, special deal," the pixie said. "Dravielle said you'd know."

"Mmmm," he said again, flipping down a second lens in front of the first. "It will be difficult. "Give me an extra five percent."

"I'm not authorized to do that!" the pixie said.

"Five percent of what?" Brittney asked, trying very hard not to push the crocodile snout away from her face.

"Of your experience, when you earn some again," the crocodile said. "The total would be twenty-percent."

"WHAT?" Brittney said. "Nobody gets twenty percent!"

The pixie was floored, she just stared at her.

The crocodile paused. "Then leave," it said.

"Oh, no," Brittney said. "Itsy bitsy whats her face over there said I'm being chased. You can bet the authorities, whoever they are, will be here soon enough. So why don't you do your job and get it over with?"

The crocodile wavered for a moment. "Oh... alright. Fifteen then, but you'd better stay still, because I won't be wasting anesthetic on you. It's only partially effective on humans anyway."

Brittney shrugged. "Whatever. Bring it on."

10

DISTRUSTED AND DISCOVERED

Max stood on the bridge of the Midnight, watching the ocean go by below. This world's sun was setting behind the ship but Max could still see the orange and pink light reflected from the tops of the waves below in little wavy lines. It was pretty, but more importantly it marked the safer part of their travels. Not only did he see far better at night, but the light airships were much easier to see and avoid with their lighthouse-sized high beams.

Despite being in Reylosian territory for more than a day, they hadn't seen a single airship. Max was starting to wonder about that. If they weren't patrolling their western borders, where were they?

Though there hadn't been any ships Max had seen a few islands today but none had featured the still smoking volcano he'd seen after exiting the Abyssal temple as a Dread Knight. They'd probably already passed that, or maybe it was farther west.

"Hey," said a feminine voice from behind him.

Max turned around to find Arinna standing in the entrance to the bridge. "How was your... entombing."

"Ha ha," she replied wryly. "I was expecting a coffin joke."

"We're fresh out," he said. "Did you sleep?"

She nodded, yawning a little. "Did you?"

"I don't need to," he said. "All it does is refill my magic."

"But you did anyway," she replied. "I saw you made a new sleep sign in the cargo bay."

"You pay attention," Max said. "You're right. I was hoping I might have a nightmare and hear some news from Vish."

"Did you?"

"No," he replied. "No dreams, nothing."

"Hmmm," Arinna said as she stepped onto the bridge. "It must be bad back home."

"I'm betting they know you're free," Max said. "I know there are demons who don't want that, one of them tried to kill me using that automaton there."

The bird headed robot looked over at Arinna and waved sheepishly.

Arinna looked away, staring out the window. "Yeah."

"Anyway," Max said. "I was hoping you could help me with something."

"What's that?" she asked, turning around and taking a seat in one of the command chairs.

"You said we need a necromancer," Max said.

She nodded.

"You're not a necromancer though."

She shook her head.

"Neither am I," he said. "I have access to all the base classes but necromancer isn't in that list."

"No," she said. "It's a prestige class, like Dread Knight."

"Great... So can you tell me how to unlock it?"

Arinna's eyes went down. "No, sorry."

"Seriously?" Max said. "Aren't you the goddess of death?"

Her expression hardened. "I told you before. I don't do magic. I kill things. I bring death, I don't play with it."

Max folded his skeletal arms. "But you know it's a prestige class."

"Yes," she said, "and?"

"Well... Obviously we need to get the class," Max said. "You don't even have a clue?"

"I remember them being relatively common in cities," she said, shrugging. "You said we were going to a city you'd been to. Did you see any there?"

"Yes... actually," he replied. "But I was told not to get tangled up with them."

"By whom?" Arinna asked, raising an eyebrow.

"Trina, actually," Max said.

"I see," Arinna said, making a face.

"You have a problem with Trina?" Max asked her.

"I don't know her," Arinna said. "I know you. You're bound to me. She is not."

"What's that supposed to mean?" he asked.

"Exactly what I said," Arinna replied. "You're an undead, you were brought here specifically to find me and deliver me back home. The girl is not. She could be from the light for all I know."

Ooh... This would not be a good time to mention that Trina had in fact come from a light family in Verian. Arinna would probably find that out eventually but it wouldn't be from him.

"She and I have been through a lot," Max said. "She's made a few mistakes, here and there, I grant you, but so have I. I trust her."

"If you say so," Arinna said flatly.

Max figured it was time to change the subject. "Even more annoying: I even have a book on necromancy. I read the whole thing. I know all the abilities and the spell components, all of it, except how to unlock the friggin' class."

"You sound a lot like my father," she said. It did not sound like a compliment.

Max was lost in his thoughts though, musing. "It has to be something simple, something easy."

"I wish there were something to do here," Arinna said, standing up. "I'm going crazy in this tin can."

"Sorry," Max said. She'd just spent an awful long time in captivity. Wanting to get out made sense. "How about we go up top?"

Arinna's eyebrows raised. "We can do that?"

Max nodded. "Yep. There's a little space to hang out up there. You can at least get some fresh air and watch the moon rise. Tela, is everything under control here?"

"Absolutely!" Tela said. "Still on course!"

"Sounds good," Max said. He waved to Arinna. "Come on."

They walked the short distance to the ladder up to the Midnight's top hatch. Then he unlocked the hatch and crawled out onto the ship's top surface. Max turned back and offered a skeletal hand to Arinna which she took, allowing him to pull her up but as he did, Max saw something in the distance.

"Those are big birds," he said, but even as the words escaped his teeth, the realization was already dawning on him. "Looks like you're going to get some excitement after all," he added.

"Oh?" she replied, levering herself to standing on the metal surface of the Midnight. Her pitch black hair and the purple scarf blowing in the wind made Max realize once again how beautiful she was. It was a shame they were probably cousins, though he still wasn't sure about that one. His dad might have been to this world but Max hadn't seen any real evidence he was from this place. Not that it mattered, he was made of bones anyway.

"Yep," Max replied. "Looks like Griffin knights and they have definitely seen us."

"Can't you use your staff?" Arinna asked, putting a hand on his shoulder to steady herself against the wind.

"I could... but they'd just go back to wherever they came from and report what we look like and that they lost us. No, there's only one option. We've got to engage and take out every one of them."

Arinna grinned, baring her pointed teeth. "Good," she said.

Bite?

Scuff was peeking his head out of the hatch.

"Scruff!" Max said. "Perfect! Run down and wake up Trina."

The creature made a quick salute before diving back down into the ship.

"Are you still a Dark Summoner?" Arinna asked him.

Max nodded, watching the birds close in. "If we fire on them with our weapons and take a few down, we'd have to chase any that broke off," Max said. "How far can the Griffins fly?"

"Not terribly far," Arinna said. "Usually they keep them on an airship and launch from there."

"Yeah, I saw one of those," Max replied. "That means the ship will be nearby, probably just over the horizon to our east. I think it's better we let them land and take care of them when they're in the ship."

"It pains me to say it, but even at level two I'm no match for a Griffin knight," Arinna said.

"No, I know," Max said. "You just don't have the health... yet. Don't worry about the knights, the Scruffs and I will make them wish they never saw this ship."

No sooner had Max finished his statement than a tiny blast of holy fire launched from the lance of one of the knights. He ducked, barely avoiding losing his entire head to holy fire. The shot slammed into the deck behind them with a clang. Because of the low angle the fire caromed off but not before it left a charred dent the size of a manhole cover.

"No more jawing," Max said. "Let's get inside, I've got to change into my super suit."

"Your what?" Arinna asked as she slid down the ladder.

Max just jumped down, hitting the deck beside her with a thump. "I've got to change and put on the Dread Knight getup. I just... thought it would be funny."

Arinna shrugged. "Meh."

"Everybody's a critic," Max said as he ran to the back bay, unequipping his mage robes and boots as he went. That was another thing he would want: some actual high tier magic gear.

"Wooo!" Arinna called from behind him. "Naked skeleton!"

Max was so surprised his skull turned back and he slammed head first into a bulkhead with a loud clang!

"Ow!" he shouted, glaring back down the hall but a chuckling Arinna had already disappeared. Four of the smaller dungeon crawlers appeared around him, all drooling expectantly.

"Hey guys," Max said as he pulled himself back up. "Get ready, we've got boarders coming. Get all those little poison sacs juiced up."

The little tentacled beasties shook with anticipation. They were very ready.

"Stop it!" Trina yelled from her room. "Max! Get this thing off me!"

"I told him to get you up," Max replied. "Griffin knights incoming. Get ready to repel boarders!"

The ship rocked from another hit.

The ullu's head popped out of Max's room. "I'm sorry! Did you say Griffin knights?"

"Yes! Just get back in your room," Max said as he selected Dread Knight. "I've got this." The change was quick and as both the classes were relatively high level, mostly painless. Only a minor headache plagued him as he equipped the Unending Dread armor. His great-swords were too big to use in the confines of the Midnight, but that was just fine, Max had the Spiked Mace of Toxic Trials to test out. He paired that with a sturdy Dark steel kite shield also stolen from one of the stone warriors at the Abyssal temple.

No sooner had he turned around to leave the bay than thuds sounded from above. The knights had landed.

MAX RAN down the hall to stand to one side of the ladder. Scruff appeared on the other side.

"You head down and cover the bottom hatch, take a couple of your buddies," Max said. "And tell me if anyone shows up."

Scruff saluted again.

"Bite em up!" Max said.

Bite! Bite! Bite!

All three of the dungeon crawlers were chanting in unison as they clambered down the second ladder to the lower level where the airship's engineering area and the bottom hatch were located. Max still wasn't exactly sure how machinery worked on unicorn blood, but this wasn't exactly the time to get into it.

Max pointed to two spots along the ceiling. The two remaining dungeon crawlers understood and clambered up the walls heading for it.

"I won't be in the thick of it," Arinna said, "but if you need me, I'll be here."

Max nodded to her but immediately noticed she had a new garment. A pure black cloak had been added to her dusk leather armor. He remembered that one. It was the stealthy night cloak he'd gotten from that stone frozen dark elf. He should have given that to Arinna earlier. That was the problem with a huge inventory full of great stuff. Things tended to get lost.

Three clangs sounded from above.

"By the Order of the Sky Sword, I command you to give yourselves up and turn over this stolen vessel," shouted a gruff masculine voice.

"Not by the hair of our chinny chin chin!" Max shouted back.

"Huh?" the voice asked as the top hatch opened slightly.

"Look, if you want this vessel, come and claim it," Max said.

"So be it!" the knight shouted. The hatch was wrenched open and an armor-clad knight slammed to the steel before Max. He carried a short arming sword in one hand and a buckler with a nasty spike in the other. Instead of striking at Max, the knight lunged, pushing both weapons out in front of him, trying to force Max backward into the hall.

As solid as his armor was, Max's bones still didn't weigh anymore than they had the first day he arrived. The move surprised him and that alone was enough for him to be pushed back three feet before he was able to dig in and use his strength to push back. He took no damage but there was now ample room for a second and a third knight to drop into the ship which happened immediately.

These guys were good.

"Shit!" Max hissed as he brought his mace to bear. Even though the spiked mace wasn't much bigger than a hammer, it was still hard to swing it with full force in the cramped hallway. No wonder these guys always carried short stabbing swords. His first attack was easily deflected by the buckler, as was the second, but his third shot hit the guy hard on his shoulder pauldron. The spikes penetrated easily causing the guy's first hit of poison.

The knight responded quickly with a flurry of stabbing thrusts. Max deflected one with his shield, but the rest hit home, not that it mattered.

5 damage received.

7 damage received.

1 damage received.

"Dude," Max said. "One damage?"

"Be silent, foul beast!" the griffin knight responded.

"Trina, Now!" Max shouted.

Half a second later, the lights inside the Midnight went out. As it was now night outside, it was completely black within the ship, and both Max and Arinna could see perfectly in the dark.

Max knew the knights would have some way to make light. There would only be a few seconds to make good on their advantage. Luckily, Max knew exactly how to do that.

It was time for a Flood of Terror.

Dark waves of hatred pulse from his body, rattling the Midnight as it passed. The griffin knights groaned and whimpered as they froze. Whether they resisted Max's ability made no difference, they were paralyzed by their own terror all the same.

Fifteen seconds was a long time for a mace in tight quarters. Max smashed the first Knight in the head four times, the second knight in the back of his head five times and he was getting ready to attack the third when he realized Arinna had already slit his throat with her curved blade.

"That's it? There were only three?" Arinna asked.

"No," Max replied. "I saw five but there might be more. And I didn't see a combat win notification, did you?"

Arinna smiled. "Nope."

Here!

"Scruff!" Max said. "Do you have it under control?"

There was no response, but there was some clanging from below. Damn! Mytten was too big to crawl easily through the hallways and there was no chance she was getting through a hatch.

"I've got it," Trina said as she slipped out of the bridge and onto the ladder to the lower level.

"Please go with her," Max asked Arinna. "She's-"

"A support class, I've got it," she said as she disappeared into the dark.

"I was going to say blind," Max replied but a thud from behind him, made him turn.

A huge knight was now standing in the hallway beneath the hatch. He took up the entire width of the passage with his thick armor and comically bulky shoulder pauldrons.

"Did you get lost on your way to Warhammer cosplay?" Max asked.

His enemy didn't respond, he only smashed his mailed fists together. Max realized the guy wasn't even holding a weapon, he was going to try to pummel him with his...

CLANG, CLANG, CLANG, BRANG!

The dark steel rang as hammer blows rained on Max's shield. He had to use every ounce of his strength just to keep it from being beaten aside. There wasn't time to even think about attacking and his terror ability would still be on cool down. This guy must have been just outside though, it was possible the terror had been nullified somehow.

CLANG, CLANG, CLANG, CLANG, BRANG, BANG, SLAM!

The beefy knight brought both arms down from above his head like a pile-driver. Max braced his shield with his weapon, angling it up in an attempt to absorb the blow. He was driven down, nearly to his knees and almost lost his footing.

37 damage received.

A single drip of the goo hit his right arm and sizzled. Max looked up. "Ok guys," he said to the two dungeon crawlers hanging from the ceiling above. "Sic 'em."

Bite! Bite!

The creatures dropped onto his enemy's back, shoving barbed tentacles in between the plates of his armor. If they got inside, the guy was in for a world of hurt. He knew that too, the knight reached back to grab at the crawler currently ripping at his neck.

That was his chance! Max launched forward, smashing his mace into the knight's bright silver helmet four times in quick succession. He wasn't going for power so much as many smaller strikes to build up as much poison as possible. Combined with the dungeon crawlers, that should mean death in moments.

The knight lashed out with a thick armored arm, knocking him back a couple of feet. Max didn't mind, he just whacked the guy's forearm with his spiked mace, driving the poisoned spikes as deep as his strength would allow.

The guy was starting to weaken. His gauntleted fingers slowed in their attempts to grab at the dungeon crawler attached to his neck as blood flowed freely from his visor. He dropped to one knee.

Max had him! Just one more blow and...

A brilliant light exploded in the air above Max's fallen foe, blinding Max and pushing him back with a gust of dry hot wind.

133 damage received.

The dungeon crawlers were squealing in pain.

Max pulled his shield up to try to cover his eyes but the light seemed to be coming from everywhere at once. There was no shadow for him to take refuge.

Another burst of light followed, this one with a bluish tone. It wasn't as bright, but Max could feel it burning his bones right through his armor. What the hell was going on?

A hammer fist slammed against Max's shield, knocking it aside. Max felt so weak. He wanted to return the favor by smashing his mace against the other guy's helmet but it felt too heavy to lift.

Two gauntleted fists slammed into Max's chest plate, knocking him backward.

37 damage received.

42 damage received.

This was followed by two hammer blows to Max's shoulders, driving him to his knees.

29 damage received.

36 damage received.

Max looked up at his assailant, trying to see through the glare. The guy was standing tall, like he'd never been poisoned at all. It reminded Max of Tesh. That first battle had been all about regeneration. Tesh had been getting it from equipment. This seemed different.

CLANG, CLANG, BRANG!

34 damage received.

41 damage received.

57 damage received.

Three solid punches rocked Max's helmet. This was bad, real bad.

11

BURNING FEATHERS AND TENTACLES

Three bright green throwing daggers shot out of the dark behind Max. He only saw them because of the glint of white light that flashed as they passed. This was followed by a sort of screeching scream that came from behind the great armored knight that stood over him.

The light faltered and Max felt his strength return. As the next fist came in for his face he used his shield to smash it aside and jabbed the head of his mace into the center of the knight's helmet. The black tines at the end of the weapon were particularly long. They lanced through the holes in his enemy's visor and broke off, leaving black poisoned spines in the guy's face. The man screamed and clawed at his helmet.

Max raised his mace for a followup blow.

"No!" Arinna shouted from behind him. "Forget about him. He's nothing without the Seto angel. Kill that!"

Angel? If he was going to do that, Max would have to get past the mass of flesh and armor before him. The guy looked a little off balance though, maybe a Raeg style bull rush would work.

He bent low and used all the strength he had to launch himself forward, shield first. With a loud clang Max bowled the knight over only to pause, astonished.

Floating in the air ahead were two... things. One was a pair of white wings that seemed to be suspended in space around an unblinking eye that appeared to be covered with white flames. The other was similar, sort of, it too had wings, but they were royal blue. Instead of an eye, the second one had a crystalline beating heart at its center that shed shining tears of pure silver.

The creatures noticed him immediately and tried to escape but the Midnight's closed in walls prevented it. One of them tried to flee to its right and slammed into a metal wall while the other bashed itself against the ceiling.

"Oh, I don't think so!" Max said as he beat the ever living crap out of the white one first. Feathers flew everywhere as the creature flapped and shrieked. The thing didn't feel at all like it looked. It was like beating a feather pillow to death with a baseball bat, only about a hundred times more satisfying. After the sixth hit, there was a burst of white light and it was gone. Even the many white feathers it had lost during its struggles evaporated at its death.

Max turned to find the blue one had managed to figure out how to start flying down the hall, only to receive another throwing knife from Arinna which pinned a wing in place. The bizarre looking thing was shrieking and flapping as Max approached, raising his mace, ready to put it out of its misery.

A red flash behind him caught his attention, causing him to turn just in time to dodge the sword thrust aimed at the back of his helmet. A new flapping winged creature had appeared; only this one had red wings, a crown at its center and two disembodied human hands that clutched a sword wreathed in brilliant red flames. The creature struck again, wordlessly jamming its flaming sword at Max's helmet.

Max swung his left arm around, beating the weapon aside with his shield but before he could come around with his mace the blade was already angling for another strike and another and another.

74 damage received.

83 damage received.

63 damage received.

"Ow!" Max shouted, finally finding an opening to swing his own weapon but the flaming sword parried his mace effortlessly, responding with a pair of devastating stabs.

114 damage received.

97 damage received.

"What the hell is this thing!" Max shouted.

"Javal Pari," Arinna said. "It's a flame angel. The sword of burning devotion."

"Great! How do I kill it?!" he yelled as he just barely ducked a slash meant to decapitate him.

"You don't," she replied as she appeared from the dark and slashed one of the creature's crimson wings. "I do."

The angel emitted a horrible warbling cry and struck back at her. Arinna deflected the first thrust and dodged the second, but the third was a feint that led into a slash that ripped through her left thigh. Black blood splattered the deck.

Arinna receives 21 damage.

"Shit!" Max said and charged at the thing, his shield up. It was true that she'd done the only damage to the creature but she couldn't take hits like that. Rekindle or no, just one drop of pure water, which that other blue winged thing appeared to be crying, and she would be a corpse.

The flame angel danced away from Max's attack, setting up in a sort of attack stance down the hall a bit near its pinned brethren. The good news was that Arinna was behind him. The bad thing was that he had no idea how to kill it.

"Will my terror ability work on it?" Max asked, glancing back at Arinna only to find Trina at her side, wrapping her wound with a salve covered poultice.

Arinna receives 13 regeneration.

Arinna receives 12 regeneration.

"What do you think?" Arinna replied, wryly. "It's an angel! The only thing it fears is its own."

"Hey! Where do you think you're going?!" Trina shouted through her Plague Doctor mask.

Max turned to follow her gaze and saw the ullu climbing the ladder. Reken ignored her and zipped up the ladder like someone had lit a fire in his pants.

Sparks flew as Max deflected the next blow from the flaming sword but the following thrust went right through his shield, stopping only about an inch from his helmet. He used it as an opportunity to twist the shield to the left, forcing the red-winged creature to slam into the wall. The blow stunned it enough for Max to finally get a good solid whack in with the spiked mace.

The angel screeched, but then seemed to shake it off. It yanked its sword free and set up for another attack, seemingly completely unharmed.

That's when he noticed the lines of blue pouring from the other one into the back of this one. It was healing it just as it had healed the big knight.

Max turned around. The big knight. Oh shit!

"Arinna!" Trina said as the huge armored guy, blood still coursing from his visor, raised his fists to smash them both.

What should he do? Trust Trina and Arinna to handle the can of beef or rush over there and help them out? Max's second of indecision cost him as the flaming sword erupted from the center of his chest having burned straight through his armor.

236 damage received.

Arinna rolled to her right and slashed at the big guy's leg, causing pinkish blood to spurt, and Trina followed up with her own weapon, a bright blue glowing dagger he hadn't seen before, which she jabbed into the knight's armpit.

He swung at Trina but she side-stepped out of harm's way, jabbing him again, this time in the thigh.

Max watched the sword withdraw from his body and tried to turn around but the blade was already coming in from above. He only barely got his shield up in time to prevent the loss of half of his head. The fiery blade dug into the shield, cutting a molten gouge four inches deep.

"I really hate this thing!" Max shouted but as he said it the two dungeon crawlers from earlier, now charred by the earlier angel, leaped from the walls and wrapped their tentacles around the crimson angel's disembodied hands.

They held it only for a few moments but it was enough for Max to get all the way around with a swing of his spiked mace. He put everything he had into this single power attack, and it probably would have done incredible damage, had it not slammed into the wall with a clang and then missed the flame angel entirely. Max then watched as the creature let go of the flaming sword with one of its hands and proceeded to cut each of the crawlers in half with two swift strikes.

"Noooo!" Max yelled. "Blade of Brutality!" he cried and twenty percent of his remaining health was ripped from his body. It flowed into his mace like a black mist that caused the weapon to glow with bright violet tinge. Then he went apeshit.

Max lunged forward with his shield up and made it look like he planned to bash the angel with it but his mace was already in motion. The shield was just that, a visual screen for his incoming mace.

The angel tried to dance away but was hampered by the close quarters. It managed to deflect Max's first attack, but the next two hit home, smashing into a wing and the creature's weird floating crown, knocking it down to the ground. Max put one dark steel boot on the creature's wing and the other on the hilt of the flaming sword, pinning it to the deck. Then he raised his mace and hammered it over and over again, bashing the crown until the whole thing shrieked one last time. There was a burst of bright red flame as the angel seemed to evaporate into flaming embers.

Max sighed.

The blue angel was still struggling, emitting its own warbling little shrieks. Max's helmet turned in its direction and he raised the spiked mace.

"Oh yeah? You want some of this too?" he asked... and then he heard laughing from behind him.

DAMMIT! Max had let the flame angel thing distract him and he'd forgotten that Arinna and Trina were handling the big guy by themselves. He turned around to see the two of them collapsed against the walls of the corridor, panting heavily. The big armored knight was dead between them. He lay on his chest in a growing pool of pink blood.

"Are you two alright?" he asked.

"Yeah," Trina replied, panting. "We got him."

Arinna nodded.

Well, that was good... but who was laughing?

Max heard laughter again but it came from above. He looked up. The sound was coming from outside the ship?

The sounds of struggling and shrieking intensified behind him. Max looked back just in time to see the blue angel evaporate into steam. What was going on?

Then a head appeared in the hatch above. It was a man in his thirties with a thin blonde chin strap beard. His expression looked pained. A second later Reken's owl head appeared next to the other guy.

"I got him," he said. "It took some work, but these nerds always have one of six weaknesses."

"What are you talking about?" Max asked.

"He's a Comedian," Trina said. "He's really good at paralyzing smart people."

"That's an extremely specific talent," Max said.

"Comes in handy more than you might think," the ullu replied as he used both clawed hands to shove the bearded guy down into the hatch. The man whimpered as he fell, crumpling in a heap at the bottom of the ladder. He didn't even try to get up, he just lay there in fetal position. The guy was wearing some kind of ornate robes with a sunburst pattern on them and a lot of gold fringe.

"Wow," Max said. "Was he doing the.. ah..." Max pointed to where the angels were.

"Yeah," Arinna said as she used the wall to get up, wincing. "He's an Emissary. They call angels from the heavens into battle."

"So like the light version of Dark Summoner," Max replied.

Reken slid down the ladder, landing next to the crumpled man. "No... that would be Dawn Caller. This man is an Emissary."

"It's more like their version of Necromancer," Arinna said.

Max looked down at the pathetic looking guy at his feet. "Will he answer questions?"

Reken frowned, the feathers above his eyes knitting together like angry caterpillars. "It's paralysis not truth magic."

Arinna stepped forward, drawing her blade. "Ask your questions Max. I can make him talk. I'll just cut things off until he-"

Reken laughed. "No! The light are trained to resist physical torture. It's what they expect."

"Then what do you suggest, bird?" Trina snapped as she removed her Plague Doctor mask.

Reken held up a single clawed finger. "Bilton," he said.

The eyes of the man on the floor shifted back to the ullu.

"Why don't you answer the good Boneknight's questions. Lest I tell everyone here what it is you like to do on the weekends."

The man's eyes widened in fear. "B-but... That's..."

"Ask," Reken said, nodding toward Max.

Max chuckled. Whatever this guy did with his comedy, it was nasty. "What sort of ship did you come from?"

"T-the Sovereign Herald, a griffin carrier of the Order of the Sky Sword," the man replied.

"Is that the only ship near us?"

"N-no," he said. "There is also a Kestrian destroyer, the Banisher."

Kestrians huh? Way out here by Reylos? "Where are they?" Max asked.

"J-just over the horizon," he said. "to the E-" his words were cut short by a crossbow bolt that shot down from above, lodging perfectly in the Emissary's left eye.

Griffin knights, Armored enforcer and Emissary of light defeated!

Trina has gained a level of Plague Doctor!

Trina has gained a level!

Arinna has gained a level of Grave Blade!

Arinna has gained a level of Grave Blade!

Arinna has gained a level!

Arinna has gained a level!

Max looked up, but he only caught a glimpse of a white cloak fluttering as someone ran off. This was exactly what he'd hoped wouldn't happen.

"Arinna," he said. "Are you healed up?"

"I could use another salve," she said.

"Consider it done," Trina replied as she called the medicine into her hands.

Arinna's health is restored.

"Whoever that was is heading back to report on us. We need to catch up to them and kill them before they get there," Max said. "Failing that, we destroy both enemy ships."

"Why?" Trina asked. "We could just escape."

"There's too little time to explain," Max said.

Trina shrugged. "Alright... TELA!"

"Yes?" Tela's voice called happily from the bridge.

Trina ran off, heading to the bridge. "I'll get her in pursuit. Can you and Arinna crew the guns?"

"You got it!" Max said.

The ullu pulled on Max's cape. "Excuse me, what do we do with all the," he gestured toward the bodies choking the corridor, "debris."

"We feed my friends," Max replied. "And we keep anything they leave behind, like armor, but usually the higher level guys don't drop much because they wear-"

"Cache amulets, yes," Reken replied, rubbing his beak like a chin.

Actually, that reminded Max. "Scruff?" he called. "Where are you?"

"He's fine," Arinna replied. "I went down to help Trina like you asked. There was only one Griffin knight coming in from the lower hatch. Trina stunned him with some gas and your little crawlers ate his face off. They didn't need me."

"Good to know," Max replied, but that wasn't the only reason he wanted to talk to Scruff.

The creature's tentacled body appeared at the lower ladder ahead.

Max?

"We lost two of yours down the hall," Max said, trying not to sound as sad as actually he was about it. He'd really loved those little guys.

No sad. Eat.

"Thanks bud," Max said, patting Scruff on the head as he passed the ever growing dungeon crawler. The other two crawlers that had gone with him were a little beaten up but otherwise seemed well. Good, at least they had survived. "The rest of the dead are yours too."

Eat! Eat! Eat!

"Do I go up or down?" Arinna asked.

"Unless you have a preference," Max said, "I went to the upper turret last time. This time I'll take the bottom one."

Arinna grinned at him, her vampire teeth showing.

"What?" he asked.

She shook her head. "Nothing, up I go."

Max shrugged and climbed down the ladder to the lower turret.

"Tela says we're gaining on her," Trina called down from the bridge. "She's on a Griffin straight ahead."

Max used the foot pedals to spin his turret around to face forward. There wasn't anything out there but black night and the many stars above. "Don't see it!"

"I can!" Arinna yelled down the ladder from her own turret. "You're a skeleton. Your night vision is poorer than mine. She's about five degrees to the right of the nose."

Max stared in that direction. He still didn't see anything. This was definitely harder when the enemy didn't have huge lights shining on them.

"Still can't see it!" Max said.

"Look!" Arinna yelled and fired her gun.

A single small spear of holy fire shot out ahead in exactly the direction she'd indicated. The shot arced out like a flare before dropping down to the waves. It worked though, Max caught a glimpse of their quarry. It was only for a second, but it was enough. The griffin was there. It did look like they were gaining on it, but slowly. Too slowly.

"Can Tela speed up?" Max yelled up.

"No," Trina replied.

"Where's a miracle working chief engineer when you need one?" Max mumbled under his breath.

"I told you!" Trina yelled down. "I'm not an technician-"

"I'm a doctor," Max grumbled as Trina said the same thing. How did she even hear him? There might be tubes that connected the turrets to the bridge. Maybe he didn't have to yell at all.

Max made a decision and jumped up out of his chair, climbing the short ladder back into the Midnight's central corridor. There he found Scruff and his two remaining spawn feasting on the remnants of the big knight. That guy must have been the 'Enforcer.' He should remember to ask about that one. He hoped it wasn't one of the regular light soldier varieties. Facing dozens of enemies like that guy would not be fun.

"Max, where are you going?" Trina asked, sticking her head out of the bridge.

"We're not going to catch up in time. I'm going to go up and get on Dwayne and follow that griffin back to its base and take down both ships," he said.

"Because you're a mad man," Trina said.

"You mean he's a Mad Max," Arinna said, stepping out of the upper ladder well.

Max laughed. "Ok... that was good."

"I'm glad you think so," Arinna said. "Because I'm coming with you."

12

SHIP-TO-SHIP AND AN ANTIHERO

"No way," Max said. "You're only level four now."

"That's more than enough," she replied.

Trina frowned. "Just make sure to leave Mytten so she points me in the direction to fish you out of the ocean."

Max pointed at Trina. "That is a good idea!" With his other hand he summoned Mytten's cattan and threw it at the floor of a nearby room. With an explosion of black smoke, Mytten appeared.

Reken made a little screech and ran toward the back of the ship.

"I assume you know what's going on," Max said to the spider. "Since you can hear most of my thoughts."

Yes.

"Great, also keep a few of your eyes on Arinna," Max said.

There is no way she won't come.

"There is no way I'm not coming," Arinna said. "I can't let you face two ships by yourself!"

"You can," Max replied.

"I won't," she said, leaning forward, her green eyes burning with determination.

"You two..." Trina said, shaking her head. "Just kiss and get it over with!"

They both turned to her, glaring.

"I have no lips, Trina!" Max said.

"Let's go," Arinna said as she strode to the ladder. "We're wasting time."

Max shook his head. "Fine."

Dwayne was stoked to be called upon again. He was flapping as hard as he could. Max got some extra speed out of him by casting Empower and Hasten. They weren't as powerful as they would be if he were one of his casting classes, but it still helped quite a bit. They were closing on the griffin.

"There!" Arinna said, pointing ahead.

She was right, there were two small lights along the horizon. Small at this distance, likely large up close. The griffin was heading for the left one. Max wondered, attack the destroyer first or the carrier?

"I say we go for the carrier," Arinna said, as if she'd read his mind. "The faster the remaining griffin knights are heading to the bottom of the sea, the better."

As the destroyer was likely too slow to get away, that made sense. "I agree," he said. "Are you sure you're ready for this?"

Arinna leaned in close to his left ear. "Absolutely," she said.

"Dwayne, can you fly up higher? I want you to dive down right onto their deck," Max said.

That will be very fast Max bro.

Max sighed. The wyvern just wasn't getting it.

You don't have a riding harness. You may fall off.

"We'll be fine," Max said.

They weren't. Dwayne used his powerful wings to drive the three of them high into the sky above the enemy carrier. Then he dove. The second the wyvern pitched down Max was almost jerked free and Arinna with him. He thought they were going to be fine after that but that didn't turn out to be the case.

As soon as they were spotted the carrier opened fire with several smaller turrets just like the ones on the Midnight, fast firing guns designed to kill fliers just like Dwayne. That forced Dwayne to dodge and weave as he plummeted downward. The fourth such juke, yanked Max right off the wyvern's back. Arinna held on to him but he knew that if she hit the deck straight on she'd die and he'd be forced to stand over her body waiting for her to revive. So Max took her into his arms, shielding her body with his as they slammed into the carrier's deck.

247 damage received.

Arinna receives 34 damage.

"Ow," Max groaned.

"Oh get up you wuss," Arinna said playfully with a wide grin. "We've got killin' to do."

"You are a monster!" he said as he pulled himself up. Gone was the dark steel shield and the spiked mace. Instead Max summoned the Taker of Will, a mottled green great-sword with a thick heavy blade.

Arinna looked back at him, a twinkle in her eye. "You have no idea."

"Fire!" someone shouted from his left. This was followed by the thunk of several crossbows. Rather than wait to be impaled, Max rolled to his right and charged the four Griffin Knights that were on their way to engage him, swords drawn.

"I've got the bows," Arinna said from behind him, and in a flash she was gone.

"We are Cerathia's sword!" the knights shouted as they charged.

Max waited until the last moment, when until his enemies were raising their swords to strike, when he activated the Flood of Terror. All four knights fell to their knees screaming as did all the support staff on the deck and the handful of griffins they were tending. The winged creatures took to the air, screeching and dragging their handlers with them.

Then he went to work. The Taker of Will slammed into each knight, one at a time. When they weren't moving it was easy to cut them down. The weapon carved through their shining white armor like butter. Max had no idea how much damage he was doing, which was a shame, but it had to be a lot. Each griffin knight went down with one smooth cleaving stroke.

Pinkish blood stained the metal clad deck as Max stepped over the bodies. A second line was trying to form a defense at the entrance to the lower decks. Max ran at them, full speed, his weapon raised. Though his ability had already worn off, three of the regular soldiers panicked and ran at the sight of him.

Max made quick work of the remaining five, cutting them apart with his greatsword. Not a single hit even glanced across his armor, which was good, that Emissary's angels had given it a beating. Max didn't know how much more it could take and he didn't really have time to dig into it.

Order of the Sky Sword Griffin Knights, Watchers, and Soldiers defeated!

Arinna has gained a level of Grave Blade!

Arinna has gained a level!

Arinna's health is restored.

"Sweet!" Max said.

"Yes it is!" Arinna replied.

This odd comment caused Max to turn and see his betrothed wiping about a pint of bright red blood from her chin. The entire front of her armor was splashed with it.

"What?" she asked. "The lower level ones don't taste as bad."

"You missed a spot," he said.

Arinna rolled her eyes at him. "Ooh," she added, pointing to the sky behind him. "More friends to meet."

Max chuckled as he turned around, thinking she meant a flock of Griffin Knights flying in. "Oh! Oh wow!" he said. It was the destroyer. The airship, which was probably ten times the size of the Midnight, was hovering directly over them, its many lower guns quickly turning in their direction. In about four seconds they would be burning in a barrage of holy fire.

"Time to get below!" Arinna said. "We can take this ship out from the inside."

Max's eyes caught something shiny on the ground nearby. "Actually," he said. "I've got a better idea. Come on!"

Max snatched the Pakheta Amulet from the ground and ran toward the edge of the carrier as balls of holy fire rained down from above. Arinna was hot on his heels, actually she'd already caught up. Was she already faster than him at level five?

The two of them jumped as Max held out the amulet and yelled. "HAMU UDACHAUM!"

Arinna held on to his elbow as the two of them raced toward the ocean's surface.

After a few seconds Max started to get worried. Had this griffin fled too far to hear his call? Should he try again?

Then, with a thump and a shriek, the griffin appeared, diving beside them its wings folded tightly against its body. The creature deftly maneuvered Max into its saddle and Arinna slid in behind him. They pulled up just before they reached the black surface of the deep ocean.

"Udana!" Max yelled, taking the reins and pulling the creature skyward. They flew around behind the carrier, ignored because of their mount, and rose up to land on the very top of the tower that jutted from the top of the destroyer.

"I'm guessing this is the bridge," Max said. "And look at that." he pointed down below. The destroyer was still hovering above the carrier, likely trying to protect it in case they attempted to return.

"Perfect," she said. "I see what you were thinking."

Max nodded. "I thought you might."

"How are we going to do it?" Arinna asked.

Max dismounted from the griffin, patting the creature's beak with his gauntleted fingers. The creature hissed, but it didn't attack. "I could switch to a magic class and pump a bunch of fire in there, but that would be a pain."

Arinna grinned. "Or we could just go in and kill everyone."

Max pointed at her. "That one."

SOMETHING SMELLED RANK. It took Brittney far too long to realize it was probably her. There was probably puke on her shirt and who knows what else. It was odd that she hadn't smelled it until now, but the crocodile had said something about that. Something about how they weren't changing her eyes but her head, so all her senses might change.

The smell was getting worse too. Ugh. Could this day get any worse? Actually, never mind that. It was a question she probably shouldn't ask.

"Janine, how long has it been?" Brittney asked instead. It turned out the blue pixie girl had the most normal sounding name she'd heard in a long time. It reminded her of that time, back during the last serious war with the dark, when she'd fought against an army of goblins and found out their leader's name was Kevin the Terrible. Kevin! What was wrong with this world?

"Only four bexels less than it was last time!"

Brittney sighed angrily. "I told you! I don't know what that means!"

"It means shut up and wait," a familiar voice said.

"The old lady?" Brittney asked. "You're here?"

Janine hissed. "You ungrateful human freak! Gravielle is the only reason you're alive right now!"

Brittney sat up, still holding the cold wet thing they'd told her to press against her eyes. "I don't care who she is! I hate this place!"

"Ha!" the old woman said. "You fool! Did you think serving the light would be easy?"

"I don't serve the light," Brittney retorted, angrily. "Didn't you hear what they said? I conspired to help that stupid skeleton free Arinna from that disgusting fat pervert... and now I'm what? A fugitive?"

"You served better than any in centuries," the old woman said.

"You're a hero," Janine said.

Brittney frowned, wishing she could see these people to know if they were pulling her leg. It didn't sound like they were but...

"The light is dying," Gravielle continued. "A cancer has taken hold of us in the form of our own hubris. Many have known for a while, it was an open secret among the learned in the white towers of Vis Vavilaya but none would risk their position to point it out. I couldn't take it any longer. I spoke up about the problems, about the corruption, the injustice, the suffering. All caused in the name of Cerathia, by our own people."

"Look," Brittney said, hopefully gesturing in the right direction. "I think you're being just a little over dramatic." At that moment she had a flashback of her mother saying the same thing to her long ago, so long ago... What had she even wanted to do? Go to a party? She couldn't remember what it was, all she did remember was that she got so angry she poured a bottle of her mom's favorite guzzling wine into the front seat of her mother's car. That had been a bad few days.

"She is not!" Janine snapped and something tiny flicked against Brittney's cheek.

"Did you just slap me?" Brittney said as she snatched at the air in front of her face. "Get over here you little-"

"Silence!" Gravielle said. "As a result of my temerity, the angelic council of Akasa demoted me, stripped me of my power. Now I shuffle papers, copying the endless laws of my brethren for all of my days."

Brittney sneered. "That's just how governments are. My father used to yell all the time about how much of his money they took and how it all went to drug addicts and layabouts."

"Stop it!" the old woman retorted. "You hear but you do not listen! This is what has happened to you. You stumbled across something embarrassing to the light so they've thrown you away."

"Like yesterday's trash," Janine added.

"I got it, thanks," Brittney replied. Her ears were ringing and her skin felt hot. These were all things she'd been told would happen when whatever they were doing to her was finished. "Can I take off this stupid blindfold yet?"

"You've still got sixteen bexels," Janine said.

"I SAID I DON'T KNOW HOW LONG THAT IS!" Brittney snarled through her teeth, swatting her free hand through the air again.

"You are wrong about governments," Gravielle replied. "The light was once a bastion of freedom and righteousness... for hundreds of years the people of Fohra were served by us but we lost our way. Now we control... everything, everyone, and what should be wondrous is anything but."

"That's why it's time," Janine said.

"It's time?" Brittney asked, starting to peel her blindfold away. Her hand was flicked.

"No, you idiot!" Janine said. "It's time for the dark to rule."

"What? But they're horrible! I remember how it was when they were in charge! I was there! There were fields of gnarly skulls and people were torn to shreds and eaten when they weren't enslaved. It was fully craptastic!" Brittney said.

"They *were* terrible," Gravielle said. "You're quite correct. But they too were at their end, as are we. Now it's our turn to fail."

"No wonder they locked you up," Brittney said. "You're insane."

"Ding, ding! Ding, ding!" the pixie shouted as she buzzed from Brittney's left ear around to her right and back again. "Time's up!"

Brittney suddenly became worried. "Are you sure?"

"Yes! As long as you aren't smelling funny things and feeling tingling and heat and ringing in your ears, then you're good."

"What? I have been feeling all those things!"

"You have?" Janine said, sounding terribly perplexed. "Oh! That's right! You should be. I got mixed up there. I'm sorry."

Brittney gulped. "So... it's Ok?"

"I think so," Janine said.

"Fine!" she snapped and pulled off the blindfold.

At first Brittney was blinded again by the brightness of the room. She was forced to shield her eyes with her fingers. Then, after a few seconds, she could see multiple moving shapes in the room. Some were big, some small, some were even floating. Then the light started to separate from the dark, and the shapes started to become clear.

"Whoa!" she said.

Janine the pixie was floating a foot away, staring at her. Before she'd been blue, but now Brittney could see so much more. She could see trails of light and a sort of glowing dust emanating from her body.

The old woman who Brittney now knew as Gravielle was behind the pixie. She was still chained at the ankle by a glowing shackle and chain, but she looked different... She had wings, golden and beautiful. Brittney could see more too... she could see through to her soul.

This wasn't the same room she'd visited before was it? The one with the papers had been tiny, barely big enough to turn around in and everything had been caked in papers. It was really much larger, she could see that now. The papers weren't papers at all, but glowing filigrees of the most beautiful ink, writing songs that filled her ears with their glorious tones the moment she beheld them.

"Are you alright?" Janine asked.

"Give her a moment," Gravielle replied. "For the first time in her life, the girl can truly see."

Wait... the other shapes. There were other people here?

"She is disappointing," a voice said. It spoke an ancient angelic dialect that Brittney had never heard before, yet now she knew it fully, like the intro to Bed of Roses, her favorite Bon Jovi song.

"This Sikari would not have been my choice," said another angelic being, a sort of circle of rings that hovered in the air. It didn't speak with words but with pure intention, but Brittney felt the truth of it.

"She'll be fine," Gravielle said. "When she returns she'll understand."

"I disagree," said another. "We've waited so long. We cannot allow this human to fail us."

Gravielle turned. "You fool! That's exactly the kind of thinking that put us here! We must put our faith in her."

"Faith for what?" Brittney asked. "What are you asking me to do?"

"Arinna is in trouble," Janine said. "She's walking into a trap."

"So what!" Brittney said. "She's evil!"

"She does not understand," said the first angel.

"It may not be possible," said the other.

"She will," Gravielle said. "Besides, I'm sending Janine with her."

Brittney frowned. "What?"

13

NO LEVEL AND NO PEACE

There wasn't a door into the bridge from where they were, so Max made one. He summoned the Taker of Will and cut a huge hole into the metal below them.

Before he could say anything, Arinna winked and jumped in. The screaming started immediately. By the time Max had stored his greatsword and jumped down into the bridge, the deed was nearly done. The inert bodies of Kestrian naval officers were everywhere. Only the captain remained. She was a severe looking woman who Max thought was a dead ringer for Charlize Theron. As he approached she stood tall, placing herself between her enemies and the control console.

"You... You undead horrors! You won't take control of this vessel," she said, raising a gilded rapier. "I won't allow it!"

"Oh we don't want it," Max said, stepping toward her. "Seriously. That would be a huge headache." He looked to

Arinna who nodded as blood dripped from her blade and her chin. "Right?"

"Sure," she replied.

The captain frowned. "What do you mean?"

"We'd have to crew it, and fuel it... and god knows what else. That's just a major pain in the ass, one I don't need right now," Max said. He rushed forward, summoning his spiked mace.

The captain used her weapon beautifully, she parried his blow and then stabbed him right in the chest. It was a perfect bulls-eye into the open hole in Max's armor left by that obnoxious flaming angel. She had to be some kind of class that was all about sword play, maybe the light equivalent to duelist.

13 damage received.

Though she wasn't very high level.

"Ha!" Max said as he grabbed her hand, keeping the blade embedded in his torso. "I'm sorry about this, but it has to be done."

Her eyes widened as Max's mace finished her. Blood splattered against Max's helmet as he let go of the woman's hand. The rapier was pulled from his body as she slumped to the floor, making way.

Kestrian crew and Kestrian Captain defeated!

"Awww," Arinna said, pouting a little. "No level."

"Crap," Max said.

"What?" she asked, appearing at his side.

"Manual controls," he replied. "I hate these."

"All you need to do is crash, right?"

Max nodded. "Good point. That, I can do."

"Throw me... uh... Dwayne is it?" Arinna asked as Max sat down in front of the two weird handles.

"Sure," he said, and tossed the wyvern's cattan to her.

"I'll be waiting up top with our ride."

Max gave her a thumbs up and turned his attention back to the console. "Down we go!" he said as he twisted the two handles, hard in the opposite direction.

Alarms screamed all around as the Kestrian destroyer twisted to the right before diving straight down into the carrier below it. The destroyer's sharp bow smashed directly into the carrier's deck, slashing the ship open like a chainsaw through a watermelon.

Now that everything was vertical, Max found it hard to pull himself free of the pilot's chair, but when he did his foot caught on the Captain's rapier and he tripped and fell onto the glass of the forward viewport. It didn't shatter immediately, which was good, but it was cracking. Max could hear that tinking, clinking sound all around him.

When he looked up, he saw three bodies falling through the air, headed right for him.

He sighed. There was nothing to do but wait.

The bodies crashed into the glass which shattered causing the bloody remains of the Kestrians to shower the carrier below. Max managed to snag the edge of the viewport and was now hanging, watching as flames shot from the two ruined ships as they twisted and turned together on their way to the ocean below.

"Well... I might as well try it," Max said as he swung himself forward and let go, trying to get some distance between the destroyer and himself, but as he did there was an explosion behind him that blasted him even farther out and set his cape fire to boot.

321 damage received.

So now he was, flying through the air in a perfect arc, streaming smoke. Awesome.

Thankfully, he had the... uh oh. The Pakheta amulet was gone. He'd forgotten to put it on. He must have just dropped it somewhere. Oops.

Then, with a crunch, Dwayne's jaws snatched Max out of the sky.

135 damage received.

Armor durability critical.

"Ow..." he said.

Sorry, bro.

"It's cool," Max groaned. "I'm good."

"You alright up there?" Arinna called as the wyvern used the hot air from the two crashing ships to corkscrew up into the sky and around back toward the Midnight.

Max finally let himself relax. They'd done it. Their ship was safe. "Yeah," he called back. "I think so."

Unfortunately the wyvern's neck wasn't long enough to turn around and place Max on his back, so he was forced to lie there and stare up at the stars and the few clouds passing above. It made him think about those ships. Why was a Kestrian ship out here? That hadn't been a big carrier like the one he saw before. This one was lighter, smaller, and accompanied by a destroyer. It made him think of when he'd played space strategy games in the past. Typically you had picket ships out at the edge of a larger fleet. They were meant to detect the enemy and report on them to the larger force, just like that Griffin rider had done.

Max hadn't seen that person again either, he was pretty sure. Though he hadn't gotten a really good look at them, he was sure he'd seen a cloak. No one with a cloak had shown up during the battle. Had they pushed on, or gone down with the ship? Probably not the latter. So maybe something bigger was going on here. Max suddenly got a bad feeling that something might have happened to his friends.

"Mytten?"

Yes, Max.

"Is everyone Ok there?"

Trina and the bird man are arguing. He is afraid of me.

"But the ship is alright?"

Yes.

"And the Scruffs?"

They have cleaned the bones of the bodies you left them and await your return.

God those little things are going to be so fat, Max thought as he sighed slowly. Despite learning that all his friends on the Midnight were safe, the worrying feeling had not gone away.

"You alright up front?" Arinna shouted to him. "We're almost there. I can see the ship."

Max waved to her. "Thanks!" he yelled back. He needed to stop focusing on feelings and start thinking about what to do next. They had precious little time to do what they needed to when they hit land. They couldn't afford to be fighting every enemy ship they came across.

No, what he needed to do was figure out how to unlock Necromancer. If he couldn't do that then they'd be forced to try to recruit someone in Ceradram, which would be a gamble.

He was sure that it should be easy though, especially for someone literally made of bones. Whatever you had to do, it would be about death. He'd touched a lot of bones in his travels here already, that couldn't be it. He'd even picked up items from that pack of gither creatures that said they were specifically for necromancy.

Actually, now that he thought about it, he should look at one of those. What were they called? He remembered the word shard. Bone shard? No. Necro... Necrotic shard? No. Was he going to have to dig through his inventory? Ugh, it was so full of crap, he really didn't want to... wait...

"Undead shard!" he said.

A small piece of bone appeared in his gauntleted hand. And that was it. It didn't look like anything and just holding it sure didn't unlock anything. Max stored it again and brought up his items screen. It took forever to dig around and find them but he did it, he had thirteen of them and they stacked like any other crafting item. Max hovered over the listing.

Undead shard: The last remnant of a soul bound undead. Necessary component for necromancy and crafting necrotic items.

Soul bound undead. Right, they had to have souls attached to them to function. Max half remembered something. It was from weeks ago, back when he'd first arrived in this world. Hadn't he seen a creature's soul? When was that?

There was Bob... But Max honestly still wasn't sure that goblin had even been a ghost, no matter what Khilen said. That guy had looked real, like one hundred percent alive.

Still, he had to figure this out. He needed to become a necromancer, somehow.

"We're here!" Arinna called.

MAX'S FEET hadn't even fully met the skin of the Midnight when a beaked owl-like head shot out of the hatch and glared at him.

"There you are! How dare you leave that monstrous hairy thing in the ship!" Reken shouted at him.

"He sounds angry," Arinna said flatly, with a bit of a grin.

"Great job Dwayne, you are the man, now come back," Max said.

The wyvern looked pleased as he dissolved into black smoke and reformed into a tiny cattan in Max's palm.

Max then turned to look at the ullu. He really didn't feel like dealing with this guy. "Write a grievance note and put it in the suggestion box," he said.

"There's a suggestion box?" Reken replied, then his eyes narrowed. "I see... giving me the brush off eh? And after I saved your boney ass from that Emissary too. You..."

Max paused, standing over the ullu. He took off his helmet so the owl-man could look his bare skull right in the glowing green eyes. "Yeah?"

Reken's words dissolved into a sort of squeak. Then he mumbled: "We'll talk later," and scurried back down the ladder.

Arinna chuckled. "You handled that pretty well."

Max shrugged. "He says he's a Comedian, but I'm gonna be honest: I don't get it." He waved her toward the hatch. "After you."

Arinna took a step but Max reached out to stop her.

"Actually... There's something else I wanted to mention."

Arinna paused. "What's that?"

This was gonna be bad, he could feel it... but he had to. "Trina mentioned that you were looking for potions."

Arinna frowned. "So?"

"I just... I've learned about those things. It's not the same as having a drink to relax every once in a while. They're more like heroin and-"

"Let me stop you right there," she said. "I asked about them because I needed healing. I didn't know we had salves. Of course those are better. Potions are cheap and easy to get, so I assumed we would have them."

"Well we don't," Max said, "and I don't want us to."

"Fine, sure," Arinna said, she was definitely upset. "Let me just say... while we are airing things, that I don't trust Trina. She gave all our gol away to those pirates because she likes their captain. She's young and foolish and she has this attitude... she acts like she's from a rich family, and the only rich, educated people left in this world are from the light."

"Noted," Max said.

"Noted? That's it?" she snarled at him.

"I get your concerns. I do," Max said. "I've done some stupid things too but you know, most of that money actually came from Trina. She did the surgery on the dragon that gave it to us. She's also single-handedly kept us stocked with healing items for basically every possible status effect, some of them I haven't even heard of before. We've been through a lot... including the loss of my first companion, my friend. What I'm telling you is... I trust her."

Arinna nodded. "Sure," she said curtly and walked off, pushing past him to get to the hatch.

Max felt anger rising... but he wasn't angry at her, he was angry at himself. Why did he have to bring it up? Now she was going to hate him. Dammit!

He found himself standing there on the top of the ship, as the wind whipped by, staring into space. What should he do? Should he chase after her and apologize? Would she cool off on her own?

Max?

A tentacle laden head appeared at the hatch.

"Hey buddy," Max said.

Good! Max home!

Scruff and his two smaller copies flooded out of the hatch and tackled him, knocking him down and licking his boney face with their poisoned tongues. It felt pretty good actually. It kind of sizzled, but in a nice way.

He let them greet him, patting a few of the creatures on their heads, until he felt a little better.

I would have come as well, but I am too big to make it through that hatch.

"I'm sorry Mytten," Max said. "I appreciate that though."

Come inside so I can give you a hug too.

Max sat up. What would a spider hug even be like?

It will be good.

Max chuckled. "I'm sure." he stood up, glad that he had friends, even if they were a little... slobbery. He slipped down the hatch just as it began to rain, storing his helmet. When his plate armored feet hit the deck in the corridor, which was now littered with skeletons, he saw Mytten immediately. She dropped from the ceiling and wrapped the front four of her eight legs around him.

I'm sorry you're angry.

"It's Ok," Max said, hugging the spider back, as weird as that was. "I appreciate you."

The Scruffs flopped down beside him as Mytten let him go and returned to her place on the ceiling, but just barely given her size. He might have to start keeping her in her cattan more often just to save space. Though the obnoxious owl-guy would like that, which made him not want to.

"You guys did a number on these bones here," he said. "Clean as a whistle."

Scruff saluted.

Eat more?

"I'll see what I can do," he said. "I think Mytten and Dwayne could use some food too."

Not me! I'm getting too fat!

"Nonsense Mytten," Max said. "You're just big boned... er... exoskeletoned?"

A long hairy arachnid leg reached down and slapped his skull.

"What's going on here?" Trina asked.

Max shrugged. "Just wranglin' my giant spider. What's up?"

"The automaton is saying we've got another twelve hours before we get to your first destination," Trina said.

Max nodded. "That's great." It seemed they were making better time than expected. Thank goodness, he'd really needed some good news.

Trina looked like she had more to say though.

"Out with it," he said. "It's not like you to hold your tongue."

She frowned. "Sorry, I just... I saw Arinna stomp by and I realized it was probably because of what I told you to say."

"Yes, it was," he said. "Is that it?"

"Uh... actually, no," she said. "I think we should turn north. I think with a Kestrian ship here, and a carrier from an order of light, the second one we've seen... It's... It's too dangerous this way. We should connect with Caerd and the Black Skulls. They're our friends. They have ships too. We'd be safer."

"You're right," Max said.

Trina was stunned. "Whaa?" Her brow furrowed. "You're joking."

"No, I mean it," he said. "It would be safer. We can't do that though."

"What? Why? Did Arinna tell you to?"

"No," Max replied. "I realized it earlier. I have no idea how to become a Necromancer, and we need to unlock that class. You and I both know there's someone who can teach me."

Trina's eyes widened. "Rachel!"

Max nodded.

"Oh, no!" Trina said. "No, Max... not her. She's... she's terrible! She'll try to control you and if she can't do that she'll destroy you."

"You and Arinna will have to help me with that then," he said. "Either we learn from her, or take her with us so she can open the portal."

"Ugh," Trina groaned, sounding utterly disgusted. "But that woman barely wears any clothes..."

Max paused. Did he hear what he thought he did? "I'm sorry, what?"

"Nothing," Trina said and turned to go.

"There's another reason," Max said.

Trina stopped, turning her head. "For what?"

"I could bring Raeg back," he said.

She turned around, "You... probably could do that! But he'd be undead. He'd be like you."

Max nodded. "I know... He really loved to eat," he said. "It would be hard on him... and..."

"What?" she wondered.

"And I read... that he has to want to come," Max said.

"He will, Max," Trina said. "If anything, he probably won't want to see me again."

"We both let him down," Max said. "I was angry at you when it happened... but... it was on me too."

Trina sighed. "Thank you for saying that."

"You're welcome. Now go back to bed. You're supposed to be sleeping."

"I'm not a child, Max!" she retorted. "I'm a trained Plague Doctor with more experience than those three times my age."

"You also gave all our money away to some pirates because you think their captain is cute."

"I made most of-"

Max cut her off, holding up a hand. "I know and that's why it's cool. Just wait until I'm around next time."

She pursed her lips. "Bah…" she said and stalked off.

Max turned around to see Reken the ullu leaning against the door to the cargo bay. "I stand corrected," he said. "It seems you're not as popular with the ladies as I thought."

"Mytten!" Max said.

Yes?

The spider appeared on the ceiling, crawling upside down into the corridor from one of the side rooms.

Reken screeched. "Ugh! Keep it away!"

"I think this bird needs a spider hug," Max said, folding his arms.

14

NEW EYES AND OLD PROBLEMS

Brittney couldn't believe it. She was finally able to see this place, this paradise the angels of Akasa lived in, with its incredible swirling energies, magnificent towers and super cool looking castle-like buildings, and they were going to force her to leave.

"Maybe I want to stay here," she said.

"Not possible," the angel beside her said. He was the flapping creature from the meeting earlier but he'd turned into something resembling a hairless bear with a very tiny face that was just loping along beside her like nothing had changed. People here were weird.

"They'll eventually find you and throw you out," Janine said as she buzzed along to Brittney's left. "Being able to see allows you to avoid them, sure, but not forever. They always find people here, always."

Brittney pointed at a floating spire that chained to another tower and another and another, until at the very top there stood a platform with a single tree and a little bench beside it. "Look at that! I wanna go up there with like a sourdough sandwich and just hang."

"There are ways to remain here," the angel said. His name was Quelal, or so he'd said.

"Don't bring that up now!" Janine shouted scornfully. "She's got a mission."

"No I don't," Brittney replied, folding her arms. "I never said I was gonna do what the old lady wants."

The bear paused, the look of surprise and sadness that poured from its tiny features was shockingly cute, overpoweringly so, even without fur. "But... But you must!"

Brittney put up a hand. "Ok, ok! I'll consider it, just stop that."

"Hey!" the pixie said. "Why don't you listen to me like that! I can pout too!"

"Because you look like Tinkerbell's slutty half-sister," Brittney said.

"Now you take that back! I don't know exactly what it means... but I know it was an insult."

"You're smarter than you look," Brittney said.

"I... uh... thank you?" Janine replied, placing a tiny finger at her chin.

"You are not very nice," Quelal said as he turned to trundle toward their destination again.

"Yeah, you're not the first person to say that," Brittney replied, "and you won't be the last. Though... uh... could you explain to me, how could I stay here? You know, just to pass the time on the way."

Quelal nodded. "You could become one with an existing resident entity."

"You mean get married?" she asked.

The bear-thing nodded. "That is... close to the same. From a human standpoint, I suppose."

"No it's not!" Janine said. "You don't just live together, you share your dreams, your desires. It's meant for bringing geniuses in this place, people that would improve the halls of Akasa with their knowledge or artistic abilities."

"Hasn't been done in ages," Quelal said. "The council doesn't recommend anymore."

"The council has to recommend someone?" Brittney asked.

"No... not technically, that's just... how it's always been done," Quelal said as he plodded along.

"The council recommended that people come here," Janine said. "That's why we're here. It was angel Manarielle the greater who said-"

"Shut up," Brittney said. "Don't care."

The tiny blue girl's face went purple with frustration. "You! You! You stinky... butt!"

Quelal froze in his tracks and gasped. "That's quite enough!" he said.

"What?" Brittney asked. "You don't swear here?"

"Of course not," Quelal said. "We're angels."

"But what if you get your thumb... er... wing stuck in a door."

"Never happen," Quelal replied. "The doors we have sense your approach and open for you. They never close on anyone, certainly not a wing."

"Whoa... like star trek?" Brittney asked.

"Is that a wonderful place where everything is always perfect?" the angel asked.

"Ummm, I mean for nerds, sure."

"Then yes!" Quelal replied.

"How can you ignore something so vile!" Janine said. "I call you a-"

"Stop!" Quelal said. "Do not do it again!"

"But what if you really hate someone, because they did something terrible and you just want to vent that out in the most powerful verbal way possible."

"Who hurt you?" Quelal asked.

Brittney snorted. "How much time do you have?"

"Eternity," Quelal replied. "The answer to your question is that would not happen here. We are calm, peaceful, placid beings. We make rules and we follow those rules... and if our leaders will it so, we impose those rules on others."

"That last part is where you get in trouble," Brittney said. "Nobody tells me what to do."

Janine was still angry and was flying with her arms and legs crossed, but she still buzzed in closer to speak. "Gravielle told you what to do, and you survived the hearing because you did it."

Brittney waved her hand. "That's... That's a special case."

"You were very lucky we heard about you," Quelal said absently as he plodded forward. "They wanted you dead. They still want you dead."

"They who?" Brittney asked.

"The council because they cover up for him, but Garem most of all, because... well... you know. You've seen."

"I only saw the one scio-"

"AUGH!" Janine shouted. "Don't say it, don't even think that word."

"Such things are forbidden here," Quelal said, scratching his hairless head with a clawed hand. "Beyond all other things. It must not be widely known among our kind that the old rules have been broken, and by our only remaining god."

"What?" Brittney said. "I thought Cerathia was here."

"Oh, no," Janine said. "She's been gone for more than a thousand years now."

"What?" Brittney asked. "Cerathia is gone? What does that mean? Missing? Killed?"

Quelal shrugged. "We don't know. Those of us who've tried to find out, have themselves disappeared."

"That's why we need your help," Janine said. "We believe that if the balance is restored, if a dark god were to make it back to the throne of the dark in Uhksaan, Cerathia may return."

"She would fix this place. She would make it all like it was," Quelal said softly, a blissful expression gracing his minuscule facial features. "Cerathia would make Akasa great again."

"Here we are," Janine said, pointing ahead to what looked like one of those tall fountains you saw in pictures of Europe. "Ready?"

Brittney frowned. If she stayed here they'd find her and kill her, or so the angels said. She could only stay if she married someone, but then, even if it was peaceful here, and it seemed to be, she'd be living in a world where nobody swore. It didn't matter how beautiful it was: screw that.

"Yeah," she said. "Let's go."

"It's right up here," Janine said.

"The fountain?"

"No," Janine said. "That would be stupid! It's the statue."

Brittney looked up, squinting in the ubiquitous warm light of Akasa. Now that her eyes could see the squinting wasn't really necessary because it wasn't too bright here, not really. It was more that the diffuse light in this place felt like it came from everywhere at the same time. What few shadows existed were soft and hard to see and that made things like marble statues hard to make out until you got close.

"Is that... a man?" she asked. It looked like it. He wasn't particularly tall or short, but he was wearing the armor of a Griffin Knight, though the helmet was held in the crook of his arm. His pose was clearly meant to be heroic but in his upraised left hand, where the statue was clearly meant to be holding a sword, was nothing.

"Very astute," Janine said.

"Look," Brittney said, pointing to a thing nearby that was shaped like a person but with no head and a giant hole in their midsection where a glowing fire was quietly burning. "Stuff like that is why I asked. All bets are off in this place."

"Few know about this," Quelal said, "but the planning department ran out of funds for the statue after Cerathia went missing. Apparently she'd ordered this one and several others, but when she wasn't around to make sure they were built... poof!"

"So even the angelic council is corrupt," Brittney said.

"Corrupt?" Quelal replied, his tiny face looking puzzled. "No, I don't think so... unless moving resources around to benefit those you know is corrupt."

"Uh… yeah!" Brittney said. "Like, duh!"

The bear creature put a claw to his miniature chin. "I… I don't understand."

"I do," Janine said, "and none of this matters. The thing is, when they didn't finish the statue they left a hole in the tapestry of Akasa. We'll just go through that."

"Whoa, whoa, whooooooaaaa," Brittney said. "Run that by me again."

Quelal was still pondering. "But… aren't you supposed to help your friends?"

"I said there's a hole where his sword is supposed to be," Janine said.

"Right," Brittney replied. "I got that part."

"So we'll go through it," Janine said.

"A tapestry?" Brittney asked. "How is that possible? And I don't see any hole."

"Yes, it's a tapestry. That's how it was explained to me long ago, an unending curling swirl of a multi-dimensional tapestry, woven by Cerathia's divine will. You don't see the hole because they patched it," Janine said.

"Then how are we supposed to get through?!" Brittney asked.

"They didn't do that great of a job," Janine said. "Just fly up there and you'll see."

"Do you see any wings?" Brittney snarled.

"All over the place!" Janine replied as she buzzed in a circle.

"ON ME!" Brittney said through her teeth. "I MEANT ON ME!"

"Oh, no," Janine said. "Then I suppose you'll have to climb."

Brittney looked up at the multi-layered fountain before them, it had to be at least thirty feet tall with a man sized statue on top that she would also have to scale, somehow.

"You'd better get started," Quelal said as he was backing away from them. "The authorities have arrived."

"How is it?" Arinna asked as she stepped into the bridge.

Max turned around. "I haven't seen more ships."

"That's good," she said.

"Is it?" Max replied. "There has to be a bigger fleet around here."

"You've been traveling in the dark with the lights off, haven't you?" she asked.

"Yeah... I know it's not likely anyone has seen us, but..."

"You're running out of time," she said.

"That's part of it," he said. "We got down here faster than I expected, that was good. But heading back up and connecting with the pirates before we go for Ghrellen will be... I don't know if I'll have enough time."

"We'll get there," she said. "We'll find a way."

"First though," Max said. "We need to connect with our allies here and train you up."

"Have you felt anything?" she asked.

Max had switched to Scavenger an hour ago, when they'd hit the coast and started climbing up and over the Valcas mountains. "Not yet, no."

"Maybe they've moved on?"

"I don't think so," Max said. "I had Tela swing north first and then turn south. I should have felt something but I don't know what the range of Rummage is. Some of these abilities are annoyingly unclear. Whoever did the balance on this game sucks."

"Heh," Arinna said. "That's something I've wondered also. There are times it seems like the dark's abilities aren't quite as strong. It's almost like we're meant to lose."

"Yeah, well, life isn't fair," Max said. "My father often said that, along with another of his favorite gems: 'wishing for something doesn't make it happen, you do.'"

"You're lucky your father talked to you at all," Arinna said as she stepped up to the front of the viewport. The sun was beginning to rise, silhouetting the many peaks of the Valcas mountains against a peach tinged sky.

"Gazric wasn't around for you?"

"It's not a big deal," she said. "So what's next?"

"Well... there's the second part of the deal. I know a huge turtle you can beat on for a while and-"

Max stopped.

Arinna turned around. "What?"

He'd felt a thump. Was it the turtle? Had his ability switched to the giant turtle just because he thought of it? But he'd been sure to tell it he was looking for only one thing: Khilen's carved wooden token necklace.

Thump. It was lighter this time, almost nothing at all.

"TELA STOP!" Max said.

"Absolutely!" Tela said and the Midnight lurched to a halt.

"Did you feel something?" Arinna asked.

"I think so," he replied. "Tela, back us up... can we back up?"

"We sure can," Tela said. "It's just slower than going forward."

"That's fine," Max replied. "I want slow."

Thump. There it was. "Ok, ok... I felt it... Now stop."

The ship stopped again.

"Turn left ninety degrees."

The mountains flowed past the viewport as the ship spun around and stopped. They should be facing roughly to the north east now.

"Done!" Tela replied.

Thump.

"Go forward," Max said. "Slowly."

"Sure!" Tela said.

Thump. Yes! This was it.

"Ok, a little faster."

Thump. Thump.

It took some maneuvering... but soon the Midnight was rising up and up and up toward the peak of a very tall mountain and Max's Rummage ability was getting faster and faster.

"What's that!" Arinna said, pointing out the front viewport.

"What?" Max asked, leaning in next to her. All he could see was snow. Huge drifts completely covered this mountain's peak like a white blanket.

"There," she said. "You see that shadow? It's small... but it might be a shelter or something."

Max could not, but it was worth a shot. "Tela, bring us closer to the mountain. I can't see it," he said. "You'll have to direct her."

"Down a little, and to the right... maybe twenty degrees," Arinna said. "Can you do that?"

"I sure can!" Tela said. "Just one second."

Thump. Thump. Thump. Thump.

"Oh yeah," Max said. "This is it. Tela, turn us around so we can use the cargo exit."

"You got it," Tela replied cheerily. "Good luck!"

"Thanks," Max said and turned to leave the bridge but he nearly ran into a yawning Trina, still rubbing the sleep from her eyes.

"What's all this turning... and stopping nonsense?" she asked groggily. "You rolled me... into the wall three times. If it's time to get up you could just say so. Ugh... I have a terrible headache."

"We might have found Khilen," Max said as he passed her. "Maybe."

"Max, we can't stay here for long," Arinna said.

He turned back, "Why?"

"Because you and I are undead," she said. "But this girl is not."

"Oh... oh shit," Max said. "The oxygen's got to be way low up here. I didn't even think about that."

"Mmmm... That's... That's..." Trina said as she tried to step forward but nearly collapsed.

"Go quickly," Arinna said as she took Trina in her arms. "Find what you can, but we need to be heading back down the mountain as soon as possible."

Max turned and ran to the back of the bay, his mind filled with concern. He should have thought about the air. It was difficult to do that though when your own ears didn't pop from the pressure change. He'd had no clue anything had changed. Still, Trina was part of his party, he had a duty to not let crap like this happen to her.

"Mytten?" he called out, but when he reached the bay, the answer was already in front of him. The giant spider had collapsed upside down on the floor of the bay, her long legs draped over several containers.

"Shit!" he snapped. "Mytten, come back!"

The spider dissolved into black smoke, returning to her cattan which Max stored. Hopefully, she would be alright.

"Well there goes my chance at a safety line," he grumbled.

Dammit! What the heck was Khilen doing way up here? The goblins were supposed to be inside the mountains, not on the very top!

Max lowered the cargo door and the entire hold filled with a furious wind that brought with it a white curtain of swirling snow. Max jumped off the end into the snow, sinking all the way up to his hip bones. It took some digging, but he managed to make his way to a lump in the snow with the ends of three sticks poking out of it.

This thing must have been what Arinna had seen from the ship. The sticks were tied at the top with leather string like a tee-pee and only the very tip was visible in the snow. It was only about four feet high, and not big enough at the base for a person to live in, even a goblin.

Max dug into the snow down along the side of the small structure. After a minute or so he found a flap in the construction and pulled it open. Inside it was empty except for a stick with Khilen's necklace hanging from it. Tied to the necklace was a small leather tube and that was it. Max double checked to make sure he wasn't missing anything and grabbed the token and the tube.

Acquired: Carved Token Necklace.

Acquired: Goblin Missive Pouch.

Max then tried to run back to the ship, which was hovering only about fifteen feet away, but there was no point. With a rumble, the snow around him released from the mountain side and started tumbling down. He stretched and just barely caught the edge of the bay door with his skeletal fingertips. The snow tried to pull him down, but luckily his legs were thin enough that they just sort of popped out on top of the budding avalanche. Max used his other hand to pull himself back in, dragging his body into the ship.

"What are you doing?!" Arinna called. "Trina passed out. We need to get out of here, now!"

"Go!" Max shouted as he pulled himself to his knees. "I'm in!"

The midnight pulled away from the mountain peak and dived toward a lower altitude. Max closed the bay door and stumbled his way down the angled corridor to the Midnight's bridge.

"I can't imagine you found goblins up here," Arinna said. She was holding Trina, keeping her from rolling along the floor as the airship descended.

"How is she?" Max asked.

"I don't know," Arinna replied. "She doesn't have a status effect, or lost health."

Max nodded. "That's good, but it's not everything. I learned early that physics work in this place just like back on Earth. You die if you drown or if you're crushed by water pressure. It makes sense that altitude sickness would be a thing too." He shook his head. "I should have realized it."

"Uhm, how far down do we need to go?" Tela asked.

"As far as we can," Max replied. "Look for a valley or something. Actually, this is a good time to go to the turtle. Do you remember that place, Tela?"

"I sure do!" she said happily. "But... uh... we might have a problem."

"What?" Arinna asked. "What problem?"

"There are ships ahead," Tela said. "A lot of them."

15

UNDONE AND UNSULLIED

Max ran to the front viewport but it was so bright out now that it was getting hard to see. There were a few shiny objects out there... maybe. Stupid sun! Why did his eyes have to suck so bad in the daylight?

"I can't see them," Max said. "Arinna, can you-"

"No!" she said. "My eyes might be better than yours, but they suffer during the day just as much."

"Hey!" the owl-headed ullu said, walking into the bridge. "I have a nasty headache, do you know if there's a storm or-"

"You!" Max said, momentarily forgetting the owl guy's name. "Can you look out there and-"

The ullu was already covering his eyes. "Ugh... too bright."

"He's an ullu!" Arinna said. "They see in the dark also."

"Dammit!" Max said. "Does anyone here see well in the daytime?"

"There are several ships," Tela said. "Though I don't know what kingdom they're from. I know they're warships."

Max turned back to the console. "How can you tell that?" he asked just as a loud thud went off outside and the entire ship shook.

"Because they're shooting at us," Tela said brightly.

"Shit!" Max said. "How many?"

"There are fifteen incoming enemy shots right now!" Tela chirped.

"Well take evasive action!" Max said. "And tell me how many ships there are, that's what I meant."

"Oh!" Tela replied. "Of course! There are seven ships. All of them are firing at once. One is quite large. It may be a Kestrian Justice heavy cruiser. I haven't seen one of those in-"

"Shut it, pegasus!" the ullu shouted. "We need to get out of here! Stop yapping and fly faster!"

"Turn us away from them, Tela," Max said. "I need to think."

The Midnight banked left, swaying everyone to the right.

"Mmmm... wah?" Trina said.

"She's coming around," Arinna said, holding the girl steady.

Max couldn't help but think that, for a vampire, Arinna seemed to be pretty good with people.

Damn! He was getting distracted again, but why? Oh... right! He was still a Scavenger. He had nowhere near the mind points he had as any other class.

Quickly he brought up his display, unequipped everything, and switched to Dark Summoner. Technically his mind points were higher as a Dark Mage, but the summoner was just a better choice, it had more options.

Only a single second after he'd changed his class, Max thought of one: Neline.

Yes, I am here.

"I'm going up top," Max said as he flipped his display back to equipment and grabbed what little magic gear he had, including the bone wand.

"But..." Arinna said. "What are you going to do?"

"I'll figure it out," Max replied. "Take care of Trina."

He ran for the ladder, passing the two remaining smaller dungeon crawlers as they were dragging their larger friend out of an anteroom.

"Is he alright?" Max asked as he paused at the first rung of the ladder.

The smaller dungeon crawlers nodded.

Ok. Scruff Ok.

That was good enough for him and up the ladder he charged. Man, he hadn't even thought that Scruff would be affected by the low oxygen but how could he not? He was a living creature after all. Was he losing touch with what it meant to be alive?

Before you ascend, tell them to close on the enemy ships.

"What?" Max asked. "They'll tear us apart! Why?"

The death spell will not work through the armor on those ships unless we are very close.

"You know an awful lot about killing people of the light," Max said.

Yes.

Why was he not terribly surprised?

"Tela!" Max called back. "Turn around! I need you to head straight for them, full speed."

"Are you a lunatic?!" Arinna yelled back. "This ship has seen better days!"

"I know! Just trust me!" Max replied. Then he ascended the rest of the ladder and opened the top hatch, sticking his torso out.

BOOM!

A holy fire exploded just to the ship's left, bathing him in heat and light... but luckily it wasn't close enough to do anything but sting. The explosion had been big, easily ten feet across, if not more. A direct hit from a shot that big would reduce him to a pile of ash. It had to be from that cruiser. Wonderful.

"Here we go again," he said, pulling the hood of his cloak out as far as he could to shield his eyes from the sun.

The Midnight was wheeling around and as bright as it was out, he could still see lines of fire streaming their way. A whole line of ships had formed below them

"Neline! You'd better be ready!"

Not yet.

"What?"

I can only exist in your plane for a short time. If you summon me too early, it will be wasted.

"What should I do then? Twiddle my skeletal thumbs?" he snarled in response.

Use a barrier spell or a deflection spell.

"I don't have either of those!" he said.

That's not my fault, is it?

Max brought up his magic screen.

```
Magic

• Ball of Flame • Bolt Lance • Dead Weight
• Flame • Freeze • Ground Slam
• One with the Void • Shock • Sleep
• Stagnation • Teeth of Fate • Void Crush
• Venom • Empower • Hasten • Thundercrack
• Undone
```

God, he really hadn't gotten anything good in a while. Wait... Undone. What was that? It sounded like a time related spell. Did he have time to try to read it? Did he have any choice?

The Midnight swerved out of the way of yet another gigantic ball of holy fire but a smaller one clipped her right side, exploding and burning a huge hole in the side of the ship.

Nope. There was no time to read. Max would just cast the spell and pray it would do something... Unless undone was an attacking spell that would tear apart whatever it was cast on. No... No he didn't think so. Stagnation was like that. It was a slowing spell to cast on your enemies. Game developers didn't stack similarly functioning spells together in an unlocked set. Then it would be boring and the chief function of any good game was to be fun.

Max put both of his hands on the bone wand and pointed it at the Midnight's metal skin.

"Undone," he said. There was a flash of blackness. A swirling sort of skin appeared around the ship and then it was gone.

"Was that it?" he asked. Had it used his magic? He flicked a finger to bring it up.

321/428 MP

Yep, a whole lot of it.

You should duck.

"Augh!" Max shouted as he flattened his body to the deck, just in time for a man-sized ball of holy fire to whiz past. When he looked up again the Midnight was already juking again to avoid more of the constant withering fire coming from the line of enemy ships ahead and below. The airship went up and down and tried to twist to the side.

"MAAAAX!" Arinna cried from below. "What are you doing up there?!"

There was another thump as a smaller shot hit one of the Midnight's left steering propellers. She curved off course, turning over into a true straight dive. A second hit followed, this one exploded on the ship's underside.

"Neliiiiine!" Max said through his teeth, gripping the sides of the hatch as tightly as he could with both of his hands.

Two more shots hit the Midnight. One detonated to Max's right and completely severed the right side propeller assembly, while the other slammed into the hull near the bridge, boring a huge fiery hole. In the debris that flew by, Max thought he saw the automaton's decapitated bird-like head.

Shit. This was it.

The enemy ships were right below them now. The biggest of them was a monster, three times as big as the destroyer they'd encountered. Its sides were bristling with smaller blister-mounted guns that dwarfed the ones on the midnight, but at its center was a huge turret with two gigantic cannons. They were aiming right at them.

Now. Summon me.

"But... we're done for. It's over."

DO IT.

"Fine! Summon Nelinex Horror, Neline," he said.

Max almost passed out from the massive pulse of magic that was sucked from him in an instant. The magic formed together and coalesced into a bright aquamarine ring through which Neline emerged. She was a bit bigger now, and every bit as grotesque as before. Tentacles squirmed and slime dribbled into the air around them as the summoning finished and the ring evaporated.

Death!

Just as before, a terrifying blackness erupted from Neline. It traveled out in all directions, the very essence of the end of life.

It is done

Max was looking ahead at the two giant spheres of holy fire coming right at them. They were going to hit. The ship would be destroyed, Trina, and Scruff, and the ullu would die in agony. Only Arinna and he would awaken and when? Days from now? Weeks? He might not wake up at all.

Activate the spell you idiot!

"What?" he asked.

Undone. You cast the first part, now do the second.

"There's a second part?" he shouted. The balls of holy fire were right on them. Max could feel the heat coming. The light was burning his eyes. It was so bright.

Just say it again.

"Undone!" Max shouted... and the whole world stopped.

BRITTNEY WHIPPED AROUND. Quelal was acting like he'd just randomly wandered into this place and was now randomly wandering out, quickly. Behind him, she saw angels, angry looking ones. They appeared as long thin winged creatures with bright red transparent skin and flaming crowns upon their heads. In the hand of each one was a long blade covered with bright red fire.

"Uh... so I guess they don't have non lethal police here, do they?"

Janine laughed. "What would be the point of that?"

Brittney shook her head. "Yeah... maybe I... uh... maybe I need to apologize to someone."

"Just start climbing!" Janine said. "I'll distract them!"

Brittney scoffed. "How? You gonna show 'em your-"

"Go!" the pixie shouted.

"Sure, fine, whatever!" Brittney said as she jumped over a thin translucent line that surrounded the fountain and landed in a patch of some kind of weird singing flower, smashing several of them flat.

Nearby someone gasped at her antics.

"Yeah!" Brittney shouted at everyone who might be nearby "I trampled 'em hella good!"

Then she stepped into the lowest layer of the fountain. Oddly, she wasn't sure what she was in was actually water. It looked blueish, but it felt too airy and thin. Walking through it wasn't a problem at all. It was like walking through something just a little bit thicker than air, but with a kind of bite to it. It was hard to describe, but she liked it.

"What are you doing!" Janine screamed.

"Sorry," Brittney said, looking back. What she saw caused her jaw to drop.

Janine, the tiny blue pixie girl with the short skirt who looked like she just got off of a job pole dancing for a bunch of Star Trek nerds, was fighting the angel cops... and she was winning!

Bright blue magic was exploding in every direction as the pixie seemed to be channeling magical power into forceful strikes that extended into ethereal fists and feet that smashed the glowing red angels who were surrounding her. A fist crunched into a flaming crown while a foot kicked another angel in its creepily thin midsection, over and over, like one of those sped up kung-fu movies.

Brittney found herself staring. No! No Janine had said go, she needed to do it. If she waited around they'd eventually come for her.

That only left one huge problem: How to get up this stupid fountain!

"You there!" an angel nearby said. "Get out of that fountain! Didn't you see it's clearly marked?"

Brittney snorted and spit into the weird airy water around her feet. "I spit on it," Brittney said. "Now it's mine!"

"But... Is she correct? I'm not aware of that rule!" said the angel.

"Neither am I," replied another. "But it could have been passed by one of the sub sub councils as recently as today."

Brittney was looking up. There were too many levels for her to climb. She'd have to jump up and pull herself up each level. Now that they'd stolen all her levels her arms weren't feeling nearly as strong as before.

"Are they in session today?" asked the first.

"I believe they are," replied the second.

"Oh my god!" Brittney snarled at them. "I can't even think! Shut up!"

The two of them just stared at her. One was very long and thin with a head like a cat and very tiny thin bird-like wings while the other was shorter with a more human face, only it had four pure white eyes and long broad wings like an eagle.

"There's no need for language!" the first angel said.

Brittney looked back at Janine, the pixie was surrounded and it was getting worse. Soon she wouldn't be able to keep up.

"Hey, can one of you fly me to the top of this fountain?"

"Why would we do that? You'll just dirty it even more!" the second angel said, frowning with disdain twice as hard with those four eyebrows.

"If you don't," Brittney said. "I'll start *really* swearing."

"You wouldn't!" the catlike creature said, flapping faster.

"You bet your feather covered ass I would," Brittney replied. "Do it and all this commotion will go away and it'll be quiet here again. You want that don't you?"

"I think I'd better Quelanielle," the one with the smaller wings said.

The other sighed. "If just to keep the peace."

"Wait... you?" Brittney said, but the cat face angel with the smaller wings had already swooped in behind her and grabbed her by the armpits, lifting her from the slushy fake water of the fountain.

"Where do you want to go?" the creature asked.

"To the very top, where the guy's hand ought to be," Brittney said. "I think."

"As you wish," the angel said, pulling her into the air, like she had no weight at all.

"I hope you're almost there!" Janine screamed from below.

"Yes!" Brittney called back.

"Humans shouldn't be here," the angel said as they passed the final level of the fountain and Brittney came to the same height as the statue. Brittney could see an emblem on the man's tabard, it was familiar somehow. A broken sword. Had she seen it before? If so, it had to have been a long time ago, back when she'd first arrived. The face on the knight was chiseled, and not just in a 'made out of stone way', in a real, this guy could have played superman kind of way.

"You don't belong," the creature added, taking her higher.

"I think you're right," Brittney replied as they continued to ascend and something wild caught her eye. Janine had been right! Floating in the air above the knight statue's hand was a sort of fold. It hadn't been visible from below, but now she could see it plainly. It was like reality itself had torn, and someone had hastily buttoned it closed, only the button was missing and the flap hung lazily open, just waiting for her to go in. She reached for it but missed as she was pulled upward.

"Hey!" she said. "That's enough. This is what I needed. You can let go."

"I don't believe I will," the angel replied.

"What?" Brittney asked. "Why?"

"I recognize you," the angel said, still taking her upward. "You're that betrayer. You got off easy for your crimes but that won't happen this time. Not with trampling the flowers, spitting your vile fluids into the fountain of unbroken will, and cursing! It'll be death for you!"

"That's bullshit!" Brittney shouted.

"Ugh!" the creature yelped, making a sound like it might actually vomit up whatever its kind ate. "No... Don't."

"Put me down now you dirty steaming lump of feather covered SHIT!" she screamed.

That was it, the arms let her go and oddly, unlike she'd expected, Brittney didn't fall. She sort of glided downward like a Styrofoam peanut. She was just close enough to snag the edge of that weird hole in the world and the knight statue's arm to prop herself up.

"I'm going!" she shouted back down.

"Thank you!" Janine screamed. This was followed by an explosion of blue light and a cloud of smoke that drove the angels back. Out of the top of the cloud emerged Janine. Like a tiny shooting star she rocketed out and slammed right into Brittney and together the two of them tumbled through the hole.

Brittney was swallowed not by darkness or by light, but by gray emptiness. She didn't feel like she was falling either, it was more like floating in a lazy river on a sunny day.

"Hello?" she asked.

"Hello," a voice replied. It was a soft voice, an empty voice, neither male nor female.

"Who are you?" she asked.

"Who are *you*?" it replied.

"Ok, ha ha, I get it. You echo everything I say. Good job, real funny. Now CUT IT OUT! I'm supposed to be somewhere."

"Somewhere?"

"Anywhere!"

"No, not anywhere," the voice said. "Here."

A circular window opened on a grassy hill. Brittney recognized it immediately. It was a park just outside of Ghrellen. She used to snooze there often, back when

Garem wasn't forcing her to help disgusting abusers by killing stupid skeletons.

"Yes, that's probably right," Brittney said.

"Or here?" the voice asked.

Another window opened. This one showed the backyard of her family's home. It was evening and there wasn't much she could see but two pastel pink pool chairs and the small glass table between them. Brittney's sunscreen bottle was still there, and still open, right next to her Chanel sunglasses. Small ripples were rolling across the surface of the pool. Had she just left? Was this right after she'd been taken?

"Can... can I go home?"

"Go home," the voice said.

Wait a second. Where was Janine? She was supposed to be helping Janine wasn't she? Brittney wasn't sure how but the angels had said they were counting on her.

She could smell the scent of cocoa butter coming through the portal. It was like a lure, drawing her in. Why not? This place could get along without her. Who cared what happened to them?

"Who cares," the voice said.

Wait a second. She hadn't said that. It was in her mind.

"Go home," the voice said again.

If there was one thing Brittney hated more than anything else, it was assholes who tried to manipulate others. She'd been through that with her mother and her father, and a string of mean, hateful boyfriends that was waaaaay too long for any one girl.

No. F-ing. Way.

She dove for Ghrellen.

16

MORE LIES AND LEVELS

Max stared at the world around him, fascinated. It had all frozen. Shards of the midnight's hull were floating by as was the top half of his bone wand which he'd inadvertently snapped when he slammed both hands down on the deck.

Perfect.

Then, as if someone had flipped a switch, everything started again, but backwards. The wand snapped back into place, the Midnight's propellers returned and her hull sucked back together, as the whole ship rose back through the sky.

Max realized what was happening, and laughed. It was resetting everything back to when it was cast, but just for the target: the Midnight and everyone in it. What a spell!

With a swirling black flash, time returned to its forward motion, at least for their own, now mostly intact ship. Below it wasn't the same. Death had consumed those inside the Kestrian vessels below which had stopped firing and were now drifting off toward the side of the mountain. If they weren't stopped, they would collide.

Kestrian naval crew, Kestrian Naval officers, and Kestrian captains defeated!

Arinna has gained a level of Grave Blade!

Arinna has gained a level of Grave Blade!

Arinna has gained a level!

Arinna has gained a level!

Trina has gained a level of Plague Doctor!

Trina has gained a level!

You've gained a level of Dark Summoner!

You've gained a level!

"Excellent!" Max said, watching his display scroll through the notifications.

"Get down here!" Arinna shouted from below him as she yanked on Max's right boot.

Do not tell her about me.

"Alright!" he yelled, answering both of them as he climbed down into the airship, closing the hatch behind him.

The second his feet touched down Arinna grabbed him by the clasp of his cloak and pushed him back, pinning him to the wall.

"Uh... hi," he said.

"What are you keeping from me?" she demanded.

"What do you mean?" he asked.

"Don't give me that crap!" she said. "That spell was Death! That's a level four spell that can only be cast by Dark Wizards and Dread Lords and you are neither."

"I didn't cast it," he said. "It was an item."

Good idea.

"Yeah?" Arinna said. "What item?"

It's called the Ultimate living death. It looks like a little black skull.

"It was a little black skull," Max said. "Ultimate living death, I think it was called."

"I've been all through our inventory, Max. I didn't see one of those," Arinna said.

"I had it in the cargo bay. I was worried it was dangerous, which, as it turns out, it was!"

Arinna stared into his green glowing eyes as if searching for something.

"I'm sorry I didn't tell you about it," Max said.

TIM PAULSON

"That other spell, that was Undone, from your bent," she said

"Yes," Max replied. "I just got it. I had no idea what it would do..." he chuckled nervously. "Looks like it worked out though."

"Yeah," Arinna said, releasing him. She still looked skeptical. "You need to tell me about powerful items like that," she said. "You're right when you say they're dangerous. There's a reason only Dark Wizards and Dread Lords get those spells."

"I have unlocked the wizard, actually," Max said. "It happened back on the beach when the Clathian's took you."

"What's going on?" Trina asked. She was hobbling down the corridor holding one hand to her head while the other was pressed to the wall.

Arinna rounded on her. "I told you to stay put!"

"I'm feeling better... and you wouldn't tell me what happened!"

"We found the amulet, but it was too high up so you almost died, but then we flew back down and there were seven enemy ships and I used a magic item to kill all the crew on the ships and now we're safe," Max blurted in one big rush.

"We flew up beyond the safe travel limit?" She asked. "Why would we do that?"

"The necklace was hidden at the top of a mountain," Max replied. "We had to."

Trina frowned. "But everyone knows you can't go above the limit or the strain of the height becomes too great on your brain and you pass out. It's in all the text books. You should have waited until I was awake!"

"I didn't know," Max said. "Well... I did know, but I didn't realize... What I mean is: It's my fault and I'm sorry."

"I should have thought of it as well," Arinna said. "I haven't been out in a while."

"It's fine," Trina said. "I've got a bit of a headache but I'm otherwise just fi-"

Blood had started dribbling out of her nose. Max and Arinna pointed.

"Oh!" Trina said, scurrying away into her room, her hands cupped together.

"Suddenly I'm feeling thirsty," Arinna said.

"Gross," Max replied. "We don't need blood, what we need is a good hot bath in some raw sewage mixed with assorted entrails."

Arinna laughed. "I'm gross?"

"It was a joke," he said.

"Well, I think it was offal," she said with a smile.

Max laughed. "I guess we ought to figure out where we're going."

"You found something?"

"You foun somefing?" Trina called from her room. A second later she appeared with a rag pressed to her nose. "You nof going to kill me aww you?" she asked Arinna.

"No," Arinna replied. "I'm well enough fed after that bridge crew a couple days ago."

"Thass goo," Trina said.

"Anyway, yes," Max said. "I found something." He summoned the carved token necklace in one hand and the tube in the other. "The tube was with the necklace. I think... yep." Max stored the necklace and used his free hand to pull one end from the leather tube, revealing a rolled parchment. "A message for me."

"Weh ree iff!" Trina mumbled.

"Huh?" Max asked.

"She says read it," Arinna said.

Max unrolled the parchment and read it aloud.

Dear Max,

I hope this letter finds you well. Ciara suggested that we place it high on Black Tooth Peak where only someone with your constitution and Scavenger abilities could come across it. I have made many friends among Ciara's goblins including the queen herself, who is quite resourceful so you need not worry about me. However, if you wish to see us again I must tell you: abandon that idea. The most important thing you can do is turn right around and go back.

As I am writing this message the newly liberated city of Ceradram has been destroyed. An armada of airships from the light came in from the north and burned the entire city to ash. Tens of thousands were killed. Those that could, fled into the mountains, the rest perished in the holy fires of the light. I begged Ciara to take in refugees and, reluctantly, she has.

You must not return to Ceradram, the light awaits you there. They expect that once you hear of their attack you'll return. Do not do so. Don't try to find us, we'll be fine. The mother of the black stone has welcomed us.

If you have found Arinna, and I hope you have, you must find a way to get her to Ghrellen. My mother once told me there is a portal there that can be used to travel to the over or the underworld but you will need a necromancer to operate it. Unfortunately, no necromancers remain in Ceradram.

Best of luck to you. May the moon rise!

Khilen

P.S. I hope you don't run into any snakes. Ha ha.

"I can't believe it," Max said gravely. "The entire city."

"There isn't supposed to be a city under Verian, you know," Trina said, pulling the cloth away from her nose. "Ceradram grew there on its own from people who had nowhere else to go." Tears were brimming in her eyes. "Those poor people."

Arinna looked disgusted. "The light talks of virtue and piety and then burns cities to the ground. It didn't used to be like this... There was a time when... when they didn't do these things."

Max's mind was racing through all the people there... the people from the dark market, that lizardman alchemist, the Arachnians, Vilnius the vampire blacksmith, and Delara and her werewolf clan. He hoped some of them had gotten out alive.

"What does she mean about snakes?" Trina asked, still dabbing at her nose.

"I told her Indiana Jones," Max said.

"Ahhhh," Arinna replied.

"What does that mean?" Trina asked. "What's an indy anna jones?"

"It would take too long to explain," Max said. "But I think there's another clue here. Maybe she wants us to find them."

"What do you mean?" Arinna asked.

"The mother of the black stone," Max said. "In high demonic, that's Kapon Taw."

"The old stronghold." Arinna said, "It was built to guard the pass south to the Ceras swamps."

"Why would you guard that?" Trina asked. "It was just a swamp. The Verian waterfall dried most of it up... until we destroyed it. I suppose the swamps have probably returned."

"This light city of Verian... It was over the Ceras swamps?" Arinna asked.

Max nodded. "Yep, and Ceradram was under it but then we destroyed the waterfall so they had to move the floating islands out. Until they came back and burned the city to the ground." Max shook his head. "They seem to care a lot about that place."

"That's because the Ceras swamp marks one of the four centers of power. We of the dark call it Bukhan Nu Yazhraal, The Shrine of Decay. When it is controlled by the dark, the power of earth sways in our direction."

"None of this is true," Trina said. "It's all goblin wives tales and jibber jabber. There are no centers of power."

Arinna folded her arms. "No? Then tell me, did you have many necromancers in your city?"

Trina narrowed her eyes. "There were a few, sure."

"We've been around," Max said. "And I haven't seen any others."

"Nor I," the ullu piped up from behind them. "Not that... I'm listening or anything."

"So there were necromancers, what of it?" Trina said.

"The power there may be swayed to the light, but the old shrine still exists beneath the swamp, waiting to rise again," Arinna said. "That is why there are necromancers there. They feel its power. They are drawn to it. It fuels them."

"But does it unlock the class?" Max asked. "Because that's what I need."

"I don't know," Arinna replied. "Perhaps."

"Perhaps?" Max asked. "That's not good enough. Khilen says they're waiting for us there. If we go, we risk everything. If they shoot down this ship, we're done. I die and they take you back to forever jail."

"I know, Max!" Arinna said. "I'm well aware of the stakes!"

"We need to make a decision," Trina said. "I say we go back and reconnect with the Black Skull pirates."

Arinna rolled her eyes.

"She makes a good point," Max said.

Arinna frowned at him.

"No, seriously," Max said. "We know there are ships looking for us. I think we should probably do that."

Trina looked surprised.

"What?!" Arinna said. "We shouldn't run! We can wait until night and take out each ship like we did with that destroyer. The light needs to pay for this Max! They need to pay for what they've done to these people, and to me!"

"They will!" Max replied. "I promise you, but getting you home is number one and we can't do that if they destroy our only method of transport."

Arinna slammed a fist against the metal wall of the Midnight, leaving a huge dent. "Aargh!" she growled. "I..."

"I know," Trina said. "I felt the same way when they took Melnax. All I cared about was getting him back. Anger... it makes you blind."

"Yeah," Arinna replied, letting her breath escape through her teeth like steam. "Yeah."

"However," Max said. "Before we head back north there are a couple things we can do."

∼

"Keep hitting it!" Max yelled from his relaxing spot atop a set of boulders.

"Oh my god!" Arinna yelled back. "But this is so boring!"

Max leaned back, putting his boney arms behind his head. "If it's not boring and terrible," he said, "it's not grinding."

"Coooommmmeeee baaaaack heeeeereee yoouuuuu!" the giant tortoise said as its head turned around for about the hundredth time, trying to get to Arinna as she attacked the top of his shell with two small low quality swords, over and over again.

So far she'd been at it for about six hours. It wasn't as long as Max had worked on his own tortoise, but that one had been much smaller. That was something he wished he'd learned before: the strength of the enemy you were hitting affected the skill experience you received. Arinna would benefit from that however. He couldn't wait to see how much.

"This seems kind of cheap!" Arinna called as she vaulted backwards over the tortoise's monstrous head.

"That's because it is," Max replied. "But it's what we've got."

"Slowwww Dowwwwwnnn!" the giant tortoise yowled as it tried to snap at her again. This time Arinna ducked it, and whacked him seven more times in the chin as he went by.

"I feel like we're just wasting time here," she said. "This can't possibly work."

"Oh it works," Max replied, watching as several puffy clouds passed overhead. The day had largely been bright and sunny, which was a little annoying, but he'd pulled his hood up so it wasn't too bad. Now the sun was already heading for the horizon. It was probably only a few hours until sundown.

"Maybe it won't work for me! Ever think of that?" Arinna asked as her swords clinked and clanked again and against the tortoise's shell.

"Sssstoooooop!" the creature said. This time it didn't snap at her. It just sort of stared and grumbled.

"Why? Because you're whining too much?" Max asked. "Do you think the universe punishes whining?"

"I am not whining!"

"Yes," Max said, "you are."

"No! I'm not!" she snapped as she rolled to her right and then stabbed with both small swords. There was a double ching of metal as both snapped in her hands.

"Pleaaasssseee!" the giant tortoise said. "Leeeeet meeeee goooooo baaaaack tooooo sleeeeeep."

"Sure thing buddy," Max said. "But besides that, you've been super helpful. Is there anything we can do for you?"

The great reptilian head swung around to face Max.

"Reeeeaaaaalllly?" it asked.

"Yeah," Max said. "Name it. If I can do it, I will."

"Buuuuutttt... Yooooou'rrrre of the Daaaaaark."

"Does that mean I don't know how to appreciate someone for services rendered?" Max asked. "What do you think Arinna, being the future dark queen and all?"

"It definitely doesn't," Arinna replied as she slid from the back of the creature and dropped to the ground.

"Ohhhh... geeeee... I doooon't knooooow," the tortoise said. His great eyes, the size of basketballs sort of unfocused as he contemplated.

"Don't think on it for too long," Max said. "We'll be leaving soon. Come on up here Arinna. I've got a sleep sign all prepped."

She was already standing next to him.

"Sheesh!" Max said, starting. "You freak me out doing that!"

Arinna nudged him with her foot. "You're going to wake me right back up?"

Max sat up. "Yep, you'll be out for around ten seconds."

"Alright," she said. "Please make it fast. I hate sleeping in the sun. My... kind... take lots of negative effects."

"You mean vampires," Max said.

She sighed. "Yes."

"Like what?" Max asked.

"The most important one is that rekindle works differently for me. I can only revive at night."

"Ah... you probably should have mentioned that before," he said.

"Yeah..." she was looking around.

"Oh, it's here," Max said as he used one hand to grab one of the boulders he'd been lying on and moved it. On the stone beneath was the sleep sign.

"I had better not have wasted my entire day," she said.

"Just do it," Max replied, standing up next to her, pausing to brush some dirt from his cloak.

She sighed and stepped on the sign. The green in her eyes went out and she dropped. Max caught her in his arms and lowered her to the ground.

It made him wonder. How did Arinna not know that you could raise your skill levels like this? It seemed common enough knowledge that when you slept you gained levels, but nobody seemed to realize that it allowed you to power level your skills. Maybe they didn't think of it as a game? He didn't know. One thing was for sure though, it definitely did work like one. These kinds of things were repeatable. He'd level Trina this way... and Raeg too.

Raeg. Max sighed. Would he want to come back if he had to be an undead like Max? There was only one way to find out.

Max shook Arinna's shoulder.

"Mmm?" she said.

"Wakey wakey," he said, bringing up Arinna's status. "Let's take a look at your... Wow."

Status	Arinna		
Level	7	Grave Blade Skill	83
Health	121/121		
Magic	1/1	Affinity	Wanderlust
Skills		Magic	

Veil of Night, Decapitate, Overwhelm, rekindle

Strength	61	Attacks x 5	67
		Accuracy	108%
Agility	70	Defense	50
Vitality	47	Evasion	46%
		Magic Defense	28
Mind	37	Magic Evasion	32%

"Eighty-friggin-three!" Max exclaimed.

Arinna's green eyes widened. "What? Are you serious?"

"I can't believe those stats!" he said. "Insane!"

"How is this possible?" she asked, frowning as she stared at her own little green undead display.

"I've been thinking about that," Max said. "I'm betting somebody wants it like this."

"Who?" Arinna asked.

"I'm not sure," Max said. "Have you ever heard of a guy called Ahrengee?"

Arinna frowned. "No."

"Sure? He's got a bird head, kind of like a vulture."

"Hmmm... My memories from before are foggy... but I think I remember someone like that. I think I saw him talking to my father."

"That would make a lot of sense," Max said. "I had a run in with him myself. It was not my best moment here, but... I did learn that he works for someone. I think that person or thing, or whatever, is why this place is like a game."

"You mean the screens and the inventory?" Arinna asked.

"And the stats and the classes," Max said. "Yeah, all of it. It might not always have been like this."

"If it was different once... I don't remember that," she said.

"I didn't expect you would," Max said. "That might also explain why none of the people here seem to treat it like it is. What we just did here, this quick leveling thing, anyone can do it, yet no one does."

"You think we're only allowed to play in certain ways," Arinna said.

"Bingo," Max replied. "In this world. God most assuredly does play dice."

"What do we do about it?" she asked.

"I don't know enough yet," Max said, "but I'm gonna keep my eye sockets open. In the meantime. We keep moving forward."

"The portal," Arinna said. Quietly she reached over to a boulder and used only her fingertips to crack it in half.

Then she took a chunk into her palm and crushed it into powder. "I feel like we have a better chance now."

"Good," Max said. "Confidence is good. We need to get you some better weapons though."

"Hummmmm," the giant tortoise said.

"Agree," Arinna said. "Why didn't you level your Dark Summoner?"

"Because I wanted to relax!" Max said.

She tilted her head skeptically.

"Ok..." he said. "I actually did. While I was waiting for you I found an arcane entity in a valley nearby. I named him Phil. Come on out Phil."

A huge toothy maw appeared beside Arinna. It was her turn to startle. "What the heck is that?"

"It says it's a Gorovan Pursuer," Max said. "I cast haste on him as many times as I could. Watch this."

Max grabbed a basketball-sized chunk of rock and hurled it as high and far as he could. He wasn't terribly good at throwing things, but the six extra strength from the signet ring helped a lot.

"Phil," he said. "Fetch!"

The giant crocodile shaped creature launched itself like a rocket after the stone and caught it before it had even begun to drop, crushing it in its jaws.

"Impressive," she said. "But does he roll over?"

"You bet your ass he does!" Max said but he didn't even have to give the command. Phil was already barrel rolling on his return trip.

"Wow!" Arinna said, laughing. "What a nice little beastie you are! How many levels did you get?"

"Got Dark Summoner up to seventy-three," Max said. "I'm happy with it. We still need to get Necromancer though."

Arinna nodded, patting Phil on his reptilian head as he floated by. "Have any ideas?"

"I do," he said. "It's our next stop."

17

IMMATURE AND BEGINNING AGAIN

Brittney landed in a field of grass in exactly the spot she'd seen through the portal. It was almost sunset and the magical lanterns that lined the park grounds were just coming. She rubbed a hand through the grass and smelled it. As beautiful as the land of the angels had been, this was better. Even if it wasn't Earth, it was real dirt and real grass.

She frowned, leaning in. Small streams of fear and joy rose from the grass like tiny streamers as she touched it. She could see them with her eyes and hear it also. It was as if the grass feared and loved her at the same time.

Brittney rubbed the grass again. More joyous screaming. Did the grass think she was going to eat it? Maybe.

It was weird... but she felt compelled to apologize. "I'm... I'm sorry grass," she said. "I didn't mean to frighten you."

More streamers rose from the tiny blades, soft cooing ones. Did they want her back?

She rubbed the grass again, but more carefully this time. Oooh's and Aaah's came from the grass.

"What is going on right now?" she said. "You don't pet grass, right?"

Had someone slipped her something? That was the only way that... oh. They'd changed her! They'd said she could see things differently. Brittney had assumed they only meant there, in the world of the angels, but maybe not. Maybe it was everywhere.

She stood up, looking around, trying to ignore the grass as it cried out beneath her feet.

"Janine?" she called. "Where are you?"

Was her voice softer? Or was she hearing it differently? Either way, the annoying blue pixie was nowhere to be found. Friggin' rad! What else could go wrong?

"You, girl," said a stern man's voice. "What's happened here?"

Brittney's first instinct was to run but when she tried, her first step caused such a cascade of screams from the grass that she shrieked and fell over. Only then, when she was lying in the grass, listening to it crying all around her, did she realize she wasn't wearing the same clothes as before. Now a sort of frock covered her, like a white frilly nightgown. She had no shoes or socks and her underclothes were... weird.

A large shadow loomed over her. "Are you... alright?" the man's voice asked. "I... I saw you..." he cleared his throat. "But... I..."

This man was acting nervous. Why? Brittney was accustomed to tongue tying men, but not like this. Perhaps it was the clothes?

"I'm sorry," she said. "I... Firion?"

The strapping man knelt beside her. "You have me at a disadvantage then," he said. "Could you tell me your name?"

He didn't recognize her? What the hell?

His golden eyes had locked on to hers, staring. He was waiting for an answer. She had to come up with a name, fast. Uh... uh...

"Arielle," she said. It was the first name that came into her head. She'd seen that movie as a girl and identified so hard with that character, it wasn't even funny.

"What a wonderful name," he replied. He was staring at her hair and her eyes. Why?

Firon held out a hand. "Please, allow me to escort you home," he said. "As I'm sure you're aware since you know my name, it's my duty to protect the citizens of this city."

Bullshit, Brittney thought. Firion's duty was to protect the hierarch and his council, nothing more. Most of his job was stamping papers with his seal to transfer the children of various rich families in and out of the guard in order to add 'Guardian of the Hierarch' to their list of titles, for a fee of course.

"If you cannot walk," Firon said. "I could certainly carry you."

"I don't believe that will be necessary," Brittney said. Her voice had become softer! What else had that angel creature thing done to her? "Please, if you'd help me up."

She took his hand and he lifted her out of the grass and into his arms despite her objection. There was nothing she could do about it either, she was so weak now. Before she would have broken his jaw and torn one of his legs off for touching her body without permission. Now that the angels had stolen her levels she was powerless.

Fear came for her, threatening to overpower her, but she fought it back. She would handle this, whatever it was.

"Where would you like to be taken, young Arielle?" the Guardian asked but he was already moving down the slope toward the entrance to the park.

Maybe this was an opportunity. She could use this to her advantage. Firion had been trying to talk Brittney into joining him on his airship, probably to take advantage of her, until he'd found out she was a sikari who could break his neck with a flick of her wrist. He'd likely be interested in something similar with her now. All she had to do was chat him up.

That might be dangerous though. She wasn't a sikari anymore. She wasn't sure what she was but her strength and levels were surely gone. Actually, she should check her display. She brought her arms together and stared at them. They were so thin... and small...

"Here you are, Loganth isn't it?" Firion asked.

"Yes your lordship," the younger guard replied, bowing his head.

"I found this little girl in the park grounds," Firion said. "Put out the call to the other stations. I'm sure her parents will show up."

What? A little girl? Brittney stared at her hands, her tiny thin fingered hands.

Holy shit! It was true!

Brittney was passed from the arms of one man to another and again she couldn't even muster the strength to struggle.

"Let me go," she said softly as she was born into a whitebrick guardhouse outside of the park.

"Of course sir. She looks high born but she's not well dressed," her new carrier said. "Perhaps she's run away from her parents."

"Look at her," Firion said, "she's an angel. I'm sure that whatever's occurred, she's not to blame. Isn't that right, Arielle?"

"I... uh... Of course," Brittney responded. It was hard to disagree with that, even if it didn't help her. Where the heck was that stupid blue pixie?

Firion then left, closing the door of the guardhouse behind him. Brittney was carried into a second room with a fireplace where she was put down upon a cushioned chair.

"There you are," the guard said.

There was another guard, taller with a thick yellow mustache seated in the chair opposite her.

"What have you brought in today, Loganth?" he asked.

"Young girl, sir," the first guard replied. "I'm told she's lost her parents in the park. The commander of the council guard brought her in just now."

"I see," the mustached man said. "She's quite something," he added. "You don't often see eyes and hair like that on girls so young."

"That may be why the commander thought she's from a high born family, sir," Loganth replied. "Only they would have the money to make changes like that."

"It is possible," his superior replied as he leaned forward in his chair. "Tell me girl, what is your family name?"

Ugh. Brittney could never remember the last names of these people. They were so weird! As a sikari she had no family name. In ceremonies the sikari were considered part of Cerathia's extended family because they'd been chosen by her angels, but they were never referred to by another name.

"Out with it girl!" the mustached man said. "I haven't got all day."

"She may be confused, sir," Loganth said as he removed his helmet to scratch his balding head. "Can you remember which of the Ghrellen islands you live on?"

Brittney shook her head. All the names were the same to her. It had never mattered before. Vita had always been there to tell her where to go and how to get there. She was completely and utterly screwed.

"You better tell us something to go on little miss," the mustached man said. "Or you'll end up carted off to one of the children's homes in the fellways. What you think of that, huh?"

"Sir!" Loganth said. "I strenuously object!"

"I'm just trying to get her to talk!" the man replied. "What have you gotten out of her, eh? Nothing! We don't have all night! She can't stay here. This isn't some charity."

Suddenly there was a cracking sound from the other room like wood breaking. Both men frowned.

"Didn't you latch the door?" the mustached man asked.

"The commander closed it when he left," Loganth said. "I heard it latch."

"Who goes there!"

A tingling noise was growing from the other room. It grew in strength until a tiny blue woman burst around the doorway and into the room.

"Janine!" Brittney called.

"So you think you're going to find something here?" Arinna asked. "It's pretty far afield."

Max looked around. "Yeah, I won't be long... Where's Trina?"

Arinna pointed behind her. "In our room. She looked upset."

"You just left her?" Max asked. "You didn't ask what's wrong?"

Arinna folded her arms. "It's not really my business," she said.

"Well maybe it should be," Max said. "She's part of the party and I know she's a little pushy sometimes but she's smart and she has a good heart. Please try to be friendly."

Arinna pursed her lips. "I'll think about it."

"Oh!" Max said, summoning an item into his hand, which he held out.

"This is Dwyane," Max said. "It's dark out so it should be safe to take him north a little. There are some mountains and on the top of the first set of peaks are some giant eagle nests where you can find lots of weapons. At your skill level, it should be a breeze."

Arinna reached for the cattan but Max drew it back.

"Take Trina," he said.

Arinna frowned. "I don't like being forced to make friends."

"There are worse things," Max said. "You've been cooped up for a long time and lots of people want you dead. You could use some friends."

She extended her hand. "I'll ask her," she said. "But I won't force her to go."

Max handed the cattan over. "Deal."

Then he turned and walked down the Midnight's cargo ramp, heading back into the first forest he'd visited in this world. Hanging to his back, like a tentacle covered backpack was Scruff. Max had asked him to leave his two smaller companions with Mytten to keep an eye on Reken, just in case he decided to wander off or steal the Midnight.

"It's just you and me buddy," Max said as he stepped into the forest.

Eat!

"Maybe," Max said. "I'm kind of hoping we run into some of my old friends."

The forest was just like it had been the first time he'd entered it. Tall trees with thick underbrush that made it necessary to push your way through. Even with night vision he couldn't see very far. The noises were the same too, clicking, chirping, and rustling, all around him.

"Come on out little centipedes," Max said, brandishing his bone wand. "Daddy's got a present for you."

Nothing. Maybe they knew he'd leveled up somehow? Too bad. One of the most satisfying parts of a game like First Fantasy was coming back to the first area and wrecking the things that gave you so much trouble at level one. Yet here he was... and they weren't coming out.

"Are you sure guys?" Max called out into the dark. "I'm just as tasty as I was before when you crunched my skull over and over."

Centipedes afraid.

"Yeah?" Max asked. "Well they should be."

Will not attack.

Max sighed. "Figures. Well thanks for telling me Scruff. Better to know I guess."

He was pretty sure the Midnight had parked to the south of the clearing Max remembered, so he kept pushing north, sort of weaving back and forth, until he sort of stumbled into it. There it was, the fire pit, a few broken bottles that Max had left behind... and the bed roll. It was now all wet and gross from being left out in the rain. Man, how did he miss that?

Something coming.

"What?" Max asked, looking up and turning in a circle.

Big.

"Not helpful," Max said.

Then the rustling in the brush intensified and the head of an enormous centipede emerged from the forest. Mandibles the size of swords clenched as a thick steaming poison drizzled from their tips. Beside it, six other smaller centipede heads slid out of the brush. These were the ones Max had met before.

"Oh I get it," Max said. "Don't attack until your big brother gets here." He pointed his wand at the array of multi-faced eyes surrounding him. "You know that just makes you look weak, right?"

They all rushed him at once, like a wave of segmented death but Max didn't even flinch, he just pointed his wand straight at the center of the big one and cast Bolt lance.

A Blue flash lit the forest as the lightning discharged, coring a perfect hole through the center of the largest centipede. The creature collapsed at Max's feet dead.

Max blew the smoke from the top of his bone wand. "Who wants next?"

The centipedes all stopped in their tracks and turned to flee.

"Now Scruff!" Max said and the creature on his back used eight of his tentacles to throw eight bags of sleep power in every direction around them. When the dust settled, Max found six sleeping centipedes which he crunched one at a time by stepping on the joint that connected their giant rounded head to the remaining segments of their body.

Southern forest Visapedes and Giant Southern Visapede defeated!

"Oh man," Max said. "That felt good."

Eat?

"Go nuts," Max said. "I'm just going to check out a cave, catch up when you're done."

Yes.

The dungeon crawler was already slurping the largely liquid insides from the nearest dead insect.

All Max had to do was go straight west. Little of the trail left by Raeg still remained, just a few broken twigs here and there, but it was enough to guide him. Soon enough, Max emerged from the woods and found himself standing in front of a familiar cave. If he was human, he might have had chills.

The entrance was empty and he couldn't hear anything inside.

"Oh well," he said.

He couldn't afford to stand around. Arinna and Trina had a short flight, they could be back to the ship in only an hour or so. Not to mention that they needed to get moving quickly if they were going to head back north. Hopefully there would be enough fuel at that town the pirates were in, because they'd be coasting in on fumes.

So Max stepped into the dark. The cave was just as he'd left it: empty. The undead rats who'd seen him to the exit last time didn't seem to be around. The githers though, evidence of their activity was everywhere. He hadn't noticed it when he was here before, but there were little circular scuffs in the sandy floor of the cave from the creatures' suction cup feet.

He'd only seen a couple of them last time. There had to be more.

Max raised his wand.

"Come on out you creepy little pieces of shit," he said. "I know you're in here."

In the distance, he heard something... the sound of shuffling and it was getting fainter. It was moving away. Apparently these creatures had also realized he was more powerful now.

"Only pick on the weak do you?" he called out, hearing his voice echo through the cavern. "Wussies," he grumbled and continued on.

The passage wound left and right more than he remembered. Though he'd been pretty scared back then. New to this world, just found out he was a skeleton, and recently killed by the guy who would later become his best friend.

Raeg.

Max missed that big tattoo covered barbarian, but more than that... he needed him on the team. Max liked the magic. He had a talent for it, he knew he did. He wanted more spells, as many as they had but for that to be the case, he needed another front liner. Arinna was nasty, boy was she, but she wasn't solid. Raeg was.

Maybe there would be a clue to becoming a Necromancer here. It was all he could think of. It might be his last chance.

More shuffling in the distance. Again it moved away as Max approached. Too bad. He'd wanted to burn a few of those spherical bastards to ash.

There it was, ahead. The room where he'd arrived in this world, this place they called Fohra.

Max paused for a second outside, letting the green from his eyes wash over the cavern nearby, looking for movement. There was none.

"Hmmm," he said. Something felt off.

He looked around again, more slowly, listening intently. A gither pattered in the distance, but softly. If they had the numbers to attack, the creatures would already have come.

Still, it wouldn't be bad to have some protection.

Max summoned a cattan into his palm.

"Bind Severing Ghoul," Max said.

Severing Ghoul Ment added.

"Ment eh?"

Yes.

Max threw the cattan at the ground. From the black mist emerged a horrible twisted creature. It was vaguely man-shaped but thinner with wide black eyes and rows of pointed shark-like teeth. Each arm terminated in a pair of long scissor-like blades and that seemed to curl and uncurl as the creature breathed.

"Welcome to the family. Just stay here," Max said. "I'm going inside this room. If anything shows up."

Shred.

"Yep," Max replied. "Perfect."

Max turned to enter the room and was immediately disappointed. It was empty. Completely picked clean. The wooden pedestal that had been there was gone as was the table and everything on it including the candles. Even the bones of the other skeletons were gone. That made sense given githers lived here and they apparently ate bones. Still... he'd hoped there would be something.

"Dammit!" he said.

He'd be going back with nothing. No unlocked class. No useful items. Not even a memento.

"This sucks."

Shred. Kill. Eat.

"Oh?" Max asked, turning around. "Is something here?" He got around just fast enough to see the ghoul take off into the dark, heading back toward the cave entrance. The creature moved soundlessly. It was pretty terrifying actually, the stuff of nightmares. He felt bad for whatever it was about to eviscerate.

"Augh!" yelled a man's voice. "Stay away!"

Max couldn't believe it, but he recognized that voice.

18

A SQUIRREL AND A BUNCH OF RATS

"Ment!" Max called into the dark, "come back."

With a poof of black smoke, the cattan reappeared in Max's hand. The smoke had come from the right, farther into the cave. The same direction where someone was in pain. Max could hear whoever it was grunting and choking back screams.

"One second," Max said as he ran off into the dark. "I'm coming."

Max had to slip around a corner and through a thin squeeze where the walls of the cave came within a foot of each other, but he found him.

"I hear you!" the man's voice called in response, though it wavered from fear. "Stay back!" He held a small torch in one hand, trying to keep it aloft even as blood pumped from an open wound in his other arm, that hung limp at his side.

"Niall, right?" Max said as he walked into the glow of the Slayer's torch. "Let me help you."

"No!" he said. "Y-you win... this... round." Then Niall's eyes rolled back into his head and the torch dropped.

Max sighed. "Oh no. No dying on me this time." He knelt down and used salves and one of Trina's Necksem tonics with the werewolf blood in it. The wound closed quickly but Niall snored for a good thirty minutes before Max finally couldn't take it anymore and poked his chest.

"Wake up," Max said. "Or I'm gonna start slapping you."

Niall started and tried to back off until he ran into a stalagmite behind him, bumping his head.

"Oh!" he said.

Max realized that now that Niall's torch was out it was probably pretty dark for a human so he used one of the black candles, placing it on the ground between them.

"Light," Max said. Dutifully,the candle complied, filling the cave with its eerie glow.

"Why did you heal me? Going to gloat?" the slayer asked.

"No," Max said. "I was wondering how-"

"How I knew you would return here?" Niall asked, with a self-satisfied half grin.

Max nodded.

"Why should I tell you?"

"I don't know... I'm up for discussion at this point. What do you want?"

"You're not going to threaten me?" Niall asked, his eyes narrowed.

Max shrugged. "Why? At this point you know what I can do."

Niall nodded, catching his breath a little. "What was that thing?"

"The ghoul?" Max asked. "He's a summon."

"It came out of the dark like a nightmare. It was soundless and so fast... its movements were a blur. I have only read of such things... in ancient books."

"Yeah," Max said. "Actually, I noticed you had the necromancy book and this." He gestured with the bone wand.

Niall nodded. "Yes. I was surprised at first... that you survived that crash. But when I heard what had happened in Gelra, I knew. I knew it was you."

"But you came back here anyway," Max said.

"I had no other ideas, to be honest," Niall replied. "This was my only lead. Why did you come here?"

"Me?" Max asked. "I need to become a Necromancer."

Niall laughed.

"What?" Max asked. "Why is that funny? Is it because I'm already undead?"

"So do I," he said.

Max leaned in. "What do you mean?"

Niall's eyes moved down to the candle flame. "I... I lost my sister."

"I'm sorry," Max said.

"We grew up together in the slop blocks of Ghalarem. She is all that remains of my family. For a long time I thought if I was faithful, if I served the light strongly enough... that... that Cerathia might grant my wish for her return."

"Can they do that?" Max asked. "Just resurrect anyone?"

"I believed they could. They tell us they can... but after many empty promises went unfulfilled... my faith wavered. I began to consider... other options."

"Necromancy," Max said.

"Yes."

"She wouldn't be the same would she?" Max asked. "She would be undead... or worse."

"I read that book," Niall said. "I know... but... you live. You speak, you think. It must be possible for her to return like you."

"Are you sure that's what you really want?" Max asked. "This world isn't exactly welcoming to people like me."

"I know."

"It's not easy," Max said. "They have to want to come back and, reading between the lines a little, I think there's something else important too but the book isn't explicit about it. It seems to me that necromancy may be more of an art than a science."

"I cannot become a Necromancer," Niall said. "I promised Eryka that I would never join the dark... but," tears rolled down his cheeks, "it's the only way."

"Hmmm," Max said. "I'm supposed to be going to the land of the dead. I could find her, talk to her about it. Maybe see what she wants."

"You could?"

Max nodded. "I could... The only problem is, I can't for the life of me figure out how to unlock the stupid Necromancer class."

"No? That's child's play!"

"It is?"

"But how could you not know it? You're undead!"

"I... I know."

"You're toying with me... you must be."

Max grumbled. "No. I'm not."

"But, seriously," Niall said. "It should be so easy for you."

"Just shut up and tell me," Max said.

"Haven't you ever experienced the soul of another creature?"

Max tilted his head. "What do you mean?"

Niall leaned forward, holding out his hands. "When any living thing dies, the ethereal is separated from the body. Do you understand?"

"Right," Max said.

"Have you ever seen this?"

"Maybe?" Max replied. Had he? He felt like he had, a while back.

"To unlock Necromancer," Niall said. "One must call a spirit back into an item. Their own body or bones is the easiest. It was their former home. This is how most with an interest in death unlock this class. Usually they are dark and of one of the Ksaya or Vicara affinities."

These were new words to Max. "The what now?"

"Um..." Niall was spinning his hand, looking for the words. "Thinking... and... ah...dying."

"Ok," Max said. "If you mean thought and decay, I'm a mix of that right now."

"Yes... those are also words you could use. As a Slayer I was taught to hunt Plague Doctors and Alchemists first. They most often become Necromancers."

"I see," Max said. He stared at the little candle in front of him. All this time, because he'd been power-leveling by beating on things but not killing them, and he'd always been on the move, leaving the dead behind... he'd been screwing himself. Max looked back at the Slayer. "I'll find your sister for you," Max said, "And if she asks to return as an undead, I'll help her."

Niall took Max's skeletal hand and leaned forward and kissed the signet ring. "Thank you."

"Ok," Max said. "That was weird. Don't do that."

"I'm sorry," Niall replied. "It's how everything is done on the light."

"Not with me," Max said. "Where can I find you?"

"Do not worry," Niall said. "When the time comes. I will find you."

Max nodded, standing up. "Good enough for me. Oh and I'd watch out, there's githers in here."

"So?" Niall replied. "They only attack undead. Why do you think we put them in caves?"

"You put them here?" Max said.

"Well not me personally, but you know, others of the light. We exterminate the dark species and spread the light ones. It's part of the purge."

"Wow," Max said. "Thorough."

"Yes," Niall said. "Let me go disassemble a few traps I left by the entrance. May Cerathia light your way."

"Uh, you too," Max said as he scooped up the black candle and pinched the flame out. "So I guess I've got to go kill something."

The first thing he did was exit the cave. Still no undead rats, and the githers kept their distance, which was fine. He emerged into the dark just as he had weeks ago, as a level one nothing, only now he had a bit more going on.

Max also stored his wand. He could cast magic without it and he expected that if he was going to kill something, a basic dagger was a better choice than burning it to a crisp. Unfortunately, he only had one dagger and it was the purity he'd gotten from Brittney, less than ideal.

Brittney. Max hadn't thought of her in a while. Hopefully he wouldn't have to deal with her again.

In the end, he was forced to go with his own bare hands.

Max!

"Scruff!" Max said. "How was the feasting?"

Good.

"Now that you're here. I've got a question my tentacled friend."

Yes?

"Do you know where I can find something alive? Preferably something with bones."

Like this?

Scruff lifted a tentacle from his back, extending it upward. Wrapped by the tentacle was a small furry creature. It was around the size of a squirrel and very similar otherwise, with tufted ears and a fluffy tail covered in white spots.

"Where did you get that?" Max asked.

Woods. Snack for later. You want?

Scruff gestured with the limp little body, pushing it closer to Max.

"Uh... I was going to kill it," he said. The thing looked so sad with its eyes closed like that. "But I think it's already dead." That was probably good. Max didn't know if he could kill something so cute and helpless.

Not dead.

Scruff shook the creature and the tiny eyes opened. The thing looked terrified. Now Max was absolutely sure, there was no way he could hurt-

Scruff used his tentacle to snap its neck.

"Ah!" Max said.

There. Dead.

Max sighed and knelt down in the dirt in front of the cave. "Bring it here."

Scruff laid the little squirrel body down in the dirt in front of Max.

Max stared at it. Nothing was happening. What was he supposed to do?

Then... he saw something. A sort of glowing form began to ooze out of the tiny body. Max leaned in and it became brighter. Then he realized... the spirit wasn't glowing on its own, it was reflecting the green light from Max's eyes. The light of death. Creepy.

"So what do I do now?" Max asked.

"WHAT IN THE name of Cerathia happened to you?!" Janine yelled. "You shrunk!"

"What was it?" the mustached man asked.

"Dunno," the other man replied as he peered around the door. "Someone opened our door and just left it open!"

"Well close it then!" the other replied.

"They can't see you?" Brittney asked, realizing what she'd done only after the words had left her mouth.

"Eh?" the mustached man asked, his thick blond eyebrows knitted together.

"They can't see how... important you are," Brittney said. She could not get over how soft her voice was. Had she actually sounded like this when she'd been a girl? It had been normal at the time, but now it just felt wrong, like someone else was speaking through her mouth.

The man continued to frown at her.

"Since they... you know... broke open your door," Brittney finished, helping him along. It seemed they didn't post their best and brightest in these guardhouses. Just like home.

Finally, the man nodded. "That's true. Loganth, go out there and have a look."

"Yessir," Loganth replied.

"Of course they can't see me," Janine replied. "I'm a pixie."

Right, of course, duh, how could Brittney not know something so stupidly obvious. All the books back home said the same thing: nobody could see pixies except little girls and crazy people. And, of course, Brittney was now BOTH.

"Haven't remembered your family name have you, girl?" the mustached man asked. He seemed a little less annoyed with her now that she'd said he was important. Men.

"Who are these people?" Janine asked.

"I don't know," Brittney said, answering both parties as best she could.

"You still can't stay here," he said as he stood up, wandering over toward where a belt with a sword hanging from it hung from a hook on the wall. "I meant it about escorting you down to one of the homes, but maybe we can stop somewhere else first."

Brittney didn't like the sound of this. She used her eyebrows to gesture toward the mustached man.

Janine didn't get it. "What?" the pixie asked.

Brittney waited until his back was turned and mimed punching him with her fist.

"Oh! You mean knock him out?"

She nodded.

"Can't," Janine said. "Used almost every drop fighting our way out of Akasa, sorry. It'll take me a few hours to recharge my magic So... what happened to you?"

Brittney glared at her.

Well, it wouldn't be the first time she'd gotten herself out of an unfriendly situation. The mustached man was strapping on his sword belt. She could ask to see the weapon... and stab him with it. No. She was too weak to handle anything that heavy now. Would he want to play hide and seek? No, not likely.

Come on, think Brittney! What would Monica do? Of all the characters from Friends, Monica always found a way to win.

Just then a sharp whistle started in the other room.

"Loganth!" the mustached man shouted.

There was no response and the whistling continued unabated.

"Argh! That idiot ran out of here and left the kettle on," he said as he turned to her. "I'll be right back. Stay here, or else."

Then he stomped into the other room. That room was on the way to the door, which was probably closed. There was no way to get past him and get it open before he could get her. That left only one option. Brittney quickly pushed herself off the chair she'd been tossed onto and ran for the stairs. She didn't even have to be quiet about it because her feet were bare and she weighed little.

"Why are you ignoring me?!" Janine snapped, buzzing around her head.

Brittney swatted at her. "Hush!" she whispered. "I need to escape this place!"

"Oh? Oh right!" Janine said as she buzzed by. "Let me go on ahead and look for a way out!"

Brittney ascended the wooden stairs as quickly as she possibly could, which is to say: unbearably slowly. The stairs were steeply pitched and her legs were not strong.

"I hate this body!" she whispered. "Whoever did this to me... I'll get you for this!"

"Hey!" the guardsman called. He'd already returned from the adjoining kitchen, holding a cup of tea. "You can't go up there!"

Oh yes I can, Brittney thought, just slowly.

"There's nowhere to go up there," he said. "You won't escape that way."

Finally, she made it to the top stair and the upper landing, which was a cramped hall with a wooden floor. This must be the sleeping quarters for the guards. Wonderful.

She ran down to the end but found only a window that was latched closed. The latch was far too high for her to reach, even jumping. When she turned around the pixie was right in her face.

"I found something," Janine said. "But you won't like it!"

The sound of boots coming up the stairs was echoing through the hall.

"Don't care!" Brittney said. "Show me."

"This way!" Janine said as she zipped through the air, leaving a trail of soft blue sparkles and then with a thump, slid under a door to Brittney's right.

When Brittney's tried the handle: clunk. Locked.

"Janine!" she hissed.

"I told you," the mustached man said as he reached the top of the stairs. "There is no way out."

A click to her right announced that the door had been unlocked and she yanked the handle. This time the mechanism disengaged and the door opened.

"Hey!" he called after her but Brittney was already inside and snapping the lock back in place.

"Here!" Janine said, pointing ahead to an open window.

"Mmmm muh?" a voice said to Brittney's right. It was another guard. He was in his bed, asleep! That's right, it was night. He must have been on the early morning shift.

"Go back to bed," Brittney said as she stepped through the window. "This is just a crappy dream."

"Mmmmm," the guard replied as his head lowered back down into his pillow.

SLAM! It was the man outside the door.

"Let me in! Germit! Get up and unlock this door!"

"Muh?"

Brittney couldn't pay attention to what was behind her, because she was looking ahead and what was ahead was far worse. It wasn't just a short drop down to the ground. That she might have been able to deal with. She probably would have sprained an ankle doing it, but she would have tried. But that wasn't even close to what she was looking at. There actually wasn't any ground, at all.

The guardhouse was backed up to a drop tube, one of the many circular holes that the floating cities had for dumping waste down below. This was a big one too, it was at least thirty feet to the other side and the bricks around the circular hole were smooth, purposely, so it was difficult to climb up or down.

"Quite a drop, right?" Janine asked as they flew out over the opening. "Looks like a long drop. I can't even see the bottom!"

"Yeah," Brittney whispered. What was she going to do now? Before she would have used one of her flying summons, but they were gone, stolen.

"Ooh, look at this!" Janine said, pointing above and behind her. "There's a cord. I think I can pull it down."

There was more muffled yelling from behind her. Whatever they were going to do, they'd better do it quickly.

When she looked up she was a little encouraged. The cord looked to be some way to adjust a rain shutter mounted far above the window. It was probably thick enough to hold her weight. There was only one obvious problem.

Janie ripped the cord free and threw the end down to her. "Here you are!" she said triumphantly.

Brittney caught it. "I can't pull myself," she said. "My arms are too weak." It was true too, she'd be lucky to hold on.

"This would be so much easier if you could just fly!" Janine said.

Brittney scowled. "Don't you think I know that?" she replied... but a thought occurred to her. There was another window to their right, which probably led into some other room. Maybe she didn't have to pull herself up after all.

"Grab her!" The mustached man yelled.

"Shit!" Brittney said and launched herself off the side of the window, trying to swing as far as she could toward the far window, unfortunately the cord gave way halfway over and she dropped ten feet before swinging back far below the window she'd been standing on. The force of the return swing was too much for her tiny hands to hold on to and she was flung into empty black space.

About ten seconds went by where Brittney was sure, this was it, that she'd bounce off the wall and fall hundreds of feet to go splat. Instead there was no wall to bounce against. Brittney's face ripped through paper that had been painted to look like brick before bouncing off an old broken bureau and landing on one of several dirty mattresses on the floor of a very dark room.

One of those weird rat people startled and ran off with a squeal.

Brittney groaned as she rolled off the mattress onto a wooden floor. "What just happened?"

"You're a lucky girl," Janine said, buzzing in from outside. "Looks like people are living here in secret, right next to the guard station. What an odd thing to do."

"These aren't people," Brittney said, disgusted. "They're big rats."

"That's not very nice," Janine said.

"Whatever, how do I get out of here?" she asked. Ugh, she felt terrible. She must have smashed her back into the bureau pretty hard when she flew in here. There would be bruises for sure.

Janine buzzed over to the other wall. "I believe this is a way out."

Brittney stumbled in that direction, wishing very much for some shoes. The floor here was coated in dusty little nubs that stuck to the bottoms of her feet. She didn't want to scrape them off for fear they would smell like she expected them to: like the droppings of something nasty.

What she found wasn't a door so much as a roughly circular hole that had been chewed into the wood. The marks of pairs of teeth were everywhere. This wasn't a home, it was a rat warren.

Just the thought made her shiver involuntarily.

Even worse, the tunnel ahead was pitch black. No candles, no lights, nothing but dark.

"Fly in here and light the way for me," Brittney ordered the pixie.

"Fine!" Janine retorted. "Come on."

But as soon as the little blue form entered the tunnel, Brittney gasped. Multiple pairs of eyes shined back from the dark, reflecting the blue light and shifting it to a greenish yellow.

"Who are you speaking to?" a voice demanded.

19

THE POWER OF DEATH AND TRANSFORMATION

Eat?

"No Scruff," Max said. "Not yet."

He was watching the essence of the tiny squirrel-like creature slide out of its body and start flitting around. It seemed to be gaining strength as it went, becoming more solid in its spiritual form. Max couldn't help but be reminded of Mytten. She'd recently molted and the process had likely been a lot like this. The little thing had cast its body aside and was embracing a new life.

If that was true, Max might have limited time.

He hated the idea of messing with something's soul... but... that's what had been done to him. Max hadn't been given a choice though, and from reading the book Max knew that he should be able to release this creature later without an issue, assuming this worked.

"Well... here it goes," he said and reached out his boney fingers.

The spirit seemed to feel him approach. Even though it wasn't yet fully formed, its movements quickened.

"Don't worry little guy," Max said as his bones closed around it corralling the creature. "This shouldn't hurt." Max then pulled it back toward its body, pushing the soul back inside.

The spirit disappeared, subsumed by the creature's dead body and all was dark and silent.

Eat now?

"Shhhh," Max said, leaning in closer to the tiny furry creature. The necromancy book had said that the union of a soul, no matter how minor, with dead flesh caused a discontinuity that called to the decay affinity. Sometimes it worked, sometimes it didn't.

"Come on little guy," Max said. "Come back to papa."

Nothing seemed to be happening at first. Max was almost ready to give up and try again... when it twitched. It was just the tiniest movement of a single claw, but it was enough.

"You can do it," Max said.

Another twitch, followed by a sort of spasm that shook the whole creature. Then... a faint green began in its eyes.

Necromancer unlocked.

"Yeah!" Max said.

The little thing was turning over and sitting up, using its little green eyes to scan around. Max knew from the book he had only seconds to complete the process. Quickly, he unequipped his cloak and boots and jumped over to the class menu.

```
Job class selection

Barbarian,  Duelist,  Tactician,  Mercenary,
Rogue,      Ronin,    Smuggler,   Trapper,
Dark Mage,  Cultist,  Shaman,     Plague Doctor,
Scavenger,  Brawler,  Breeder,    Alchemist,
Knave,      Fool,     Charlatan,  Scoundrel

Gladiator,  Dusk Rider,  Dark Summoner,  Defiler,
Necromancer

Note: Upon changing your job class you will receive
a penalty.
```

There it was, after all this time: Necromancer. Max selected it. The change was instantaneous, and marked only by a minor pulse of nausea that passed in only seconds.

"Alright..." he said. "Let's see if I can remember this," he said as he put a hand over the little creature with the glowing green eyes. The green was starting to soften. Soon it would go out and the spirit would move on.

"Anchor," Max said.

Anchor what?

Right, right. He had to know what the thing was. Wait... how was that possible? It was already dead. Scruff had killed it and Scruff wasn't technically in his party, so he hadn't received a notification. Crap!

"Anchor... tiny fuzzy squirrel... thing."

Invalid Anchor.

"Dammit!" he said.

The green lights in the tiny creature's eyes were winking out now.

"I'm sorry little guy," Max said. "I screwed up."

The creature's soul emerged for a second time. It was better formed now, more like the body it had before. It seemed to pause and regard Max and Scruff before it floated off.

"Maybe it's for the best," Max said. He wasn't sure what he would have done with an undead squirrel thing anyway.

Eat?

"Yea... No," Max said. "This little guy helped me out. We're gonna give him, or her, some respect."

Max used his skeletal fingers to dig into the dirt and he placed the little creature's body there before covering it over and patting it a few times.

"Let's go Scruff," Max said, standing up. "We got what we came for. I've been here long enough."

As he was walking back through the woods Max was thinking about bones. Specifically, skeletons. The necromancy book had been clear: you leveled the class by raising undead and using them to perform tasks. Combat was one of those tasks but as the book had specifically mentioned combat Max was other tasks counted too, but how much did they count? That was where the book was vague. That was kind of the problem with the skill books in general, they told you how things worked, but kind of glossed over the details. It made him wonder if they'd been written before this place started working like a First Fantasy game.

Whatever the reason, it was annoying. Max would have to experiment with the skeletons back at the ship. He needed to find the quickest way to get some levels. Necromancer wasn't like Dark Summoner which had access to the same spells as the Dark Mage while also having its own set of interesting summoning abilities. No, the necro was limited to only tier one spells but that cost was offset by an ability to summon increasingly powerful undead that grew to truly insane numbers at the higher levels.

When the girls got back, he needed to ask Trina to craft some more of those magic refill potions, or, failing that, they needed to find some rancid filth somewhere. That shouldn't be a huge problem given what Khilen had written about the light.

Oh! He'd been so stupid! Neline had killed all those Kestrian navy people and they'd just let the ships crash without harvesting the bodies. Though, Scruff and his little friends probably would have eaten all the flesh off. Those things truly had an endless appetite.

Max!

He stopped. "What?"

Humans ahead.

It had to be Arinna and Trina. That was impressive. He was sure they'd take longer than him given the flight time up to those mountains.

No.

"Huh?" That was odd. There was light ahead. Had that stupid Comedian turned on the ship's lights?

Others. Many others.

Max was pushed forward as Scruff vaulted from his back into the brush.

"Hey!" he said. "Where are you going?"

"You there!" a stern voice yelled from up ahead. "Hold your weapons up and step forward into the light."

Oh... shit. Light soldiers! But how? Why had Mytten not warned him? The answer was that she would have, if she wasn't incapacitated some how. Mytten! If they'd hurt his spider he would rip them to pieces.

"Come out! NOW!" the voice ordered.

"Fine!" Max yelled back as he summoned the Shadow staff into his right hand. Ruse was a tier two spell, but it was part of the staff, and that meant anyone who could use a staff, could use it. He cast the spell on himself and walked to his left while his two clones walked ahead.

It was night still, and dark inside the forest so he was practically invisible.

"You!" the voice called. "Stop right there!"

The person doing the yelling was a Sun paladin, Max was sure of it. He recognized that gaudy golden armor anywhere. The paladin was flanked by more than a dozen soldiers of various types. They all looked tough. Behind them stood a tall woman in flowing robes. She wore a tall hat with a wide brim. Light Mage or Wizard, had to be.

"That's not him, you fool!" she shouted. "It's a shadow."

"Crap," Max mumbled, moving faster. He was kind of screwed right now.

"Fan out!" the paladin shouted. "It's here somewhere."

Max had to get back to ship quickly. If by some miracle they hadn't already killed Mytten, they would soon. Quickly, he brought up his class screen and selected Dread Knight. The headache was nasty, but it could have been far worse if he didn't have so many levels. The Unending Dread set was in bad shape, luckily Max had a second armor set, one that gave him several particularly useful bonuses. He slapped the Arcane Overlord set on and turned around just in time to see something wild: an elf archer!

"He is here!" the elf said, his long pointed ears hanging out from a pointy hat. "I can sense his dark presence."

"Boy, you elves just love pointy stuff don't you?" Max asked as he called the Taker of Will into his right hand.

With lightning speed the elf rolled to the right, firing a string of magical arrows in seconds. The points clinked against Max's armor.

23 magic absorbed.

21 magic absorbed.

27 magic absorbed.

26 magic absorbed.

19 magic absorbed.

"Take that you fiend! May the light of the mother tree guide you to oblivion!"

"Actually," Max said, from inside his helmet. "I don't think you actually did any damage."

"Liar! Fell spawn like yourself can never be trusted!"

"Man," Max said, shaking his head. "I'm starting to feel like Sauron might not have been such a bad dude." He swung the great green blade of the Taker of Will, slashing through two trees before he caught the elf as he was trying to leap away. The blade severed both of his enemy's legs.

"Ooh," Max said as the body spun to the ground. "That's... that's a nasty one."

The elf was crying out and trying to drag himself back toward the clearing, leaving a trail of his blood on the leaves behind him. Max finished him with a quick second swing, further covering the green blade in that weird white blood of the light.

"It looks like I've been chopping bottles of white out," Max said.

"Get him!" the paladin yelled as he charged at Max, flanked by six others.

THREE OF THE six other soldiers rushing at Max screamed as a thin blade shaped like a crescent moon shot out of the dark and ripped through their necks one by one. Each fell half a second later, having dropped their weapons to try to stave the fountain of fluid gushing from their own neck.

This was followed by a pair of bombs that exploded in their midst, knocking even the paladin to the ground.

Max laughed. "I thought you'd never get here!"

"We ran into a few... issues," Trina said.

"But it's all good now," Arinna added, raising a long thin curved blade. There was a slight whistle sound as the weapon swung with incredible precision, decapitating another soldier who was running in from her right.

"Can the two of you check on the ship and Mytten?" Max asked. "I'm worried about her." He couldn't recall the summon to her cattan unless he was close enough for the command to be heard. Stupid rules!

"There's a wizard over there," Arinna said as her long blade flicked again, cutting the weapon hand from another enemy. "Are you sure?"

"Don't worry about me," he said. "I'm good."

"Don't be long," she said, suddenly standing very close to him. Her finger ran along the edge of his spiked shoulder pauldron. "You look nice in that armor."

Max chuckled. "You always look nice," he said, "and deadly."

She smiled, showing her vampire teeth, and was gone in a flash.

Trina ran past, her Plague Doctor mask shaking from side to side. "You two," she mumbled.

Only a single second after Trina passed a huge bolt of bright magenta lightning lanced through the smoke left over from Trina's bombs. It caught Max right in the center of his chest with a whack. It felt like he'd been hit with a two-handed hammer but the actual damage wasn't that bad.

37 damage received.

148 magic absorbed.

The wizard was taking pot shots. Cute.

"You!" the paladin said, using an ornate two handed sword to help get himself back up to his feet. This made Max pause. Anyone with a high enough level to become a prestige class like Sun Paladin would have huge stats right? They wouldn't leave their skill level low would they? That would be stupid.

"Die!" the paladin added, swinging his sword with as much fury as he could muster... but it wasn't that much. Max used the Taker of Will to deflect the attack with ease. His next blow slammed into the paladin's shoulder, knocking him backward.

"Your armor's pretty good," Max said. "But you don't hit very hard."

"Yes I do!" the paladin retorted as he raised his sword high above his head.

Max stood still as the blow came down and slammed into his helmet, clanging off.

31 damage received.

"Just what I thought," Max said. "I'm not gonna tell you how to live your life... but... you suck at this." Then he spun around in a wide swing. The paladin tried to block it but it was too slow. The Taker of Will slammed into the guy's left knee. The armor there was too strong to cut through, but that didn't matter, the weapon was so heavy that the hit drove through both of the paladin's legs, upending him.

A large ball of holy fire arced in from Max's left, slamming into his shoulder and almost knocking him over, almost.

173 damage received.

371 magic absorbed.

Alright, that was some damage. Seemed like she was trying different things to see what he was weak to. He definitely needed to deal with that wizard quickly.

"That was a low blow!" the paladin protested as he stepped up to one knee, panting as he did. "I expect nothing less fro-"

There was a loud clang as the Taker of Will slammed into the paladin's helmet, knocking the man down again. This time he was having a hard time getting up.

"Yeah," Max said, standing over him. "You were weak when we started this, but I bet you're feeling really weak now."

"You... disgust... me," the paladin said.

"Crap," Max said. Sun Paladins had a lot of hit points to chew through. It would take him a while and eventually that wizard would realize he was dark and hit him with something ugly.

There was a hiss from nearby as Scruff swung from a tree branch and landed on the paladin's chest with a wet sloppy thump.

Eat!

Max chuckled. "He's all yours."

The paladin screamed.

"Overwhelm!" a female voice called from his left.

Max turned just in time to receive a pulse of golden light and glowing symbols as it smashed into him... and dissipated into nothing.

Resisted.

148 magic absorbed.

"Sorry, better luck next time," he said as he strode toward the wizard.

She was backing away, feverishly preparing another spell.

"You should give up and run," Max said. Behind him, the paladin's shrieks became muffled. Scruff did like to go for the face.

"Ice over!" the wizard shouted as pure blue crystals exploded from her hands. The ice grew together into steaming sphere razor sharp crystals the size of a beach ball that slammed into Max's chest. Crystals formed all over his armor, hissing and popping with extreme cold.

143 damage received.

216 magic absorbed.

"But... you're a Dread Knight and an undead!" she stammered. "I don't understand! How can you resist so much? That should have been devastating!"

"What can I say?" Max said with a shrug. "Holy fire, ice, lightning. You seen one, you seen em all."

"The dark has never been this strong!" she replied, trying to cast something else.

"Times change," Max said. Then he raised his sword and finished her with one solid blow.

The last few soldiers fled, leaving Max on the field.

Light Wizard, Sun Paladin, Vanguard, and light soldiers defeated!

Arinna has gained a level of Grave Blade!

Arinna has gained a level!

Trina has gained a level of Plague Doctor!

Trina has gained a level!

Trina has unlocked Arcane Surgeon!

You've gained a level of Dread Knight!

You've gained a level!

Max?

"Mytten!" Max said. "Are you alright?"

Yes. Come quickly.

He turned back to Scruff. "Coming?" It was unnecessary. The dungeon crawler was already on his way. The creature leaped onto his back, wrapping tentacles around his neck and waist.

Max broke into a run. "I'm on my way!" he said as he barreled through the forest, smashing through saplings and bushes and reeds.

The situation was every bit as dire as he expected. Four large airships hung over the Midnight.

Arinna was mopping up the troops on the ground, but more would arrive shortly. If not from the ships above, then from the rest which were surely on their way.

Trina ran out of the Midnight. "Max!" she called. "Mytten's fine. They had her knocked out and in a cage. I think she was someone's prize."

"Is she on the ship?"

Trina nodded. "There's a problem though. They smashed the automaton, he's in pieces all over the cargo bay, but that's not the worst of it."

"Do tell," Max said as a crossbow bolt clanked off his arm. He stored his greatsword and brought out the damaged kite shield, holding it up in front of Trina "Come on, back to the ship, get behind me."

"They took all the fuel!" she said. "The ship only has what's in it."

"Do you think it's enough to get to Kapon Taw?" Max asked. "Maybe they have fuel there."

Wait... why wouldn't he use Neline? She could use Death and empty those damned ships. Then they could take their fuel back, plus some.

No. You told her it was a single use item. I can't do it again or she'll know.

"What?!" Max hissed. He knew she was right though. Stupid deals. Max was definitely getting sick of contracts and sneaky deals.

"What is it?" Trina asked just as a ball of holy fire slammed into them from above. It hit Max square in the chest, blowing him back a solid ten feet.

Dark steel kite shield durability depleted: Item lost.

The first thing he did was check on Trina and Scruff. Both looked Ok, if a little charred.

"Come on you two," he said. "Back to the ship."

"Where is Kapon Taw?" Trina asked as he helped her up.

Max paused only to scoop a steaming Scruff into his arms. "It's underground to the west of your school. Remember where we fought the lady with the spear and those two freaky looking dogs?"

"I don't know," Trina replied. "Assuming we can shake the four airships hovering over us, it means going over two sets of foothills and traversing the entire southern kingdom."

"We'd better," Max said, "because walking that far would be a bitch."

20

CULINARY ALLIES AND RISKY DECISIONS

"Uh... no one," Brittney said.

The rat creatures were stepping out of the dark and moving to surround her. She'd always hated the musa. Of all the talking animal people in this world, the rat ones were the only ones that made her skin crawl every time she saw them.

The lizard people weren't that bad, they loved the sun so you were always guaranteed warmth when you entered one of their inns. Neither were the werewolves, in all honesty. Brittney had always thought of them as big puppies, though she'd been much more powerful then. However, the rat people swarmed the gutters and docks of more cities every year, working as cooks and coachmen, and porters. It felt like they were slowly taking over, one place at a time.

"She lies," said one, as he sniffed at her with a long pointed nose.

"She finds us distasteful," said another.

"Yes," said a third. "Like all the children of the light. They sneer at us, kick us when they can."

"Yet we make their things work," said another.

"Nothing but ingrates," said a voice behind her, causing Brittney to turn.

She was now surrounded. "I-I'm sorry for bothering you," she said, hoping her child-like voice and size would help her. Maybe the rats would have pity on her.

"I say we take her up the chain," said one, licking his two front teeth. "Chop her up and feed her to the hierarch. The old bastard would never notice."

The rest all cackled with laughter.

"Enough," said another voice, an older voice. A staff clacked against the stone and the crowd parted to reveal an old rat. He wore hooded robes and his staff had a lantern affixed to the end. Inside was a black candle. It had been a long time since Brittney had seen one of those. She knew what it would do before the old rat held it aloft casting the violet light out, seeking.

Janine's tiny blue form was revealed and all the rats gasped.

"What's that?" asked one.

"A tiny human?" asked another.

"No! It can't be... it has wings!" said a third.

"What's going on?!" Janine whined. "How can they see me?!"

"Silent!" the old rat said. He held out a hand to Brittney. "Come girl. We should speak. Bring your puny companion."

Not knowing what else to do, Brittney accepted his offer and took the old gnarled fingers in her own tiny hand. She was led down a corridor, past many other rats, into a small room no bigger than a broom closet. The door closed behind them.

"Tell me why you've come here," the old rat asked.

"You're a Shaman," Brittney said.

"Mmmm," he replied. "You know a great deal for one so young."

"I'm older than I look," she said.

"I get that feeling also," he replied. "Answer my question."

"I actually don't even know myself," she said.

"I told you exactly what you're supposed to do," Janine said, folding her arms.

"No, you didn't," Brittney replied. "I only know it has to do with Arinna."

The old musa's eyes widened. "What do you mean?"

"Don't tell him!" Janine said. "He'll turn you in!"

"Why would he do that?" Brittney asked. "He's of the dark."

"They can't be trusted!" Janine said. "That's just how the dark is."

Brittney's eyes went back to the old rat. He sat there on a small cushion, watching her converse with Janine. Could he even hear her?

"She seems unhappy with you," he said.

"She is," Brittney said. "She doesn't trust the dark. Her people had a bad time with them, I guess. She didn't go into details and I didn't ask... because I kinda don't care."

Janine huffed in annoyance.

"I don't know who you are, or what your people are doing here hidden away in the bottom of this Ghrellen island," Brittney said. "But I need you to let me go. I'm supposed to do something to help Arinna. There's a trap somewhere, or something."

"What can you do?" he asked. "You are a little girl."

"My best," Brittney said with a shrug.

The old rat threw his head back and laughed. "I like you, girl. My people will help you."

"But.. you don't even know who sent me, or what I'm supposed to do," she said skeptically.

"It doesn't matter," he replied. "Now tell me: How do we help Arinna?"

So that was how Brittney ended up riding a rat man as he climbed the connecting chain to the upper island of the hierarch, trying not to barf.

"Hold on," he said. "We have to swing to the bottom."

"We what?" Brittney replied just as the rat she was holding on to dipped to the right, swinging around to the bottom of the chain in order to pass through a hole that had been carved in a circular metal plate.

Brittney dug her fingers into the creature's neck fur, but it was the leather belt that wrapped her waist that truly held her in place, not her pathetic strength.

"They place these here so we cannot climb," he said. "But they don't check their integrity very often."

Brittney didn't understand why it was so important until she realized that by ascending to the higher islands via these chains, the rat people avoided passing through the gates that detected the dark. They could move and work among the most prestigious people of the light. It was pretty slick.

"I'm sorry for suggesting we put you in the hierarch's soup," the rat said as he swung back around to the top of the giant chain.

"It's alright," Brittney replied. "I kinda barged in on you. Would he really not know?"

"The man is an imbecile," the rat said. "He does nothing but eat and pleasure himself with females. When you eat as he does, taste loses its importance. Only quantity matters."

She laughed. "I'm Brittney," she said. "Or maybe I should go by Arielle? What do you think?"

"I'm Lenert," he said. "I have always been Lenert. Do as you wish. Life is too short to have a name you don't like. If you wish to be Arielle, who am I to say no?"

She nodded. "I like how you think."

"Thank you," he said. "Here we are."

They climbed from the chain onto a small ledge that had been traveled many times before. Even though it was now deep into the night, bright lights blazed above on the streets and towers, as in most light cities, but none illuminated where they were. They traveled in shadows until they came to an old rusted door that the musa pulled open before slipping inside.

Inside it was too dark for her to see. Worse, people, or maybe musa, were chatting amongst themselves in a language she didn't know. It sounded dark and scary.

"Aren't you going to untie me?"

"No," Lenert replied. "You need to hold on. I'll be heading up to the kitchens with you under my uniform."

"What?" she snapped.

"It's the only way," he said. "I'll sneak you through the kitchen to a meeting with a friend. She will get you to the Svarako Dhoka."

Those words... they meant heaven door. The portal! Was it the same one that obnoxious angel had used to send her for her punishment? That was the last place she wanted to see again.

"What if I don't want to go there," she said softly.

"Yes you do!" Janine shouted from the pouch affixed to her waist. "That's where the trap is!"

"There are times," Lenert said. "When we must do things we do not enjoy for the greater good, no?"

Or in this case the greater bad, which was what Arinna was. Brittney remembered fighting against the dark, centuries ago. She'd sent countless demons back to... whatever they called hell here. She wasn't the greatest of the warriors of light, but she'd done her part. Now here she was, about to help unravel it all. As weird as it seemed, it kinda felt good.

"Let's go," she said, digging in.

"That's my girl!" Lenert replied.

A cloth robe was put on over her, though she only knew by feel since it was still totally dark wherever they were. At least in this case, it helped that Brittney was now so small and thin. With the stooped way the rat people walked around. Nobody would even notice.

"Alright," Lenert said. "Here we go. Be sure to be silent. We musa try to stay unseen and only speak when spoken to in the halls of the light. Understand?"

"Yeah," she said. How many times had she walked these very halls as a sikari? Hundreds, if not thousands. Not once had she seen one of the rat people here. Had things changed, or had it always been like this?

"Good!" he replied and stepped out into the light.

~

"MAX!" Arinna shouted. "It's not doing anything!"

"Keep shooting!" Max yelled up the ladder in response. Then he looked down toward the bottom turret currently manned by Trina. "I couldn't find it!"

"I told you!" Trina replied, annoyed. "It's in the pile on the right!"

"In your room?"

"Yes!"

The ship rocked from another hit.

"Max!" Tela offered sweetly from the bridge. "The Midnight is taking a great deal of damage."

"I know, Tela!" Max said as he ran back to Trina's small room. There were three piles of items gathered haphazardly on the floor. Max had already searched the rightmost of them, and the center pile. So now the only choice was the left one. He pushed a couple of things out of the way and...

"Bingo," he said. One single vial of the black liquid.

Are you alright?

Max looked up to find Mytten hanging from the ceiling above him.

"I am," he said and stored the potion. "Or I will be once I make those ships very unhappy they chose to pursue us.

But you have to change your class again. Will you be alright?

"I have no choice," he replied. "A skeleton's got to do, what a skeleton's got to do."

That makes no sense.

"I know," he said as he unequipped his armor and selected Dark Summoner, "but it was fun to say."

The pain was immediate and sharp, like an ice pick to the temple. Max doubled over, falling to his knees.

Max!

He held up a hand, letting the pain start to pass. "I'm good... It's... ah... it's going away. It can't last too long... This class is... high level."

Something is wrong.

"No..." he said as the ship was rocked by another hit. "It's... fine." It wasn't fine though. He was still dizzy and his head hurt. He wasn't recovering fast enough.

What can I do?

"The... sleep... sign," he said.

Mytten grabbed him with the hooks on her pedipalps and dragged him out of Trina's room and into his own where the Ullu was currently hiding in the corner.

"Get out!" he shouted but his eyes widened as he saw Max in her jaws. "By Gazric what did you do, you horrible thing? Did you kill the skeleton?"

"You... idiot..." Max said. "Get... out..."

"What? No!" Reken shouted.

Mytten hissed and the ullu shrieked with fright and bolted out of the room. Then Mytten dropped Max on the sleep sign and everything went dark. Instantly he was being slapped by a big hairy spider leg.

Max wake up!

"I'm up, I'm up," he said. The headache was gone and the dizziness with it. He checked his magic.

438/438 MP

"Let's rock and roll," he said. "Thank you Mytten. You're the most amazing spider I have ever met."

You're just saying that.

He laughed. "No... seriously. It's true," he said. "But I want you to come back into your cattan. I shouldn't have left you before. I don't want you getting hurt."

No, don't. I want to help.

"Sorry," he said. "Mytten, come back."

Max!

The spider disappeared into a poof of black smoke, reappearing as the cattan in Max's hand, which he stored. "I can't let anything happen to you," he said. "You've suffered enough for me."

He could feel the spider's anger and frustration from inside the cattan.

Max! Please!

The ship shuddered again.

"Right," he said. "Combat time."

He ascended the ladder and opened the top hatch just as a very large ball of holy fire shot by.

"Neline," he said. "Is there anything else you can do to help?"

Not right now. Perhaps later.

"Awesome," he replied as he turned to face the enemy ships. Guess it was up to him then.

The four enemy ships had fanned out in a staggered line to the Midnight's left and right. They weren't gaining, but the Midnight wasn't getting away very quickly either. That was surprising because the Midnight was much sleeker than the ships pursuing her.

Now wait a second. If casting Undone had worked on the ship, wouldn't Hasten work too? Wait, that spell specifically said it impacted travel speed. Shit! That must be how those bigger ships were keeping up. Two could play that game.

Max cast Hasten on the Midnight and he followed that up by using his Staff of Shadows causing phantom ships to split off in different directions. Finally, he lined up the closest ship and cast Thundercrack three times. The second one missed, but two was enough, the enemy airship burst into flames and began a slow pitch downward.

Holy fire kept coming from the other three ships, including the really big one to his right, but Tela was doing an excellent job weaving around it, especially now that the ship's speed was greater. That pegasus soul did not get enough credit. She'd saved them like a dozen times now. Max wondered if there was some way to reward her.

Finally they were starting to pull away.

"Alright," he said. "I burned through a good bit of my magic. But I think we're-"

"Max! There are more of them ahead!" Trina yelled.

"What?" he said, sticking his head back up. "Holy shit!"

It was a whole line of them, dozens of ships of all sizes stacked in two rows and they were coming in fast. They'd be in range soon, too soon.

Max slid down the ladder and ran for the bridge. "Tela!" he yelled. "We need to turn left!"

"That is not a great solution!" she replied happily.

"Why?"

"There are more enemy ships to our west," Tela chirped. "Also, the Midnight is getting low on sustenance."

"It's almost like they knew we'd be coming this way," Trina said dryly as she entered the bridge.

Arinna followed her. "I'm sorry Trina. We should have listened to you. How bad is it, Max?"

"Bad," he said. "Ships to our left, ships to our right, ships behind. I think the ones up ahead are the trap though. They're three times the size of the other two groups."

"We're being herded toward them," Arinna said. "Like gogs to the slaughter."

"What should I do?" Tela asked.

"I..." Max looked at Trina. "So... how long can you hold your breath?"

"What? Why?"

"No, Max," Arinna said. "I can't allow that. She almost died last time."

"I'm just trying to think. The only way I know that we can go and they can't follow, is up."

"I passed out," Trina said. "I didn't die."

"No!" Arinna said again.

Trina had her finger to her chin. "If I was asleep, I would be inhaling less often and the strain on my brain from the height could be much less-"

"No!" Arinna repeated.

"Actually," Max said. "She's kind of right... she *would* be breathing more slowly. It should affect her less."

"Max, no!" Arinna said.

"Then YOU tell me what to do!" he replied. "I'm out of ideas! In about thirty seconds those ships are going to blow this little stolen Kestrian patrol boat to pieces. I can only hold them back for so long. My magic will run out and they will win. Tell me! Do you have a better idea?"

Arinna frowned, her green eyes filled with burning frustration... but rather than respond. She looked away. "I... don't."

"I'm willing to do it, Arinna," Trina said, taking her hand. "It'll be fine. Just don't stay up above the safe limit for very long. I really hate nose bleeds."

"We won't be able to stay up above the safe altitude for very long at all," Tela said. "We'll run out of sustenance after only a few minutes."

"One problem at a time," Max said.

"That problem... I may be able to solve," Arinna said.

"Good," Max said. "Take us up Tela."

"Alright," Trina said as she summoned a bag of sleep powder into a gloved hand. "Please make sure I wake up."

"I will," Max said. "I promise you that."

Trina nodded and opened the pouch near her face, inhaling the power. Her eyes closed and she dropped. Arinna caught her and directed the girl into the corner, next to the smashed remains of the demonic automaton.

Max had no idea how he would keep that promise, but he sure as hell was going to. He put both hands on the deck. "Hasten!" he said as another wave of teal colored magic left him, pulsing into the ship.

"Did I hear something about going above the safety limit?!" Reken asked, poking his head into the bridge. "I strenuously obj-"

Arinna snatched the bag of powder from Trina's hands and flicked it into the ullu's face with one swift motion. There was a thump and a poof and the owl-headed man slumped against the doorway before flopping onto his back in the corridor, snoring.

"Thanks," Max said.

"Least I could do," she replied.

Up we go!" Tela said as the Midnight pitched up hard, screaming into the night sky. The angle was high enough that Reken started sliding backward down the hall, snoring as he went.

The midnight was forced to dodge several large shots from the ships up ahead, but it was quickly apparent the enemy wasn't willing to join them. They were passing right over the enemy airships.

"They've stopped firing!" Tela said happily.

Max sighed heavily. He turned to Arinna. "You said you had a way to deal with the fuel problem?"

She nodded. "I do, but you're not gonna like it."

Max shook his head. "Tell me."

21

BLOODY SOLUTIONS AND TRICKY PROBLEMS

"My blood," Arinna said.

Max threw up his hands. "Somehow I knew you were going to say that."

"Arinna," Tela said. "You're of the dark."

"Correct," Arinna replied.

"Then I'm sorry to say, but that's impossible," Tela replied. "Kestrian ships, like all airships of the light are only approved for the use of light aligned sustenance."

"I was around when these things were designed," Arinna said. "They can run on either fuel."

"That is not true!" Tela said. "We were told specifically that-"

"I know that's what they would say," Arinna said. "But I'm telling you: it will work."

"I don't care!" Max said. "We're not draining your blood to use as fuel. Do you have any idea how insane that sounds?"

"Said the talking skeleton," Arinna replied, folding her arms.

Max pointed at her. "That's beside the point!"

"It's not!" she said, "That's exactly the point. I know it will work. I've seen it done. There's just one problem."

Arinna led him to the cargo bay where a single empty fuel drum remained. Arinna tipped it over until a single drop of pearlescent white fluid fell to the metal floor. Then she used a pointed tip of the moon-shaped throwing weapon to pierce the skin of her finger. A single black droplet formed there. She squatted down and held her finger over the drop of white before turning it over.

Max watched as the drop of pure black hit the white. There was a flash and a sizzle as the two reacted, leaving behind a nasty looking gray foam from which a single tendril of steam curled into the air above.

"Whoa," Max said.

"Touch it," Arinna said.

Max did. It was hard... and hot as hell. "Ah."

"Yeah," Arinna replied. "That's why we can't put my blood in while there's even a single drop of that left."

"The whole thing would seize up," Max said, nodding. "How do you propose we get it out of there?"

"There's one way I know," she said. "We used to do it when we had to steal an enemy ship way back when and we only had our own fuel."

Max grit his teeth. "And that would be?"

"Blow it out," Arinna said. "But the ship has to open the fuel dump."

"I don't like this," he said. "Are you planning to... do that?"

She nodded. "I have to, I'm the only one with the strength who has lungs."

"But you'll be drained," Max said. "You'll have the bled status tag."

Arinna tilted her head. "Do you have a better idea?"

Max clenched his skeletal hands into fists. "I really don't like this."

"Max!" Tela called from the front of the ship. "We're almost below the threshold now. And... uh... I'm very sorry to mention it again, but the sustenance need is now critical. We will begin dropping soon."

"Ok!" Max yelled back. "Just keep heading north. I'll be up there in a minute."

"Wipe out that drum," Arinna said. "Fast."

Max pulled the top from the drum and Arinna threw him a ripped rag. He did the best he could.

"How's this?" he asked.

"Bad," she replied, peering in. "Luckily, the really pure stuff evaporates pretty fast." She took the drum and blew into it.

A stench came out that made Max reel back. "Ugh!"

"Yeah," she said as she placed the drum back down. "Light and dark don't mix." The weapon re-materialized in her hand, ready to cut.

Max backed away. He couldn't look at her dumping her blood... wait... Trina's necksem tonic would stop Arinna from getting bled status, which would halve her strength, making blowing the light fuel out much more difficult. He opened his palm and summoned one. Nothing happened. He was out of them. Of course he was.

"Crap!" he said.

Arinna winced as she slashed at her forearm. Black blood began running into the barrel.

"I've got to get something," he said. "Please don't pass out and die on me."

"Already dead," she replied, "but thanks for the sentiment."

Max then ran from the cargo bay forward down the main corridor, jumping over the snoring ullu. The ship lurched, causing him to slam into the wall, leaving a skull shaped dent.

"The midnight is officially starved!" Tela called. Her usually cheery tone had been replaced by a nervous trill. "I hope you know what to do!"

"We're working on it," Max said as he arrived in Trina's room and tore through the three piles looking for the little red vials. He couldn't see any. There were a few vials with reddish liquid in them, but he didn't think it was the right color and when he stored them the wrong name came up.

"Crap, crap crap!" he said and tore back out of Trina's room. She had a separate hiding spot right? Maybe she had a couple of those items in there.

Max arrived on the bridge just in time to see the ship pitch even farther downward. They were definitely angling for the ground now. That might actually be fine except there were mountains ahead. Why couldn't anything be easy?

Max grabbed Trina by her robes and shook her. "Trina!" he said. "Wake up!"

She was not waking. Max slapped her wrist. Still nothing.

What the heck? Was she breathing? He put an ear hole next to her face. Yes. She was breathing, but even more slowly than he'd expected.

Max brought up her status.

Status	Trina		

Level	16	Plague Doctor	
Coma		Skill	22
Health	364/364		
Magic	95/95	Affinity	Thought

Skills	Magic
Analysis, Prediction	Spotted leeches, Item bomb, Tonic, Poultice, Surgery...

Strength	10	Attacks x 3	58
Agility	19	Accuracy	79%
		Defense	10
Vitality	15	Evasion	18%
Mind	27	Magic Defense	25
		Magic Evasion	29%

Coma?! What the heck? That was a status? How did you even cure that?

"Max!" Arinna said. "I could use some help."

"Damn!" he said. "I'll be back for you!"

"Max, don't leave!" Tela said. "The hills are getting very close!"

Max ran back down the corridor but this time he wasn't paying attention and his foot clipped the ullu's head, knocking the creature in a circle along the floor so that he whacked his head a second time against the wall.

"Ow!" Reken said.

"Sorry," Max said as he ran by, "kinda."

He arrived in the cargo bay to a horrific sight. Arinna's head was lolling to the side as black liquid was still pouring from her arm into the barrel.

"Ah!" Max yelped.

"Can... you.... tie... that off?" she asked, her speech slurring badly.

"Ok, ok," he said as he took the only thing he could think of, the scarf he'd gifted her, and wrapped it around Arinna's arm, trying to stop the bleeding. As he did so he noticed the barrel was now three quarters full. What did you DO?" he asked. "That's like... all the blood you have... plus like a lot."

"Nah," she said, smiling languidly. "I'm jus.... fine." She patted his face. "You... have nice cheekbones. Cute."

"Shit, shit," Max said as he tightened the scarf again, wrapping it a third and fourth time.

Arinna's eyes closed.

"Arinna!" he shouted.

Nothing happened. He slapped her face.

The green eyes opened. "Oh... hi," she said.

"I need you awake. You have to blow into the system."

Arinna giggled.

"You know what I mean!" he said as he slapped the top onto the barrel and threw her over his shoulder with one arm and took the barrel with the other. Thank goodness for that signet ring, because otherwise he'd be making two trips.

He carried them both down the short ramp into the engine area.

"Tela!" Max yelled. "Dump the feeding system!"

"I can't do that Max!" Tela replied, actually sounding pretty upset. "We'll lose the last fumes the ship has left."

"Just do it!"

There was a thunk followed by a sort of sputtering whine. That had to have been it.

The ship started dropping even more.

Yep.

"Wake up!" Max said.

"Mmmm... huh?" Arinna said.

Max flipped to her status. Bled. Awesome. Her strength had been halved too... hold on. He had Empower! Max put both hands on her shoulders and cast the spell, pumping some semblance of life back into her.

He checked her status again. Ok, back to the usual strength stat. Her health was horrible though. His eyes went to the barrel. It was all in there.

"Max... gotta... cast..." she murmured.

"Cast? Cast what?" he asked.

"Shock, you imbecile," Reken said.

Max turned around. "What?"

"To fix the blood, dark magic must be sent through it. The shock spell is typically used. Do you have that one?"

"Yeah," Max said. He could find out how the owl knew about that later, first, he'd give it a shot. Max pulled the barrel lid off. "Here's hoping I don't blow us all to hell."

"I... gotta blow," Arinna said.

Reken's feathered eyebrows rose.

"Just help her get to the feeding tube," Max said as he held his fingers over the black blood and cast the weakest of his lightning spells. Blue lighting arced out into the liquid, filling the short lower corridor with the acrid smell of ozone. The black liquid had begun to change as well, it was taking on a pearlescent sheen just like the white fuel.

"Not too much, skeleton," Reken said. "Or you really will fry us." The ullu had positioned Arinna next to the opening.

"Here... goes..." she said and took a deep breath.

The ship shook.

"Maaaaaax!" Tela yelled.

"Now!" Max said.

Arinna blew as hard as she could for an entire breath and then fell back into Reken's arms as the remaining fuel in the airship's internals exploded outward, filling the ship with that same rancid stink.

Max was sure his eyes would be tearing if he had the ducts for it. He lifted the barrel. "Here it goes," he said.

"Wait!" Reken said. "It has to be closed!"

Duh! "TELA!" Max yelled. "Close feeding system again. It's about to be filled!"

"It's about time!" Tela replied as the system clunked.

Max poured every drop into the open tube and closed the catch.

"Tela! Punch it!" Max said. "Thank you," he added to the ullu as he stepped over and took Arinna into his arms.

"Anything to save my own skin," Reken replied.

"Truth," Max mumbled as he ascended to the main corridor just as a loud bang rocked the ship.

"WHAT'S THAT SMELL?" Janine asked from the tiny pouch at her waist.

"It's food," Brittney whispered in reply. "Please be quiet!"

"It's... It's intoxicating!" Janine said, a little quieter this time. "I've never smelled something so luscious before."

"It's just food," Brittney said as softly as she could. "Shush."

It was so bright and hot and steamy in the kitchens of the hierarch's palace that Brittney felt like the rat man she was clinging to had just entered a sauna. Only in this sauna everyone was yelling commands back and forth at the top of their lungs. Though, that last part was probably the only reason Janine hadn't been heard.

"Lenert!" said a booming voice. "Wonderful! Good of you to come in on short notice. As you can tell, we're swamped!"

As much as Brittney wanted to see who was addressing Lenert, if she adjusted herself even a tiny bit someone might see the musa's back moving.

"Of course, sir. What's going on?" Lenert asked.

"Big banquet for some important whats his face. It's been going since the damned afternoon."

"It's the middle of the night!" Lenert replied.

"I know! I thought they'd be wrapping up but they just ordered three more courses and they have new entertainment coming in."

"I wouldn't want to be those guys," Lenert said.

"Oh yes," said the other man with no small amount of annoyance. "I tell you, I don't need this sort of aggravation! I don't need it! So can you take the top prep station? I've got a mip berry drizzle that they keep screwing up."

"You've got it," Lenert replied. "Just let me wash up and I'll be right there."

"Excellent," replied the other man.

"I want some!" Janine shouted.

"I'm sorry?" the deep voice asked.

Brittney was surprised, apparently not everyone was deaf to the voice of her pixie companion.

Lenert stopped and turned back. "Oh... yes... I want some soap..."

"Should be some by the wash station," replied the other man. "Don't crack up on me yet, Lenert, we're just getting started!"

Lenert laughed and walked off. When they'd gotten a few paces further he hissed back toward Brittney. "What's going on?"

"I don't know!" Brittney whispered through her teeth.

"I want some of that food!" Janine said. "Please! Let me out! No one will see me!"

"I said shut up!" Brittney replied. "We talked about this. There could be angels here," Brittney added. "It's not safe."

The pixie was struggling to escape the pouch. "That's stupid... I just want a taste."

"Stop it!" Brittney said, reaching for the leather cover on the top of the pouch but Janine grabbed her finger and bit it.

"Ah!" Brittney said, jerking her hand back.

"Please!" Lenert pleaded. "Stop what you're doing! You'll get us all killed!"

"It's not me!" Brittney grumbled. "It's her!"

"Come here you little... ah... One of you rat cooks is it?"

Lenert stopped dead. Brittney could feel him shaking. Something was bad.

"Y-yessir," he responded. "Y-Your lordship."

"That's more like it," the man responded. "What are you doing here?"

"J-just washing up," Lenert said.

"Come back later. I've business here with this young lady."

"O-of course your lordship," Lenert replied as he turned around and rushed back the way they'd come.

"What's happened?" Brittney whispered.

"We can't go that way," Lenert whispered in response.

There was a snap as Janine tore through the strap that held her pouch closed. This was followed by a swish as she flew out of the uniform that camouflaged them both.

"Shit!" Brittney hissed. "Janine is gone."

"You! Rat man!" this was the same voice as a moment ago. Lenert nearly fell over from fright as he turned to face the voice. In doing so, he backed into something metal behind them which banged painfully against Brittney's lower back.

Lenert was shaking like a leaf. "Get off... get off," he whispered. "Quickly."

"What's that?" the man roared.

Brittney ripped at the belt that held her in place, trying to find the catch but found her tiny fingers fumbling at the task.

"N-nothing your lordship," Lenert replied.

"Who are you?" the man bellowed. "I don't believe I've seen you before."

"I..."

"Speak up RAT!" the man shouted.

Finally, Brittney's fingertips got the purchase she needed and she yanked the belt from its catch hook. It released and she slid down Lenert's back to the floor, landing directly on his tail. The poor Musa jerked in obvious pain, but somehow managed not to cry out. "I'm... sorry lordship," he wheezed.

Peeking out from under the bottom of the uniform, Brittney realized that what had hit her was a serving cart. Perfect! Her diminutive size made slipping into the bottom of it a breeze.

"What in the name of Cerathia is going on here!" shouted another familiar voice. "Lenert! I told you to wash up for the service! What are you doing out here?"

"I-I'm sorry sir," Lenert replied.

"This rat works for you?"

"Of course!" the man replied. "I'm Brenard D'el Gerilon, head of this kitchen! Who are you?"

"I'm Gaon of Dalinor, paladin of light and a member of the esteemed Order of the White Rose. I'm here to oversee this affair-"

"Yes? By frolicking with the serving girls in my washroom?"

"That's-"

"Just leave," Brenard said. "Leave my kitchen now and I promise I will forget about you."

"You have a great many rats in this kitchen," the paladin said, changing the subject.

Brittney sighed. She'd been worried about Lenert.

"Haven't you heard?" Brenard replied. "Musa are the best cooks on all three continents."

There was a clang against Brittney's cart.

"Someone get this cart out!" Brenard said. "It's full!"

"But..." Lenert started.

"Lenert, go finish washing," Brenard said. "Immediately."

Brittney's fingers curled into fists as she pulled her legs in even tighter against her body. Things had not gone as planned. Janine had ditched her and now Lenert could no longer guide her. She was on her own. Not good.

Footsteps quickly arrived and her cart started going. Brittney didn't understand exactly how shitty her situation was, until she realized where the cart was going. The cloth that was draped over the cart was white but it wasn't thin enough to make out more than moving shapes, even if she put her face right up next to it. That was a problem because she'd never know when it was possible to escape.

Janine! You idiot!

There was a clang as the cart passed through two wide doors and Brittney was amazed that the noise out in the banquet room was easily three times as loud as the kitchen. Some kind of weird harp and lute band was playing while a choir of women sang along but nobody was paying attention because it sounded like every single person was talking at the same time. There had to be hundreds of people.

Brittney couldn't remember if she'd ever been invited to dine with the hierarch. She'd visited the palace many times, but... No, she never had. Did they have insane all night parties like this often? If so, why hadn't they invited her?

The cart was pushed for what felt like forever, with two turns. Brittney had the feeling it might have skirted around the wall. When it came to a stop and it sounded like things were being taken from the top, she took the opportunity to bend down and pull up a corner of the cloth.

The first thing she saw was that she was right. The cart had been parked next to a wall. It was right there, on the opposite side of the cart. That was a good start, the next thing she noticed is that, even though there was a huge table in the center of everything, there were lots of other tables and people were wandering around chatting with each other all over the place. Finally, and most important:

there was a door out of the room straight ahead. The crowd was actually pretty thick so...

Oh no.

In the distance at the center of the big table, just to the right of the hierarch himself, was Vita. She was in her human form, looking like a petite girl of sixteen and wearing a pure white dress covered with pink and blue flowers. Brittney recognized her immediately. That turned up nose had never gone away, no matter how many times the angel tried to change it.

The angel was sitting next to a tall young man wearing some kind of military uniform. Besides his height, there wasn't anything else remarkable about him, except maybe his cute hair. Was this boy her replacement?

Whatever. It didn't matter. She had to get out of here. Somehow.

A loud sound drew her peeping eyes back toward the kitchen where a hapless server had just dropped his tray. All the other guests looked too, and most laughed.

Brittney realized this was her chance. With most heads pointed in that direction, she could make a break for it and that's exactly what she did.

Carefully, quietly, she slipped out from beneath the cart and made for the exit. She had no idea where she would go after that, but she didn't care. She had to get out of here before Vita saw her.

She hadn't gone four paces before Janine buzzed in from under the big table.

"Heya!" Janine said. "Where are you..." The pixie let out a large belch. "Off to?"

"I have no idea except out of this room!" Brittney snarled back. "Why did you leave like that!"

"You don't know... you didn't eat the food in Akasa," Janine said.

"No! I didn't! I didn't know they HAD food!" Brittney said. Just twenty more feet.

"Well it's tasteless, bland, and it's always the same," Janine replied, belching again. "I just... tasted at least ten things I never knew existed!"

Ten more feet.

"Good for you," Brittney replied. "Don't get used to it or you'll get fat."

Five feet. The guy in the suit next to the door was eyeing her.

"I will not!" Janine snapped. "You don't know what you're talking about! Do you have any idea how much energy I need for these wings?"

Two feet.

"No!" Brittney said and reached for the handle of the exit door. "But I'm sure you'll tell me."

A gloved hand closed over her wrist.

"I'm sorry, who are you with?" the stern looking man asked. He was dressed like a waiter, except that he also wore a few pieces of sun steel armor and carried an estoc in a scabbard at his hip.

"Uh... Michael Jackson?" Brittney replied, using the first name that popped into her head.

"You're right! It's an awful lot," Janine said. "Why, I once-"

"Janine! Help!" Brittney said.

"Who's Janine?" the man asked, his glove tightening on her wrist.

The pixie frowned. "Fine! Sure!" she retorted and used her magic to summon a small fist that slammed into the center of the door guard's crotch.

"Ooof," he said, doubling over. The fingers released Brittney and in only two seconds, she'd slipped through the door and into the hallway beyond.

Brittney sighed heavily and turned to go, almost running head first into someone else in the hall. Her heart sank when her eyes went upward and she realized who it was.

"Hello," the new sikari said.

22

FALLING AND RISING AGAIN

"This is going to be bumpy!" Tela said brightly.

"What else is new?!" Max replied.

"That's it!" Tela added.

Max turned back to Arinna. "How is she?"

"Not well," Arinna replied.

The ullu was completely fine and the vampire goddess had recovered quickly after dumping literal gallons of black blood into the ship, something that ought to be completely impossible, but it seemed Trina, their only healer, was still in a coma.

"Awesome," Max said. "I hope they have another doctor at the stronghold."

"Can't you become a doctor?" she asked.

"No, I..." Max stared at her. How could he be so stupid? Of course he could! "I'll be right back!"

Max ran into the back, grabbing Reken by a feathered arm as he went.

"What do you want now?" the ullu demanded angrily as Max dragged him toward the room with the sleep sign.

"Come with me," he said.

One class change and quick sleep later, Max returned. "We're screwed!" he said.

"Why?" Arinna replied.

"I have to go harvest my own leeches and..." he looked down at Trina's belt, where a small glass container was filled with a variety of the tiny worm-like creatures. "Never mind."

"Tela, how are our friends?" Max asked as he uncorked the jar and selected three leeches, the necessary amount for a third tier status effect. He didn't know how he knew that, he just did.

"If you mean the entire fleet that's been trying to destroy us since we took off, they're still there," Tela said.

Max pulled up the sleeve of Trina's robe and applied three of the leeches to her arm.

Trina receives 3 damage.

"How long will we have?" Arinna asked.

"I don't know. Maybe thirty minutes after we land? I would say you should ask the mechanical one," Tela replied. "But I believe I heard he is no more."

"That is true," Max said, looking over at the pile of broken metal parts in the corner. Poor guy.

"We should take him with us," Arinna said. "Few of his kind remain, and I know someone who can fix him... if we make it back home."

Trina receives 3 damage.

"We'll make it," Max said, "somehow."

"Why isn't she awakening?" Arinna asked.

"It's a tier three status," Max said as the leeches hungrily guzzled on Trina's blood. "It'll take a while."

"Here we go!" Tela said. "Everyone, brace yourselves!"

Max and Arinna grabbed onto the back of a nearby console chair. The Midnight finally hit the ground with a thud and a ripping, grating, tearing sound as she dug into the hard surface of the plain above Kapon Taw. The force of the crash tore most of the metal and structure from her bottom half. It took almost a minute, but the ship finally ground to a halt.

"I'm sorry I couldn't get all the unicorn blood out of the ship," Arinna said.

"Don't say that!" Max said. "I've been trying to forget what that stuff's made from. It wasn't your fault. You weren't exactly in the best shape. And look, somehow Tela was able to get us here anyway. She really is the greatest pegasus I've ever met."

"Thank you Max!" Tela said. "That's so nice of you to say!"

Arinna's eyes narrowed. "She's the only pegasus you've met, isn't she?"

Max held up a single boney finger. "Actually, no."

Trina receives 3 damage.

Trina's eyes opened and her head shot up as she gasped for breath. "Gah... Wha? Max? Arinna?"

"We made it," Max said, "kind of."

"To Ghrellen?" Trina asked.

Arinna shook her head. "No, the stronghold at Kapon Taw and we must move quickly, the ships that have been following us will arrive soon."

"I have bad news," Reken said, peeking his head in. His arm was pointing ahead, with one long claw indicating something out the front viewport. "The light is already here."

"What?" Max asked but when he looked, he saw that the ullu was right. There weren't any airships in evidence but there were quite a few tents and many soldiers, hundreds of them. A contingent of them were already grouping up to head in their direction. "Wow... that is..." he stood up and kicked the metal wall behind him. "Just... friggin' great!"

"Max... are you a plague doctor?" Trina asked.

Trina receives 3 damage.

"Just let him have his moment," Arinna said, "and you might want to get those off you."

"Damn, Damn, friggin', fraggin', Shit!" Max shouted as he slammed his skeletal palm into the metal of the wall.

"You done?" Arinna said. "We need to get out of this wreck."

Max sighed, running a hand over his skull. "Yeah... Let's go."

"Please, don't leave me," Tela said.

"Absolutely not!" Trina said as she crawled over to a panel on the forward console.

Max was still staring into space, fuming about their luck. Stupid light soldiers were everywhere. It didn't matter what they did or where they went. They were waiting there.

Every. Damned. Time.

"Max!" Arinna said. "Get it together. Grab whatever you want to keep. We're leaving."

"Uh... Yeah," he said. What was there to bring? The dungeon crawlers and Mytten... but he had Mytten.

"Have any more hidden treasures?" Arinna asked.

"What are you talking about?" Max asked as his eyes scanned over to the automaton. He should grab the parts, if for no other reason than they might sell well.

"The ultimate living death," Arinna said.

"Hmmm? The what?" Max said.

"The item that cast the death spell," Arinna said. "Do you have anything else like that hidden around here?"

"You had a what?" Trina asked as she stored the little box with Tela's soul in it.

Arinna had folded her arms. "An incredibly powerful single use spell."

"No," Max said as he bent down and stored the parts of the robot. "Let's get out of here."

Acquired: Demonic automaton parts.

Arinna was frowning at him.

"What?" he asked.

She didn't say anything.

"Scruff!" Max called. "We're leaving, get your friends and any of your favorite chew toys and let's go!"

"What is going on?" Reken asked. "Where are we going?"

"Come or don't," Trina said. "I don't care."

The four of them, with Scruff and his two smaller copies hanging on to Max and Arinna, marched from the crash site to the north west and a big circular hole in the plateau.

"Are you mad?" Reken asked. "I'm not going down there!"

"Then stay up here," Arinna said. "I'm sure those riders will be glad to give you some tea and cakes."

"You don't have to be sassy about it," the ullu snapped.

"They'll kill you," Max said. "Is that better?"

"No," Reken said flatly.

They jumped down into the water at the bottom of the cave. Max took a few points of damage but he emerged from the water to find spears pointed at his face. Ahead of him stood a half dozen angry looking goblins.

"Hey guys," Max said. "Got any sugar I can borrow?"

"Max?" a familiar voice called from the gloom.

"Yep," he said. "It's me."

"You shouldn't have come here," Ciara said, emerging from the darkness. With a wave of her hand, the goblins lowered their spears.

"Ciara, Queen of Goblins," Max said. "Meet Arinna, Queen of The Dark."

Arinna smiled as Ciara's large goblin eyes widened.

"No! No!" she said. "This is terrible! We're under attack here," she said. "We're just trying to buy enough time for our wounded to flee before the Kestrians overrun us."

"It's going to get worse," Trina said as she pushed past Max. "I'm Trina by the way, a doctor. I can help."

"Rich," Ciara said. "Show her to the tents."

One of the goblins took Trina by the hand and started to lead her away but she looked back.

"Go," Max said. "We'll catch up."

"What did she mean?" Ciara asked.

"She meant that we have an entire fleet of airships behind us. They'll be coming."

"How soon?" the goblin queen asked.

"Thirty minutes," Max replied. "Maybe less."

Ciara scowled. "So you've killed us then."

"No," Max said. "I'll be joining your defense."

"As will I," Arinna replied. "If we're going to make a stand, we might as well make it here."

"The skeleton has returned," a tall, very scantily clothed woman said as she stepped out of the dark behind Ciara. "You were right, girl."

"I'm not a girl," Khilen said as she too emerged from the dark behind Ciara. "I'm decades older than you."

The woman stepped forward and extended her hand. "We've met before, in Ceradram," she said, "but I doubt you'd remember it."

Max completed the dark handshake. "I'm Max," he said. "This is-"

The woman bowed low, taking a knee before Arinna. "My queen," she said. "I am Rachel K'el Allein, Necromancer, at your service."

"I never thought I'd actually see you," Khilen said, bowing her head. "Your highness."

"Rise, please," Arinna replied. "We must shore up our defenses. Ciara, please tell me how we can help."

Ciara shook her head. "I don't know how that's possible. Unless you're level thirty or something."

Arinna laughed. "I'm not," she said. "Not yet. However, he is." She said, pointing at Max.

"Uh... Level forty actually," Max said. "I know I don't look it, being you know, a naked skeleton and all. I'm currently not in my best class."

"You can change class?" Rachel asked. "You're a chosen undead!"

"He is," Arinna said. "A warrior of the dark and one of the greatest I've seen."

"We'll need him," Ciara said. "What *is* your best class Max?"

"Actually," he said. "Now that I think about it, I kind of want to use this battle as an opportunity."

"For what?" Arinna asked.

All eyes turned to Max.

"Tell me, do you have a retch pool?" he asked.

Rachel smiled knowingly. "Oh yes, we do."

"Excellent," he replied.

"THIS WAS GIVEN to me by my great grandfather," Rachel said, extending a folded robe. "It's Necromancer only." As she stepped forward the stacked bones beneath her feet cracked and popped.

"What does it do?" Max asked as he poured the final bucket of filth into the newly moved retch pool before storing the bucket and accepting the item.

Acquired: Vile Illumination Robe.

"It bolsters your magic points and lowers the cost of necrotic summons," she replied.

"That's cool," Max said. "Thank you. I wish there was something that gave me magic regeneration all the time though," he added as he switched class back to Necromancer and equipped the new robe. A wave of class change sickness followed that hit him like a brick.

"Here," Rachel said. "Let me help you."

"No... I think I'll do that," Arinna said as she stepped in and took Max's elbow to help him into the bathtub sized pool of rotting gore.

Rachel folded her arms, looking to the side. "Of course, my queen," she said.

Max sat down into the pool and the pounding headache and the wooziness just melted away. He sighed as a warm tingling feeling soaked right into his bones. "I forget how good this feels."

Health and magic restored.

"Everyone has retreated to the tunnel entrance," Arinna said. "They think you're insane. Nobody believes you can do this."

Max chuckled. "Good. Then it'll be even funnier when it happens anyway."

"I would help you," Rachel said. "But... and it seems strange to say so... I'm only level seven."

"That's fine," Arinna said. "We need Necromancy to survive. Go with Khilen and Ciara and the rest."

"Oh..." Rachel said. "I nearly forgot. There was a vampire asking if we'd seen a 'Boneknight.' He was badly hurt in the last attack but he asked us to give you this." A huge double-bladed black axe appeared in her hands. The thing looked wicked, with spikes and barbs and a sort of sharp ribbed handle that reminded Max of... a dragon.

"Holy crap, is that... was that vampire named Vilnius?"

"Yes," Rachel said as she handed the axe to Max. "He was the smith at the dark market. He and Delara's werewolves are among the few remaining survivors."

Max nodded. "That's good to hear."

Acquired: Dark Dragon Tail Greataxe. Damage 393, Durability 900/900, Triples durability damage to shields, ignores 30 points of DR.

"Sheesh," Max said. "This thing is a beast. Thank you for passing it on and not selling it."

There was no going back now. Now that Max had the axe, he needed a barbarian to wield it.

"I might have," Rachel said. "If there was anyone who would have bought it without killing me just for having it."

Max chuckled. "Noted. Well, I'd better get started here."

Arinna backed off, looking around at the skeletons beneath her feet and the many more that stretched off into the distance in both directions. "You going to raise all of these?"

"Yep," Max replied. "As many as I can. According to the book, I only need the shards for the greater undead, but for skeletons, all I need is the bones."

"Good luck!" Rachel called as she ascended the trail back toward the top of the fissure.

Max waved to her.

They're nearly here.

"Thanks Mytten," Max said as he looked over to Arinna. "They're coming."

"Then you'd better get to the summoning," she replied.

Max started with one skeleton by gathering just the small amount of soul energy he needed by expending his magic points. It took all of his points just to raise the one, and one health point also, but that was just fine, because the retch pool instantly refilled his magic and his health. Then Max raised another skeleton, and another, and another. Soon ten skeletons stood around him like silent sentries, their green eyes glowing just like his own.

Arinna was handing them what weapons and shields they had, which wasn't a great deal. The goblins had wanted to retain their best equipment, but that was fine. Skeletons didn't win because they had great weapons. If they won at all it was because of overwhelming numbers.

Twenty skeletons. Thirty. Fifty. Max kept generating them as fast as he could.

They have entered the caverns.

"Mytten says they are inside now," Max said.

Arinna nodded. "I'll go slow them down a little."

Max nodded. "Be careful."

"I'm always careful," she replied with a slight smile before ascending the wall of the fissure with leaps and bounds.

"I can see that," Max said as he went back to raising skeletons. He must have had more than a hundred now, standing together, waiting for his instructions. There wasn't any more room to make them. That meant it was time.

"Are we good, Mytten?" he asked.

Yes. Do it.

Max stood up in the retch pool. "Alright you mooks!" he said. "Go kill the light!" he then pointed up the long path to the upper part of the cave. Wordlessly, the crowd of skeletons ran at full speed up the incline.

Ready?

Max jumped out of the pool as the bone horde ran past him and turned to face Scruff, who was waiting by the wall. "Yep," Max said as he made a sleep powder appear in his hand and slapped himself in the face with it.

Max awoke to Scruff beating him in the face with a wet slimy tentacle.

Max?

"Yeah!" he replied, quickly bringing up his status.

Status	Boneknight	Betrothed

Level	43	Necromancer Skill	1
Health	2291/2291		
Magic	8/8	Affinity	Dark
Skills		Magic	
Rekindle, Summon lesser undead		Dead Weight, Teeth of Fate, Void Crush, Flame, Chill...	
Strength	0	Attacks x 2	0
Agility	0	Accuracy	70%
		Defense	0
Vitality	1	Evasion	0%
Mind	1	Magic Defense	1
		Magic Evasion	1%

"Skill level fourteen. Not bad at all. I think we can do better, don't you?" he asked Scruff.

The creature shrugged.

"That's... that's not the right gesture," Max said as he ran back to the tub and jumped in with a splash.

Eat?

"Not yet," Max replied. "When I'm done here, it's yours."

Scruff nodded. The two remaining smaller versions were over in a corner chewing on some bones. Max turned back and proceeded to summon more skeletons. Ten, twenty, thirty, forty more. He was carving nicely into the mass of bones at the bottom of the pit.

"I knew this place would come in handy," he said.

Arinna receives 13 damage.

Arinna receives 11 damage.

Arinna receives 17 damage.

Max didn't wait, he sent the next wave with fifty in it. They looked stronger though, their eyes were brighter and their movements quicker. The book had said that would happen though: the strength of the summons was linked directly with the necromancer's skill level.

"Go my pretties!" Max yelled with a cackle. "Take up the weapons of your fallen comrades above and crush the light."

The skeletons ran up the ramp again, crowding together.

Many paladins are here. They are killing your skeletons easily.

"Yeah? Max said. "Wait till they see the next wave." He made another sixty and sent those in one third the time when he realized that now that his skill had raised, his magic points had gone up and he could summon three at a time. He did sixty three times and then jumped out of the pool and slept, raising his Necromancer skill to twenty.

That allowed him to raise ten even stronger skeletons at once, which he did, turning the endless sea of bones around him into a thousand skeletons in less than a minute. Max ordered them up the ramp. Then he summoned another thousand and sent them after the first thousand.

While those were on their way to fight the light, he jumped out and slept for a third time. When he awoke, he was now Necromancer skill fifty-seven.

"Perfect," he said, checking his status.

Status		Boneknight	Betrothed
Level	43	Necromancer Skill	57
Health	2291/2291		
Magic	1254/1254	Affinity	Dark
Skills		**Magic**	
Rekindle, Summon greater undead		Dead Weight, Teeth of Fate, Void Crush, Flame, Chill...	
Strength	18	Attacks x 2	0
Agility	16	Accuracy	78%
		Defense	33
Vitality	33	Evasion	8%
Mind	36	Magic Defense	38
		Magic Evasion	25%

There it was: Greater undead summoning. That was what he needed.

"Scruff and friends," Max said. "The retch pool is all yours."

Three jubilant dungeon crawlers launched themselves into the tub of rotten gore.

"It's too bad we're going to have to flee this battle," Arinna said, having just appeared next to him. "Do you have any idea how many Paladins I just killed?"

"Two?" Max asked, wishing he could smile. He was starting to get used to the Grave Blade's silent movement. It really was just like having a ninja in the party.

She laughed. "Ha! Funny. No... it was more than that!"

"Like one more, or..."

Arinna just smiled.

"How are my bone men doing?" he asked as the dungeon crawlers slurped offal from the retch pool behind him with incredible intensity.

"They're like a sea up there," Arinna replied. "You should come look. The light don't know what to do. For every one they kill, ten more show up. It's pretty funny."

"Good," Max said. "Screw those guys. Did you get what I asked for?"

"Max!" Trina called from above and behind him, on the stronghold side of the chasm. "The evacuation is complete!"

"Awesome!" Max shouted back. "We're coming."

"Yes," Arinna said. "Behold:" She turned and gestured to a beefy looking knight on the ground behind her. "The biggest, burliest body I could find."

"Perfect," Max said. "Mytten, come get us."

"I can't get myself to the top of this thing," Arinna said.

"I wasn't talking about you," Max said as he threw the bulky dead body over his shoulder. "I was talking about us."

Mytten appeared, jumping down along the walls of the chasm until she arrived at Max's side.

Climb on!

"Scruff!" Max called back. "We're going." he took a moment to admire the continuing procession of skeletons working their way up the side of the chasm and the screams echoing from above. If they didn't want to meet a horde of undead, they probably shouldn't have come, Max thought with no small amount of satisfaction. This one was on them.

23

ROD'S LEGACY AND MAX'S
INHERITANCE

Max arrived at the top of the chasm to find Trina waiting, her Plague Doctor robes covered in dark blood. Behind them soldiers, paladins, and many others were drowning in a sea of angry green-eyed skeletons.

"That is... ghastly," Trina said.

"I know, right?" Max replied happily, glancing back over his shoulder. "It's easily my favorite thing so far."

Arinna jumped up from below. "Trina, will you be switching out to Surgeon? I saw you unlocked it."

"Why does that happen, just when you start to get competent at the class you have?" Trina wondered.

Arinna laughed. "I don't know."

"Ha!" Max said. "I've had the exciting opportunity to suck at half a dozen classes, including yours. You get used to it."

"Is that Raeg?" Trina asked.

Max patted the corpse hanging over the front of Mytten's body. "It will be."

"We'd better get inside," Trina said, gesturing behind her. "Reken has already gone with them. They're about to blast the tunnel closed. It's going to be a big explosion."

"I saw that," Max said, " but we're not going with them."

Trina took a moment to process what he'd said as she turned to go and then turned back. "I'm sorry?"

"The job isn't to flee into the goblin tunnels," Max said. "I need to get Arinna to Ghrellen and I have... just a few days left."

"But you don't even have an airship!" Trina replied.

"I have to try," Max said. "We might be able to steal one of their airships."

"You don't have to come," Arinna said. "You're alive and young. Don't throw your life away."

"For the dark? For you?" Trina said. "Absolutely!"

"Alright, then let's go. I think there's another way out of here," Max said.

"Wait," Trina said. "That turs girl..."

Max nodded. "Khilen, what about her?"

"She told me to tell you that the mother of the black stone wants to meet you. She's said she's inside Kapon Taw."

"Why did you wait to tell me?" Max asked.

"I... think she's kind of kooky," Trina confessed. "But now that we're not going with the goblins... I figured I might as well."

A loud boom sounded from a far off area of the wide cavern.

"Crap," Max said. "I forgot to give her the shaman stuff."

Mytten carried them all the way to the center of the cavern where the great black fortress of Kapon Taw hung over a massive precipice. A single thin bridge had once connected the outer ring to the fortress entrance but that had long since fallen away leaving another vast chasm. Max might have summoned his wyvern to fly across had Mytten not just walked right up the wall and climbed up along the ceiling while the rest of them held on for dear life. At last the spider jumped down in front of two monstrous black doors carved of a slick stone that reflected the light from Max's eyes.

As soon as they'd landed the doors began to creak open.

"Someone knows we're here," Trina said.

"Do you know what this is?" Max asked Arinna.

"No," she said. "This fortress used to be the domain of a Dread Lord, one of my father's closest allies."

"Olroth," Max said. "I thought I remembered that from the last time I was here."

"Exactly," she replied as they walked forward with Mytten trailing behind, the corpse still draped over her thorax.

Once they'd entered, the doors began closing behind them.

"We should go back," Trina said. "We don't know what's in here."

Max shrugged. "Why? Maybe there's pizza and ice-cream."

Arinna laughed.

Trina took off her plague doctor mask. "Are you making fun of me?"

"Nah," Max said. "I just figure, at this point, what do we have to lose?"

"Were you going to do something with that body?" Arinna asked.

"Oh!" Max said. "You're right! If we're going to walk into Oz, we need our cowardly lion!"

"What is he even talking about?" Trina asked.

Arinna shook her head. "It would take too long to explain."

Max grabbed the body from Mytten's back and placed it on the dark stone floor. He pointed his hand at it and said the words. "kharan khuin khüchir kheg süns bosokh. Minii amiig, khüchiig mini avaad dakhin amidar." They meant: Arise powerful soul of the dark. Take my life, my power, and live again.

"Raeg!" Max shouted, his voice echoing into the dark. "I need you back."

"*We* need you," Trina said, tears in her eyes. "I... I'm sorry for getting you killed. I was stupid."

1532 damage received.

Max's bones shook like he'd been hammered in the chest and he nearly fell. "Gah!"

Brilliant green light poured from the eyes of the corpse and without any warning, it sat up.

The head turned and took in each of them at a time, pausing only on Arinna. "Nice goin', boney." he said. "She's a looker." Though the face was not Raeg's the voice most definitely was.

"Nice to see you too," Trina sneered.

"This is your friend?" Arinna said.

"Yes," Max said as he stepped forward and offered Raeg a forearm. "Arinna, Meet Raeg."

Raeg took it and Max pulled him to his feet. Even as he did so, Max saw changes occurring. It was just as he'd read in the Necromancy book, souls with enough power would force the dead flesh around them to rearrange into the look of their living form. As Max watched, a deep red beard started sprouting while the hair on the corpse's head started falling out.

Raeg shivered and tore the knight's tabard and armor from his body, growling as he did. "Augh!" he shouted.

"Look!" Trina said. "The tattoos!"

She was right, Raeg's black tattoos were appearing on the dead flesh, just as if it was his own.

"Nice to meet you," Arinna said, extending a hand.

"Named after the goddess huh?" Raeg said. "Sorry to hear that. You don't look half bad though, probably not a big problem for ya."

"Raeg," Max said. "She is Arinna. That's why I brought you back. I need your help to get her to Ghrellen."

"Bah!" Raeg said, scratching at his buttocks. "Why you wanna go there? Hierarch lives there, and every other paladin with a mace up his ass." He looked down at his hands. "Wait... why's my skin so pale?"

"You're dead," Trina said, looking down at her boots. "Sorry."

"Forget about it," Raeg replied. "Being dead's not half bad. I got to try Max's bacon, which was great. And I ate about seventeen demons. I'll bet my level's higher than it was."

"You did what?" Arinna said.

"It's a civil war down there," Raeg said. "Demon against demon, soul against soul. Eat or be eaten." He stuck a thumb toward his chest. "You know me, Max. I like to eat."

Max nodded. "That is true."

"We need to get back there Max," Arinna said. "If I lose too many demons it will be impossible to keep peace in the underworld. Everything will fall apart."

"Too late for that sweetheart," Raeg said, "but sure... let's go back. I got more demons to eat." He looked around. "What is this place?"

"COME FORTH!" a female voice called, echoing down the hall ahead.

"Shit," Max said. "I think-"

Everything went dark around him. Max turned in a circle, looking around. There was like a misty fog around his feet. Arinna, Trina, and Raeg were nowhere to be seen. He reached out, swishing his skeletal hand through the blackness. It swirled like ink.

"Hello?" he asked.

Two giant almond shaped eyes opened in the dark before him. They had long lashes and bright purple irises and they were just hanging there.

"It's been a long time since you've been here," the same feminine voice said.

"I'm sorry, what?" Max said. "I've never been in here before."

"Don't be coy with me!" she said, with a sultry pout. "That's my job."

Max held up his hands. "Look, lady... fortress lady? I really don't know who you are."

"Oh," she said, as the two eyes widened with surprise and distress. "I thought... uh..."

Max put his hands on his hips. "You thought what?" he asked.

"I thought you were someone else."

"I got that," Max said. "Who? How many damned talking skeletons do you see down here?"

"None, not for a long time... I thought... I thought you might be him," she said. "But I was wrong. I'm sorry."

"Who?!" Max asked again.

"Rod," she said softly, with an air of reverence.

Max's jaw dropped. "What did you just say?"

"Rod," she repeated. "He said it was short for Rodney." She let out a long sigh. "He's an artist."

"Are you serious right now?" Max replied.

"Of course," she said. "Oh... Are you a new dark warrior? Do you know what's become of him?"

"Yeah I know," Max replied. "He's my dad."

The eyes widened again. "I don't believe that," she said but then her eyes focused on him again, staring. "Although, you do look like him."

"But I'm a skeleton!" Max protested. "This makes no sense. Also... my father was a warrior of light!"

She laughed. "No! He was Rod the Destroyer! Rod the Conqueror... We did many things together. Many glorious things."

Max held up a hand. "I don't need the details."

"So be it," she replied.

"So I'm not from this world then," Max said. "My father was brought here too."

"Yes," she replied. "If you see him again... please tell him Perilla is thinking of him."

"Sure," he said.

Huh. So that meant he wasn't Arinna's cousin. That was a relief. But if that was true, why did the signet ring work for him? "Is that why you called me here?" Max asked, "Because you thought I'm my father?"

"Well... partly," she replied. "I spoke to a turs girl, a shaman. She said that her people needed to escape and I told her that if she had a mage in her party with the magic to power it, I have a transmission portal here. She said she might send people my way to use it."

"But nobody had the magic points for it huh?" Max asked. "How much does it need?"

~

"Where did you go?" Arinna asked. "You were suddenly just gone."

"I spoke to the... whatever she is... that runs this place," Max replied. "Also, you and I need to talk."

"Yeah?" Arinna said.

Max nodded. "But first, let's get you home."

Arinna's eyes widened. "There's a portal here?"

"Yes," Max said as he walked up the corridor. "This way... and we turn left here."

"This is gonna take us back to the underworld?" Raeg asked.

"No," Max said as they walked up to what looked like a twenty foot tall full length mirror. "She said it's a transmission portal. This world only."

"But it will take us to Ghrellen," Trina said.

"Exactly," Max replied. "Now I just need a recharge of my health and magic and-"

SPLASH.

Health and magic restored.

Max looked down to see coagulated blood and rancid remains running down his front.

"I kept a buck of filth," Trina said. "Just in case."

Max laughed.

"By Barghel's beard!" Raeg said. "That stuff smells great! Got any more?"

"But your health is full," Arinna said.

Raeg shrugged. "So?"

Max touched a small panel on the top of a pedestal near the portal and pumped a hundred magic points into it, not even a fourth of his current total. How things had changed. For so long he'd had one single solitary magic point. That had sucked, but it had led him here: to the precipice of victory.

With a loud whum the portal opened, creating a black fluid membrane across its entire oval surface.

"Into the heart of the enemy's stronghold," Raeg said with fervor. "If only I had a worthy weapon."

Max laughed. "Trina, why don't you do the honors?"

Trina nodded and in her hands appeared the Dark Dragon Greataxe. She handed it to Raeg.

"Is this from that smith?" the barbarian asked.

"Bought with your own blood," Max said. "It's a part of you."

"Never thought I had the talent for a two-handed beauty like this," Raeg said, hefting the weight of the weapon. "But things have changed."

"Yes they have," Max said. "Let's go."

The four of them, with Mytten and the dungeon crawlers following behind, passed through the portal. They arrived in a well lit courtyard surrounded by scores of bright white towers and arches. Ahead was a circular dais that looked a lot like what they'd come to find: the way to the underworld. There was only one problem: dozens of enemies turned to face them.

"They've come!" shouted a sentry nearby, pointing his spear in their direction.

"Sound the alarm!" cried a second.

Arrows and bolts started streaming in from all sides. The battle for the portal had begun.

"Is that it?" Max asked as Mytten scooped him up and placed him on her back.

You're coming with me.

"Yes!" Arinna said. "We head straight for the portal. Kill everyone who gets in our way and protect Max, he's our key to opening it."

Scruff and his two smaller friends jumped up beside Max. They'd been clinging to Mytten's abdomen since the trip over the chasm but now they moved up to surround him.

Protect!

Bite!

Kill!

"Thanks guys," Max said. He didn't want to be useless though. There might not be skeletons here but there were a few things he could do.

Raeg bellowed a challenge to the nearest group of knights and sentries running at him and swung his heavy axe. The weapon cut three of them down in the first strike, causing the rest to back away. Then an arrow slammed into Raeg's bare chest.

Raeg receives 2 damage.

Max laughed. "Raeg... You're a beast!"

"You're goddam right I am!" he roared.

"Mytten," Max said. "Swerve in behind Raeg."

Sure.

The spider deviated to the left and Max summoned an undead shard into his hands. "Kharan kuin Comool." he said. The shard evaporated and the three enemies Raeg had cut down with his first swing, began to move.

"Huh?" Raeg said.

"Giving you some back up," Max yelled as the spider went by.

"Ha, ha, ha!" Raeg shouted. "I'll take it!"

Arrows were pouring in from all sides but Trina used a smoke bomb to slow down their aiming and Arinna, well...

she was off doing her thing like the goddess of death she was. Heads rolled behind her as their enemies fell, cut down like nothing. Max used up several more shards, reviving as many dead as he could. The portal wasn't actually that far. It seemed they were about to make it.

Then the reinforcements arrived.

A gigantic airship appeared overhead, a carrier, its bright lights beaming down on them from above. Griffin riders launched in waves from its surface as two dozen lines dropped to the ground. Paladins, Enforcers, Guardians, Wizards, and many more classes of enemies Max had never before seen were deployed directly before them, preventing their advance.

Raeg and Arinna attacked, flanked by dozens of Max's undead. Swords rang and shields clanged in the dark.

"The dawn is coming," Trina said as she lobbed an explosive into the center of the oncoming hordes. "We need to get this done."

"Why does that matter?" Max asked, but his brain answered the question for him. It only made sense. You've got a portal that goes to this worlds heaven or hell... it would probably only work during the right time of day. "Oh shit!" he said.

"Just get there!" Arinna said. "Raeg and I can handle this."

That was clearly not the case though. Even as Raeg and Arinna cut down soldiers, sentries, knights, and freelancers, more came and they were followed by paladins, enforcers, and guardians. Griffin knights dropped in behind them, firing balls of fire from their lances. Things were getting crowded quickly.

Max felt helpless behind them. He would raise undead warrior after warrior to join the fray on their side, only to have them swarmed and dismembered in moments.

"Destroy them!" shouted a Sun Paladin wearing incredibly ornate armor. "Keep them from the portal!"

"Shut your fat ugly bacon hole!" Raeg howled as he raised his heavy axe and beat it against the paladin's shield, driving him back. Wham, wham, WHAM, and the axe tore the shining white shield to shreds, ripping through to sever the Paladin's left hand at the wrist. The man fell to his knees, screaming. He dropped his fat golden war hammer and clutched at his wrist as pinkish blood spurted from the ragged stump.

Raeg decapitated him with his next blow and the head flew through the air across the field, only to be caught by Garem, who crushed it in his fingers.

Resplendent in a flowing white robe, Garem, god of light, strode through his many soldiers, carrying no weapons. A white headband with the symbol of the shining sun was wrapped around his forehead, radiating light like a beacon. The forces of light made way for him, likely happy to avoid decapitation at the hands of Raeg's greataxe, or Arinna's wicked blade.

Voices cheered as Garem passed, except for Arinna who stood before him, and booed.

"Ah," he said. "Good to see you again, beloved."

"You," Arinna said. "are and always will be, a loser."

"Look around," Garem said. "We outnumber you ten to one. You will never make it to the portal. Your friends will be captured and tortured until they go mad, including that pathetic weakling who calls himself the Boneknight."

"Gogshit!" Raeg shouted as he rushed in. "I'll kill you!"

With one hand Garem parried the axe and then punched Raeg in the chest, rocketing him back into the crowd of light soldiers as black blood exploded from his mouth.

Raeg receives 673 damage.

"My turn," Arinna said as she flew forward at incredible speed and slashed at least a dozen times at the god of light but Garem avoided them all, even as several knights to either side of him fell.

With his own lightning movement, he snatched Arinna out of the air, holding her by the neck.

"You're not what you were," he said. "You're weak!"

Arinna responded by driving her blade into his chest. White blood sprayed outward, sizzling against her leather armor.

He laughed. "Weak," he said again.

Max looked up into the sky and couldn't believe his eyes.

Is that?

"It might be Mytten," he said. "Let's go antagonize him."

Is that wise?

"Probably not," he replied. "But it might be fun."

"Hey shit bag," Max said. "I heard you... ah wield an extremely small sword... is that true?"

Garem's face twisted with rage.

"Like, literally impossible to see. Minuscule," Max added, pinching his fingers together. "How does that codpiece stay on? Is it magic or is there, like... a whole box of tissue inside?"

The god threw Arinna aside and started stomping toward Max.

Mytten and the dungeon crawlers all hissed together.

"I'm going to kill that spider, and those disgusting creatures and then," he said. "I'm going to make you wish you'd never come here."

"Whoa, whoa," Max said. "Stay back!"

Garem paused, frowning. Then he decided it was a trick because his face changed and he started to take a step. That was when a foot the size of a tractor trailer landed on him.

The sound of it was incredible. Three giants had slammed into the field, causing the entire floating island to dip for a second from the shock of it. All the soldiers of light fell over as a result. Meanwhile holy fire was raining from several ships high above, cutting griffin knights right out of the sky. The Black Skull pirates had come, and they'd brought help.

"Great timing!" Max yelled.

"GLAD TO HELP!" Willa replied. "WE'LL CLEAR THE WAY! YOU GET TO THE PORTAL!"

Willa, Rog, and his father Ordan then proceeded to stomp on every soldier, archer and mage they could find, shaking the entire island with every thunderous impact.

Trina was waving at the sky. "I knew he'd come!" she said. "I knew it!"

"Ok, Ok," Max said. "Let's get to the portal!"

Mytten took off, snatching Raeg, Trina, and Arinna as she went by with the hooks on her pedipalps and dragging them along the stone surface.

"Hey!" Raeg said as his head kept knocking into lumps of stone.

Max summoned the skull of Akran Tayne into his right hand. "Tayne," he said. "Help us clear the way."

A flash of black and bright green announced the arrival of a huge ethereal Dread Knight seated upon an armored undead steed.

"So be it," Tayne replied, in his deep resonant voice. He drew a monstrous curved blade and charged, cutting a wide swath through the enemies ahead. Pure pink blood poured to the ground by the gallon. When the field ahead had been cleared, Tayne dissolved into nothing.

Mytten raced behind him. It took only a few moments for them to arrive in the center of the portal platform.

"Ok," Max said. "We're here. The sun hasn't risen. What's next?"

Arinna stood up. "Put your hands on the ground and say the following in high demonic: May the moon rise!"

"Oh," Max said as he jumped from Mytten's thorax. "For once, it's easy." Then he kneeled and placed both palms to the stone. "Sar mandakh boltugai."

Nothing happened.

Then, from behind them, there was laughter.

Max, Trina, Arinna and Raeg, turned to see Garem walking toward them. "You fools. Did you think I wouldn't lock the portal from your influence?"

Raeg roared and attacked with his axe but Garem appeared to blur out of existence. When he reappeared he was behind Raeg where he chopped him in the back of the neck. Raeg fell to the ground, shaking.

Max frowned. "What's that? Paralyser? Do you guys all use that?"

Arinna attacked, slashing with her long blade but again Garem was too fast, even for her. He appeared and reappeared, kicking her legs with a sweep before smashing a palm into her chest.

Arinna receives 147 damage.

Both Raeg and Arinna were now down and non responsive. "Trina!" Max said.

"I can't!" she replied. "He's too close he-"

Max turned to see Garem behind Trina. She too had been rendered unconscious with a single blow. That was when Max saw it. The same amulet from before. Garem had it in his left hand. It bore the same symbol as his own ring.

"Where did you get that amulet?" Max asked.

Kill!

Attack!

Bite!

"No!" Max said, gesturing to Mytten and the dungeon crawlers. "Do not attack him... get behind me."

Garem chuckled. "This is an artifact of great power," he said. "I can see why you find it interesting as you now have none."

"I don't know how, but I think that's actually my dad's," he said.

The god of light frowned. "Not possible. This is an artifact of the light, you fool," he said and dropped it on the stone. The metal clinked against the stone.

Then Garem opened his palm and the amulet flew back up from the ground and into his white gloved fingers. "See?"

Should he give it a shot? Why the hell not.

Max raised his own hand. "Come to daddy," he said.

The amulet shivered in Garem's hand and then it shot straight into Max's palm with a clink.

"No!" Garem cried. "That's not possible! That's not possible."

Max walked over to Arinna, giving her a slight kick. "Hey sweetie," he said.

"Mmmm..." she responded, moving a little.

"You like jewelry?" he asked and placed the amulet on her neck.

"This is an obscenity! Return that at once!" Garem ordered as he marched toward Max. Then he stopped and looked down. Arinna's long blade had been jabbed into his gut.

Arinna then sliced his arms off at the elbows, one at a time. Garem fell to his knees.

"Y-you still can't leave," he whispered as his pure white blood gushed onto the stone. "M-more of m-my soldiers will come... Angels... also..." Arinna grabbed him and tossed him bodily off of the portal platform.

Max leaned down and put his hands out. "Sar mandakh boltugai." he said but nothing changed. "He's right."

"There!" a high pitched voice cried from nearby. "You see!"

Max and Arinna turned to see a young girl with pure white hair and white eyes. She was standing next to an armored up youth with a very choice looking sword and a shield.

"My god, you're right!" the youth said. "They've killed Garem."

"You can destroy them now! Do it!" the girl said.

There looked to be a little blue light floating over her shoulder. Was that a light? Max thought it kind of looked like it was shaped like a person. Was it a pixie or something? They had those here?

"For the light!" the boy said as he used his sword to smash a small box attached to the side of the portal.

"Max!" the little girl called. "The limiter has been destroyed. Go now!"

Max looked at Arinna, who shrugged.

"Sar mandakh boltugai," he said, one more time, but this time, with a flash of swirling black the portal opened, and Max, Arinna, Raeg, and Trina, all passed through.

THE END

BONE KNIGHT BOOK 8: Max has accomplished his goal... or has he? Arinna has returned, but her journey to the throne is far from finished. Powerful demonic forces will line up against her and they'll do anything to remain in power. Max must recruit an army and scale a shattered tower to earn the ultimate power of the dark. Can he accomplish it all before his final moments fade away?

A Brutal Clash and A Bitter Rival is available now on Amazon.

ACKNOWLEDGMENTS

Thank you to everyone who helped make this novel possible but especially my extraordinary wife and sons. Additional thanks to the following invaluable people, places, things, creatures, artificial beings and human like entities:

Blizzardlizard

Milo

Mary

Scruff

Tiny obnoxious dogs

Rowan Sebastian Atkinson

Spiders